EXTINCTION CRISIS

BOOK THREE

JAMES D. PRESCOTT

Dedication

As always, there are so many people to thank for helping to make this series a success. First off, a shout-out to my intrepid consultants Dr. Ricki Lewis (<u>DNA Science blog</u>), Joel Rubin and Ethan Siegel, who always strove to keep the story closer to science than to fiction. To Kim, Darja and the whole cover team at Deranged Doctor Design, and my editor RJ, who has never met a sentence she couldn't fix.

But without a doubt, the greatest thanks goes out to you, the readers, who make all of this worthwhile.

Books by James D. Prescott

The Genesis Conspiracy
Extinction Code
Extinction Countdown
Extinction Crisis

Note to Readers:

Once again, I've included reference material on Salzburg along with a brief recap of important plot points from earlier in the series. There's a lot that's happened in the Extinction universe and for many of you it will have been months since you read books 1 and 2. I hope this helps.

Happy Reading!

Book Description

With the doomsday ship only days away from impacting the Earth, humanity's demise seems all but assured. In every corner of the world, news of the impending destruction has led to chaos, looting and the collapse of the rule of law.

As the foundations of civilization crumble around them, Jack and Mia must race to find answers to perhaps the most important questions of all time. Why have the Ateans repeatedly eradicated life on our planet? And could the key to ending the cycle of extinctions be locked somewhere within the Salzburg chromosome? Unraveling the mystery will mean journeying deep into the heart of a perilous alien world and facing off against the very beings who created us.

Returning Characters from Book Two:

Jack Greer: A geophysicist in his early forties, Jack is at times impulsive and irreverent, but dedicated to pursuing the truth, no matter where it might lead him. His main weaknesses include cigarettes, gambling and anything else that requires a modicum of willpower.

Mia Ward: A brilliant geneticist in her mid-thirties, Mia has struggled to get her life back on track. She is determined to do everything in her power to save her daughter from the ravages of Salzburg syndrome.

Anna: An android powered by artificial intelligence, Anna is the first of her kind. She is caring and highly competent and struggles to understand the irrationality of human behavior.

Gabby Bishop: A matronly figure and accomplished astrophysicist in her early fifties, Gabby is Jack's closest friend and colleague. Her level head is often a strong counterpoint to his tendency to jump in with both feet.

Dag Gustavsson: A Swedish paleontologist in his late twenties, Dag is a deep thinker who is quick to hide his vulnerable side with humor.

Grant Holland: At fifty-nine, Grant is a British-born biologist who's not afraid of exploring the vague boundaries between science and mysticism.

Eugene Jarecki: A theoretical physicist in his early forties, Eugene masks his fears and insecurities with arrogance and bravado.

Admiral Stark: In his mid-fifties, Stark comes from a long line of Navy men. He may be a hard man to impress, but he's exactly the kind of guy you want on your side.

Ollie Cooper: Rugged and some might even say handsome, Ollie is a fifty-year-old former Sentinel agent eager to right his past wrongs. His greatest strength is loyalty. It might also be his greatest weakness.

Sven: Former member of Sentinel who intercepted Mia in Argentina. His large size and deep voice overshadow his soft side. After Tom's death on board the Atean ship in the Gulf of Mexico, Sven has sworn an oath to avenge his friend.

Recap of Books 1 and 2

While searching in the Yucatán Peninsula for the meteor that killed the dinosaurs, geophysicist Jack Greer and a team of scientists stumble upon an alien spaceship, millions of years old. Once onboard, they discover the ship crash-landed on Earth 65 million years ago, killing 70% of life on the planet. More startling still, the aliens behind the devastation then proceeded to seed Earth with new life. One of those ancient life forms would eventually lead to *Homo sapiens.*

At the same time, a geneticist named Mia Ward receives a package from her murdered boss claiming the appearance of a strange new chromosome called Salzburg syndrome may not have an earthly origin. Mysteriously, pulses of light emanating from the alien ship in the Gulf of Mexico appear to be adding harmful genes to the Salzburg chromosome. With her own daughter suffering from its terrible effects, Mia is determined to stop it.

Meanwhile back in the Gulf, when a secretive anti-alien group called Sentinel learns of the ship's discovery, they dispatch a group of agents to extract whatever extraterrestrial technology they can and destroy what's left. A battle ensues on board with Jack, Mia and most of the others narrowly escaping with their lives.

Things go from bad to worse when NASA discovers another diamond-shaped alien craft hurtling toward Earth. And when new blast waves beginning emanating from beneath Greenland's ice sheet, it becomes clear there may be a second ship.

To that end, Jack and the others are dispatched to the site, only to discover the enemy has gotten there first. When they descend beneath Greenland's ice sheet, they discover a lost city millions of years old. DNA analysis on ancient bones soon reveals the beings who lived there long ago were genetically related to modern dolphins. They push through the complex of frozen ruins, aware they're in a race against time to reach the ancient city's secrets before the enemy does.

Soon it becomes clear—the creatures that lived here once possessed a thriving, technologically advanced civilization, but it was destroyed by the same cataclysm that killed the dinosaurs. Understanding begins to crystalize in their minds that each of the major extinctions throughout Earth's geological history was likely tied to the impact of one of these alien ships. But many questions remain. Chiefly among them, why is an alien civilization repeatedly destroying life on Earth? And is there a way to stop the cycle?

Back in America, a young reporter named Kay Mahoro learns of a conspiracy to kill President Taylor. Crumb by crumb, her source leads her down a maze of intrigue that eventually points the finger at the president's own cabinet.

Kay's work exposes the Cabinet and leads to their arrest. Soon, however, she discovers that Sentinel was behind the whole thing and used her to clear a path to the White House.

Still on the run from Sentinel agents, Mia continues to unravel the mystery of Salzburg. With 30% of the population affected, societies across the globe begin to crumble. A host of discoveries, however, begin to shed new light on this mysterious illness. While the genes in the first part of the chromosome were incredibly harmful, new genes offer some benefits, such as increased bone mass, strength, intelligence, and healing. But perhaps Mia's most unusual find is a pair of twins in Rome, each with a copy of the final and most mysterious gene in the Salzburg puzzle. Called *HOK3*, it appears to enable telepathic communication. Mia's final discovery comes when Sentinel agents corner her and she learns the head of the nefarious organization is really her old boss, whom she thought was dead—Alan Salzburg. Beneath Greenland's ice sheet, Jack and the others at last reach the source of the blast waves. But instead of finding a ship, they uncover what looks like a portal. Uncovering who put it there and where it might lead is where book 3 begins...

The day science begins to study non-physical phenomena, it will make more progress in one decade than in all the previous centuries of its existence.

—Nikola Tesla

Chapter 1

Rome, Italy

Ollie Cooper stared at the cloud-grey walls of his cell
wondering about fate. Not his own. No, that particular
boat had sailed a long time ago. At least what felt to him
like a long time.

He caught the slow, deliberate sound of someone
approaching. Each footfall seemed to echo in his ears.
Fear had a funny habit of stretching things out, didn't it,
making a person feel like they were circling the event
horizon of some ravenous black hole. The truth was, in
only a handful of days, millions of tons of alien
engineering would punch a hole through the upper
atmosphere and give the earth the kind of shiner she
hadn't felt since T-Rex roamed the planet. But a lucky
few—or unlucky, depending on one's point of view—
would survive the impending cataclysm.

Ollie wondered about Mia, where she was and whether
she was safe. The last he'd seen, she'd been thrown into
an interrogation room right before he had. After hours
of intense questioning interspersed with occasional
beatings, Ollie had been tossed into this cell. Judging by
the dried blood on his lip he had been here a day, maybe
two. But sitting inside a concrete box with less than eight

feet of room in either direction, it was hard to be sure of anything.

Three pairs of shoes stopped outside his cell, followed by the echoing clank from a metal latch being turned. The heavy door swung open, bringing with it a painful shaft of light that pierced his eyes and stabbed at his brain. Ollie squinted, blinking with the force of a man trying to crush walnuts with his eyelids.

"It's about time you lot showed up," he complained. "I'll have pasta primavera with a glass of your finest red wine. And hold that sorry excuse for a bread roll you tried to give me yesterday, bloody thing was as hard as a rock with about as much taste."

Commissario Vicario flashed the hint of a smile. Distinguished and always dapper, he looked less like a cop and more like a pitchman for Black Label or overpriced tequila. Flanking him were two men wearing dark suits and sunglasses. From Ollie's spot on the floor, they looked like giants, staring down at him with cold, humorless expressions.

"Very sorry to disappoint you, Mr. Cooper," Vicario said. "We are not here about lunch."

The two gloved men stepped into the room. Dark suits, shades and matching gloves. Something told Ollie they weren't there to sell him nonstick skillets or one-piece blankets you could wear as a nighty.

Ollie noticed the corner of a thick yellow envelope poking out of Vicario's breast pocket.

"I suppose everyone has their price," the Aussie said, appraising the situation.

Vicario smiled. "If it's any consolation, I've been assured you will not suffer." His eyes flicked down to the cut on Ollie's lip and then back up to the bruises ringing his left cheekbone. "At least not any more than you already have."

"You're a real sweetheart..." Ollie started to say as one of the men reached into his suit jacket and came out with a silenced pistol. He felt the blood drain from his face. Distaste flashed across the commander's face as he pushed the barrel of the man's pistol down. "Not here. Not like this. The last thing I wanna do is give the cleaning crew another excuse to complain. 'Commissario,'" he mocked in his heavy Italian accent, "'there's blood and brains all over the walls. Do you expect us to get down on our hands and knees and pick itsy-bitsy pieces of skull up off the floor?'" He straightened up, swiping his hands down the front of his finely pressed suit. "I'm telling you, they're worse than my first wife, God rest her soul." Vicario reached behind him and came out with a pair of handcuffs. "Take him out of the city and do it there." His gaze settled back on Ollie, who was grinning. "What the hell are you so happy about?"

"Me? Oh, nothing, mate. It's just I've always loved the country. Seems like a fine place to say goodbye."

•••

They led Ollie out of the police station and into the back seat of a white Toyota. The men in dark suits got in the front and started the car.

"I'm being driven to my grave in a sedan?" Ollie quipped. "Don't you think I at least deserve a Maserati?" He caught the driver's head snap up, eyes piercing him through the rearview mirror. They made their way out of Rome, Ollie eyeing the goon in the front passenger seat as he attempted to work his wrists out of the cuffs. They had thought enough to secure Ollie's hands behind his back. What they didn't know was that at thirteen years of

3

age, Ollie had broken his right thumb playing rugby back in Brisbane. The injury had healed, but it had left him with the sickening ability to dislocate the digit completely.

Ollie was in the middle of subtly working the cuff down his wrist when he caught the guy in the passenger seat snort and flick his fingers up the front of his nose. It made a sickening whickering sound, one Ollie recognized all too well. These weren't Mafioso hitmen or corrupt Italian cops. They were Sentinel agents Ollie recognized from his days in the organization.

"Sean? That you, mate?"

The muscles on the man's face tensed.

"Sean O'Rourke, you son of a bitch, I thought it was you." Ollie leaned forward just as the man spun around and slugged him in the face. Ollie was thrown back into place, bouncing around before coming to a stop. A thin trickle of blood ran from his nose. He grinned. "You always were an asshole. And a pig, the way you flick that nose of yours. You really should get that checked."

Outside, they passed a row of trees along a narrow country road, the sun poking out behind a thick blanket of clouds. They couldn't be far now.

"You had your chance, Cooper, and you blew it," Sean said, his voice low and filled with contempt.

Ollie continued working the cuffs, shifting gently from side to side, making it look like the bumpy road was tossing him around. "Chance at what? I can already see your future. Soon as that ship hits you boys will be barbeque meat. Least I'm going out the easy way. Bullet to the back of the head."

"Don't kid yourself," Sean said, half turning and lowering the rim of his shades. His eyes were grey and

4

bright, like a husky's. "We've got the situation under control."

"Oh, you mean now that Sentinel has control of the White House? Throw a few nukes into space, that your big plan?"

"Maybe, but I don't see why it matters, you'll be dead in the next five minutes."

They were coming to an intersection, the opposite road lined with a row of stone pine trees. An audible click sounded as Ollie's hand broke free.

Damn it!

Sean's head snapped back just in time to feel the heel from Ollie's boot. The car swerved as the driver reached back with one arm to fight him. Sean reached into his jacket for the silenced pistol. Ollie lunged forward, only dimly aware his seatbelt was still on.

Double damn it!

Sean's pistol came up right as the impact shattered the driver's side windows, sending the Toyota rolling into the ditch. Shards of glass hung suspended in midair for a moment as the car tumbled. Ollie caught the sound of twisting metal as the roof caved. A split second later, the car flipped again, ejecting the driver out the broken window, as though he'd been sucked out of an airplane at thirty thousand feet.

An eternity later, the car came to a rest upside down. Ollie was dazed and not entirely sure what had happened or whether or not he was hurt. Nearby, a cow bell sounded. Glancing out the shattered remains of his window, Ollie spotted the animal, which paused and regarded him briefly before going about its business. Ollie was in the middle of trying to take his seatbelt off when he heard the distinct sound of gunshots. Sean, upside down, struggled to do the same. The assassin's pistol was lying on the ceiling, a few feet away. Sean reached for it, his fingernails scraping against the grip when the passenger door flew open. Three more shots rang out and Sean went limp. Then it was Ollie's turn. What was left of his door hung on at a weird angle. A second later it was ripped from its hinges and tossed aside. Ollie stared into the barrel of a rifle, uncertain if the large silhouette before him meant to be a friend or an executioner.

Then the man spoke and the deep and familiar timbre of his voice gave Ollie his answer. "Sven?"

Chapter 2

Greenland

Jack Greer made his way along Northern Star's battered corridors. Signs of the fighting that had taken place here were still clearly visible, the wounds of those they had lost still painfully fresh. While the holes in the three giant modules had quickly been patched and the spilt blood wiped away, doors kicked off their hinges and walls blackened from exploding grenades remained. Northern Star had become a charnel house.

The advance team had been the first to lose their lives at the hands of Israeli special forces. Not long after, the Russians had suffered a similar fate when Admiral Stark and a team of Navy SEALs and Delta Force operatives had swept in to take the facility back. Now, close to a mile beneath their feet lay a tear in space, a doorway perhaps to another planet, another dimension. Nobody knew. Not yet, anyway.

Jack arrived at the electronics lab and rapped at the door. When there was no immediate answer, he knocked again, this time with more force.

"Come in, Dr. Greer," the soft female voice instructed him.

Jack pushed his way in. "How'd you know it was me?"

Anna was hunched over the workbench busily soldering something. She stopped and spun at the waist to face him, her feet pointing in the opposite direction. It was a sight that still took some getting used to. "You always knock twice, softly at first and then loudly when you don't hear a response."

"Am I that transparent?" he asked, smiling as he surveyed the replacement leg and arm from DARPA that had arrived yesterday.

She grinned. "I believe in poker they call it a tell, do they not?"

"They do, but my poker days are over." He noticed the soldering iron projecting from a tiny port between her second and third knuckle. "Is that new?"

Anna dropped her gaze to her outstretched hand. "Since they were replacing my damaged arm, the people from DARPA asked if I requested any additions or modifications."

"And you asked for a soldering iron."

"For my work, yes. The people from DARPA are very nice."

The expression on Jack's face changed ever so slightly. Anna tilted her head. "Do you disapprove?"

"I don't have a problem with them," he clarified and then hesitated, uncertain if he should finish the thought. "But I know Rajesh did."

Anna's eyes dropped and he noticed her shoulders droop. For something that didn't breathe, she sure looked as though all the air had gone out of her. He went up and rubbed her cold metallic shoulder. "It'll get easier with time," he said, trying to somehow lessen the pain. He had a hard enough time with human emotions, let alone the robotic equivalent. He eyed the jumble of wires and logic boards she'd been working on. "Seems you've been keeping busy."

She spun around, all the while avoiding his gaze. "I find the pounds per square inch of pressure greatly reduced when I engage myself with an important project."

"We call it grief," he told her. "That's what the pain feels like when you lose someone important to you. It comes in waves, sometimes crashing against you all at once."

Jack was about to bring up the portal and the reason for his visit when he caught the sound of barking coming from the closet. Puzzled, Jack looked at Anna before his gaze settled on the remains of a shattered Roomba on the workbench. "Did you destroy another robot vacuum cleaner?"

"My apologies, Dr. Greer, but I was short on parts," she said, sheepishly.

Jack stalked over to the closet and pulled open the door right as Gabby and Grant appeared in the electronics lab doorway. A tiny robotic dog shuffled out of the closet, its delicate feet scrambling for traction on the slippery linoleum floor.

"Wha, wha," it bleated. The animal was a mad assortment of disparate parts.

Gabby swooned, dropping onto her hands and knees and calling after the little electronic beast. Grant laughed, clapping his hands together, showing no sign he'd suffered anything like the bullets he'd taken to his chest and left wrist only two days earlier. The dog stopped by Jack's feet, squatted over the toe of his boot and began tinkling. Now all of them burst into a gale of wild laughter as Anna came over and scooped it up, running her padded fingers over its small head.

"Do not worry, Dr. Greer, Tinkerbell's bladder is little more than a thimbleful of water."

"Tinkerbell?" Gabby said, surprised. "Are you a fan of Peter Pan?"

Jack shook his head. "No, but she's a fan of Paris Hilton, who also had a dog named Tinkerbell. Don't ask me how I know these things."

Grant leaned against the doorframe, wiping the tears from his eyes and then clutching his abdomen. "Oh, thank you kindly. There's no telling how much I needed that."

Anna set the dog down and it ran straight into the edge of the table, knocking itself over in the process.

"Grant, are you sure you should be walking around?" Jack wondered. "I know you like to think of yourself as Hercules, but you're a mortal man and one who was shot less than forty-eight hours ago."

Grant unbuttoned his shirt and revealed his bare chest. "If you can find a bullet hole, old chap, you'll be doing much better than that bloody doctor."

This still wasn't making sense. "What about your wrist? I saw the blood spray out when you were hit."

Swinging an awkward hand into the air, Grant displayed his left wrist and rotated it above his head like an overaged cheerleader.

"Have they offered any kind of explanation, other than your manliness? I mean, we knew you were getting better and faster than usual, but to go from lying in bed riddled with holes to walking around hole-free in less than twenty-four hours, well, that's not normal."

"I've been thinking about that myself, Jack," he replied, the humor gone from his voice. "I'll give you this, it is quite perplexing and I can think of no other explanation other than Salzburg syndrome. I wasn't the only one hit. Captain Mullins was flown to a naval hospital in

Maryland and is still in serious condition. And he was one of the lucky ones."

Grant didn't quite speak Rajesh's name, but Jack noticed the flicker in Anna's eyes all the same.

"First Salzburg nearly kills you," Jack noticed, running through the puzzling sequence of events, "and then it practically doubles your muscle and bone mass and heals you in record time."

"I'm not complaining, Jack."

"Nor should you," he said, rubbing his fingers together. "But I suspect you're not the only one displaying strange and even amazing symptoms. The real question is what it all means."

Gabby, her silver hair tied back behind her head, looked from them back to the dog. "So you built this out of parts scavenged from a Roomba?" she asked, impressed.

"Mostly," Anna replied, unable to hide her pride. "Although many of the parts were cannibalized from other, shall I say, less successful projects."

"Seems it still has a ways to go to catch up to you," Jack observed, watching the dog's legs kick at empty air.

Anna bent over and righted Tinkerbell, who proceeded to run around the room.

But Jack knew she hadn't torn apart that vacuum to build an intelligence to rival her own. She had done it for a simple reason. She missed Rajesh and was trying to forget.

The radio on Jack's belt came to life. "Jack, any word from Anna on those drones?"

"I was right about to ask her," he replied, wiping the water off his boot.

"Well, hurry up. The teleconference with the Joint Chiefs is in less than five minutes and we still have no clue what's on the other side of that portal."

11

Anna was watching him. Already, she had remotely piloted six drones through the opening, but had yet to produce a report for them.

"That is correct. I was waiting to see if I could reacquire the signal," she explained.

Grant's brow furrowed. "Did they manage to beam any images back from the other side?"

It was a question each of them had been wondering. Standing before the swirling energy mass, it was difficult not to see shapes moving on the other side. Jack had thought he had seen his deceased mother. He wasn't the only one. Apparently, after staring into the eye of it, some had reported seeing loved ones, others relatives, long since dead. Rumors had spread faster than a fire at a matchstick factory that they had uncovered a doorway to heaven.

Anna shook her head. "To date, Dr. Holland, nothing has come back."

Chapter 3

The conference room on Northern Star was spacious and decked out with a single, long, oval table and twenty plush chairs. The seven humorless faces of the Joint Chiefs of Staff stared back at them from a sixty-inch television at the far end of the room. Those gathered grew silent as the chairman, General James F. Dunham, addressed them.

"I'm sure it will come as no surprise to any of you that the Israeli government has denied any involvement in the attack on Northern Star. Secretary Myers—excuse me, I mean President Myers—is at the U.N. right now giving them a piece of his mind. Seems they felt we were denying them access to salvaged alien technology. Our assurances that Sentinel was the only group that came away with anything useful fell on deaf ears. But it isn't the Israelis who worry us. Russian agents are scouring the planet in the hopes of finding an alien ship of their own. We've vetted every member at the Greenland site, but we can't deny the possibility that one or more personnel are working for the enemy. The president has ordered three carrier strike groups to cover every possible approach. Short of a full nuclear war, I can assure you, no Russian forces will get within a thousand miles of your position."

Talk of nuclear war made Jack and everyone else in the room justifiably uneasy.

"Your latest sitrep said the blast waves have subsided," the general said, glancing down at a paper before him.

"That's correct," Jack informed him. "Which has given us a chance to clear away the ice and debris near the doorway underground." He was referring to the storage area where the gun battle with the Israelis had taken place. "We're using that location as a forward operating base for any exploration through the doorway... or whatever it is."

The edges of the general's mouth turned down. "Admiral Stark has informed me that our initial attempts to reconnoiter beyond the doorway have not been successful."

"That's correct, General," Stark replied. "At this point, we aren't quite certain what we're dealing with. The simple robots we've sent in have not be able to communicate from the other side, nor have they returned. Our lower-tech solutions have proven more successful in some regards, but in others they've only raised more questions."

"Low-tech solutions?" one of the other generals asked.

Stark swallowed hard. "Well, you see, when the drones failed to report back or to even return, one of the technicians suggested we push a cellphone through at the end of a selfie stick."

The room erupted in a spate of laughter.

"Admiral," Dunham said, leaning forward, "you have at your disposal the greatest technology the United States has to offer and you're using selfie sticks?"

"I know how it looks, but so far it's the only thing that's worked. At least partly. There's a distorting wave around the opening, so the images we took were blurry, but

14

we've managed to clean them up a touch and it's clear there is something on the other side."

Dunham leaned back and cleared his throat. He was a wiry man in his early sixties who didn't like anything fuzzy. He expected answers and it was apparent this deficit was not sitting well. "So here's the situation and I want to make sure you folks are reading me distortion-free. That incoming craft has just passed Jupiter. By NASA's closest estimates, in the next seventy-two hours, it'll strike one mile off the coast of Newfoundland, Canada. At its present speed, the devastation will be like nothing we've ever seen, scorching the surface of the entire planet and killing anyone who isn't deep underground."

They knew what was coming. All the same, to hear it in such specific terms made chills dance up the back of their necks.

As though to drive home the point, a clock behind General Dunham ticked away the time until the human race would be no more. It read: 72 hours, 13 minutes, 52 seconds.

"As you can see," General Dunham told them, "there isn't a moment to lose. If the answer to the current crisis lies somewhere beyond that energy field, then we need to find it. And if your electronics aren't giving you answers, then I'm sorry to say you're gonna have to put some lives at risk and send some people in there. I suggest you begin with members of the Delta team currently on location."

"I'm not certain that's such a good idea, General," Jack chimed in.

"Excuse me? Who is that?"

"Jack Greer, sir. What I mean is that we have no idea what's behind that door. For all we know, it's a portal to

15

another world. If we send through a team of armed men, I can't imagine it'll be good for intergalactic relations." The room burst into a jumble of overlapping conversations and arguments.

"If anyone should go, it should be me," Jack said. "I'll go in unarmed and secured with climbing equipment. At the first sign of trouble, the team here can pull me out." The room settled down just as a single hand rose into the air. The general's expression changed when he caught sight of it. "Yes? Would you like to say something?"

"Thank you, General Dunham," Anna said, lowering her hand and folding her arms on the table before her. "As the only artificial person at this facility, I believe I should be the one to go through. Unlike my colleagues, I am uniquely equipped for the challenging environment that may exist on the other side."

"Anna, don't do this," Jack told her, gripping her arm. She put her hand gently over his and squeezed. "Please, Dr. Greer. This is something I need to do."

Chapter 4

70 hours, 45 minutes, 12 seconds

Base Camp Zulu was nothing more than a series of Quonset huts — steel composite frames wrapped in a sturdy fabric membrane. Undoubtedly, they looked like something straight out of World War II, but they offered the scientists and military personnel working under the Greenland ice sheet a warm place to eat, work and rest. As Jack had informed the general, once the Army Corps of Engineers had removed the debris from the storage area, they had quickly set about erecting the camp. Military efficiency had seen the huts put up in record time. They had also been equipped with everything Jack and the other scientists would need: labs where they might conduct research and experiments, rows of bunk beds where weary members of the team could steal a quick nap whenever an opportunity presented itself, and a mess hall with an endless array of hot meals.

"A man could get used to this," Dag said, his breath pluming out before him as he snacked on a veggie wrap. They were out in the open: Jack, Gabby, Eugene, Grant and Anna. The humans were dressed in their biosuits, their helmets slung under their arms. Far above their

17

heads, the same hole punched through the cavern's icy ceiling now exposed a night sky packed with stars twinkling in the clear frigid air. Tinkerbell yapped a number of times before Anna reached down and scooped her up.

"Tink, I need you to behave," she told it. "I will not be gone for long."

Jack led them through a stone archway and up a series of steps that led to the pyramid's main chamber. He glanced back now and then, watching the joints in Anna's mechanical legs lift her gracefully from one riser to the next. They made eye contact for the briefest of moments and she smiled. In spite of the brevity of their exchange, Jack saw the hint of something in her face. He couldn't help but wonder if it could be fear.

The group arrived in the pyramid's main chamber to find Admiral Stark and a host of other military and scientific personnel. A monitoring station had been set up to the right of the entrance, positioned behind a transparent blastproof wall. A similar configuration was visible on their left.

Before them, however, was the real star of the show: the portal itself, swirling in that slow, hypnotic fashion. Just as Jack remembered it. He hadn't been back since his very first encounter, but the image of what he had seen and the mystery of who had built it and where it led had stayed with him ever since.

"Does she have everything she needs?" Stark inquired, eyeing Anna up and down.

A soldier approached and handed her an M4 rifle. Anna stared down at the object in confusion and handed it to the first person standing next to her. Unfortunately, that

18

person happened to be Eugene, who took the weapon eagerly.

"Cool!" he exclaimed, looking like a little boy left alone in a toy shop.

His finger was in the process of sliding over the trigger when Grant snatched the rifle out of his hands, the distinguished biologist scowling his disapproval.

"Young man, you were well on your way to shooting yourself or someone else."

"No guns," Jack said. "Not until we know what exactly is on the other side."

One of the techs came and wrapped a rock-climbing cord around Anna's waist, tying off the end with a figure-of-eight knot. He yanked on it a handful of times to ensure it would not come undone. The other end was tied to an electric winch. In an emergency, she could be pulled back to safety.

Dag finished his wrap, licked his fingers and moved in to hug her. The others gathered and did the likewise. Finally it was Jack's turn and he fought to choke down the terrible feeling in his heart that he was never going to see her again.

"Dr. Greer, would you watch Tink while I am away?" He took the mechanical dog in one hand and hugged her with the other.

"See you soon," he assured her, willing himself to believe his own words. Rajesh had asked him to watch over her and here he was sending the man's beloved creation into undeniable danger. But over the guilt came another little voice, one that kept reminding him that her offer to go had really been a selfless act designed to spare the lives of those she cared about. Surely even Rajesh would have been proud.

One of the techs approached with a clipboard, waving an electromagnetic detector over Anna's head and around her torso. "Her bio-mechanical readings are in the green and coming in clearly."

"Good luck," Gabby said, squeezing her arm.

Everyone in the chamber watched Anna head towards the swirling vortex. What looked like a layer of fine mist was being thrown off the hovering object's spin. The closer she got, the fuzzier she became. Jack's heart pounded in his chest as he watched her turn around, wink an eye and then step through.

All at once, Anna's signal flatlined.

"What do you mean she's gone?" Jack said. His worst nightmare was coming true.

"She was fine going in," the tech replied, his panicked fingers swiping back and forth. "Then, nothing."

Another technician activated the winch to reel her back in. But they could all see the rope was loose, tangling as it attempted to spool. What remained of the cord emerged from the portal a moment later, the ends frayed. Jack swore, threw on his helmet and ran for the portal before anyone could stop him. He caught the faint sound of Gabby's terrified voice shouting after him. A violent burst of pastels assaulted his optical nerves. He pushed forward, a buzzing sound growing in his ears and building to a painful pitch. The first step had been the easiest, but wherever he was going it seemed he would need to force his way through, like a child pushing out of its mother's womb. He felt a giant pair of hands shove him from behind and all at once he lost his balance, his forward motion arrested by a rather inglorious faceplant

20

on the ground. Jack stood and wiped at his visor, his own breathing heavy in his ears. He spun in amazement and confusion. He had stepped into the looking glass. But even so, the sight before him was hard to believe.

Chapter 5

Kay Mahoro stood in line to get a loaf of bread, a carton of milk and a jar of peanut butter. Wasn't much of a list, she realized, looking down at it. Short as the list was, she was doubtful they would even have anything left by the time her turn came around. She'd been waiting three hours already, baking in the hot D.C. mid-afternoon sunshine. In all that time the line had barely moved a full block. Which left at least three more to go.

While Salzburg had been difficult and in several cases deadly for the human population, for farm animals around the country, the chromosomal disorder had proven downright disastrous. Millions of cows, pigs and chickens had been destroyed out of hand, days before there was any sign that some had begun to recover. Not that it mattered much. No one wanted to get milk from a cow who was seen as sick. At least, that was the general attitude as it stood a week ago. Today, however, Kay was more than certain any of the desperate people in this line would not bat an eye at the prospect. Was the cow still alive? Well, then that was all that mattered.

That very human tendency toward knee-jerk reactions had also led to a serious run on the banks as folks worried they might lose access to their money. Ironically, the mass of withdrawals that had followed had all but triggered their worst fears. And not only in America. The same had happened in China, India and nearly every other industrialized—and even semi-industrialized—country. Those nations still tied to an old agrarian way of life were the least affected. Over there, if the family cow got sick, you didn't kill it, you tried to heal it. And in many cases that worked, or seemed to when the poor creature emerged from its stupor and came back healthier than ever.

The third pillar to show serious signs of cracking in the western world had been the food supply. Most never really appreciated that upwards of seventy percent of the goods and items we consumed were delivered by truck. With a massive shortage of labor and streets jammed with people in cars attempting to flee to the country, it was only natural that catastrophic disruptions were bound to take place.

Kay couldn't help remembering her days as a college freshman studying classics, a full semester before she'd transferred into journalism. One thing from those early days studying Carthage and Rome had stayed with her. Two thousand years ago, Rome was a bustling metropolis of over a million people. But the surrounding countryside didn't grow enough grain to feed such a massive population. So Egypt, then part of the empire, was tasked with picking up the slack. On account of the fertile lands around the Nile, the area was known as Rome's breadbasket. It was during a time of turmoil in the capital that a shrewd general named Vespasian used this to his advantage. He threatened to cut off the grain supply because he understood one very important truth. If you controlled the food, you controlled Rome.

Two thousand years later society was still skating along that thin line between order and chaos. Sure, there were

23

police and National Guard troops protecting the grocery stores and rationing out what remained. But even Kay knew it was only a question of time before that veneer of civility disappeared and a full breakdown occurred. The thread that bound the sweater of civilization might be holding, but it was frayed.

During her meeting with Sentinel's mystery man, Kay had been told in no uncertain terms to let this go. Without intending to, Kay had done their bidding, releasing false information that had helped indict five members of President Taylor's cabinet and put Secretary Myers, a Sentinel operative, into the Oval Office. There was still no telling what would happen to the cabinet members falsely accused of conspiracy, nor to President Taylor, still in a coma following the attack on Marine One. With only days remaining before the doomsday ship arrived, there simply wasn't enough time for proper trials, and certainly not enough time for Taylor to wake up and take back control of the country. That left Sentinel's man in charge, which in more ways than one meant Sentinel was in charge. Given the propaganda going around, Kay had heard two-thirds of the country was now against contact with an extraterrestrial race and, by extension, in favor of blasting the hell out of the incoming spaceship. Would knowing what had really happened make a difference in people's minds? She wasn't convinced it would. But either way, this was still a democracy and the people deserved to know the truth.

That was precisely the reason Kay had decided to write an article blowing the lid off the entire Sentinel conspiracy—a full exposé on how Sentinel had masterminded one of the most brazen coups in modern history. Of course they had threatened to embarrass her father with lies about sexual improprieties. She knew that wouldn't work. They'd tried it with her and had failed and her father was made of much tougher stuff by far. She had finished the article earlier today and fired it off to the newsroom right before she'd come to stand in this breadline from hell.

Kay was in the middle of sending an email when her phone rang. It was the newsroom editor, Ron Lewis.

"Please don't ask me to reveal my sources," she said preemptively.

"I just got out of a meeting with legal," he said in his usual curt and rather insensitive tone. "We can't run your story."

Kay felt the breath catch in her throat. "Excuse me? You can't run my... why the hell not?"

"From a legal point of view, the risk to the paper would be far too great."

"Legal?" Kay repeated, incredulous with what she was hearing. "Ron, it's possible in a few days there won't be a paper at all. I've just given you a conspiracy that's bigger than Watergate and the JFK assassination put together and you tell me you're worried about getting sued. Do you realize that by even writing that story, I've put my entire family at risk?"

"It's not a lawsuit we're worried about," he replied, cutting right through everything else she'd just said.

"Then what is it?"

"In the last week alone the government's put an injunction on five newspapers and two television stations."

The line advanced a few feet and Kay followed along, switching the phone to her other ear and trying her damned best to stay calm. "I heard about that. They were tiny backwoods news outlets, Ron, I don't see—"

"They were a proof of concept," Ron shouted back, stopping her short. "The government wanted to see if they could get away with it or whether a federal judge would have the balls to stop them, especially given what's going on. Predictably, everyone's so busy looking for aliens they weren't paying attention. Now I hear the White House is ready to put the kibosh on any news outfit that doesn't toe the line. CBS, NBC, the *New York Times*, they're all just one unflattering story away from being shuttered."

"I got lab results on the missile debris they found mingled in with the president's downed helicopter that proves some of the missiles were from a Ukrainian military base. This wasn't some half-baked plot cooked up by a bunch of disgruntled cabinet members. It was the work of an international organization desperate to unseat an existing president in order to further their own aims. The *Post* has faced bullies before. Remember Nixon and the Watergate story. We almost didn't run that for fear of losing the paper, but we did and we were proven right."

"I don't know," Ron said, stubborn as always.

All the same, there was a strange quality in his voice. On some level, she couldn't explain, she sensed she was getting through to him. She just needed to push a little harder.

"What about the truth, Ron?" she said. "Isn't that why we got in this business in the first place? It's one of the reasons I begged, pleaded to trade my lifestyle beat for the newsroom. You know my story's bulletproof and that's why you're scared to run it. But just ask yourself one question. Do you really want betraying the *Post* to be the last thing you do on this earth?"

26

"All right, dammit!" he screamed. "We'll run it. But if this goes south it's on your head."

"If this goes south," Kay repeated, "we won't have heads to worry about."

Chapter 6

68 hours, 22 minutes, 45 seconds

Jack spun around, marveling at his exotic surroundings. Not only exotic, but lush. He was standing in a forest. No, forest wasn't the right word. He was standing in a jungle and easily the strangest one he had ever seen. Thick clumps of dragon blood trees rose hundreds of feet into the air on long thin yellow trunks. High above him, giant red and orange palm leaves choked the sky, eagerly soaking in the rays cast from an alien sun. And by all appearances, it was a sun much more powerful than the main sequence variety he knew back on earth. A beam of light bled down through the dense canopy, bathing him in warmth. But it wasn't long before Jack activated his gold-layered visor assembly. The skin on his face was beginning to burn.

Nearby, violet tentacles protruded up from a nearby patch of undergrowth, waving back and forth in a delicate breeze. He approached and they withdrew at once, pulling back into their protective home.

Jack paused to stare down at his now mud-stained biosuit, a consequence of the tumble he'd taken after falling head first through the portal. There was something unusual about this mud. He bent down and scooped some up with the tips of his gloved fingers, examining it. Could it be shimmering? He held it up to the sun's rays and, when that didn't answer the question, spun his back to the light and snapped on his head lamp. Whatever this was, it seemed to be pulsating with light. His eyes were drawn back to the trees. Like the wispy violet strands, they too appeared to be swaying back and forth, the giant photoreceptor leaves flicking up and down like enormous kites. The sight certainly explained the movement they had detected earlier staring through the portal.

"Control, you getting any of this?" he asked, breathless. No reply came, but that was hardly a surprise. There was no sign of Anna either, who he reminded himself had been the very reason for his mad dash into danger. But the sheer majesty of his surroundings had quickly done away with all that. Jack turned back and stared at the portal, now swirling in the opposite direction. On the other side were distorted shapes that didn't look human. "Anna, do you read me?" If she was still in one piece, then Jack was sure she should be getting his signal. Uncertain, he pushed ahead, calling out to her over and over. There was no clear path visible in this world of vibrant fall colors. The ground was also uneven, and Jack found himself scrambling over ten-foot-high berms where the landscape seemed to rise and fall like waves in the deep ocean. Except these waves were covered in dense fronds that glowed magenta and cyan until he approached. Clearly the environment was reacting to his presence, although he wasn't sure just yet whether or not it approved of his intrusion. Jack was breathing hard, pushing aside an assortment of bizarre-looking foliage as he struggled forward.

"Anna, are you there?"

Jack ran his OHMD glasses through every spectrum of light available—infrared and ultraviolet among others—and yet he still wasn't having any luck. The auditory sensors in his suit detected a sound in the distance and played it for him. He stood rooted for a moment, puzzled. It was a crashing sound, like that of a falling tree striking the forest floor. Surely it was too far and too loud to be Anna.

Suddenly Jack felt something pull his right foot from under him. He fell back into a patch of violet wisps, which retracted to safety at once. Worried, Jack stared down where he'd been standing to see a long thin form crawling along the ground. Less than a second later it disappeared into the undergrowth. He scrambled to his feet. Had that been a snake? He wasn't sure, although there had been something even more unusual about the creature. The tail end had been frayed.

Then understanding came all at once. It was the severed end of Anna's rope. He chased after it, stomping through the dense jungle, through beams of light and shadow, trying to catch sight of the cord. A ripple of movement in a patch of yellow bushes to his left caught his eye and Jack bolted in that direction, scrambling over the damp soil. He entered an open space about five feet square and that was when he saw what he was looking for, peeking out from a thicket. He lunged and grabbed it with both hands, working one fist over the other.

A black object buzzed his head, then another. Moments later they returned, hovering ten feet off the ground, red lights blinking. They were the drones Anna had sent in earlier, the ones the science team at Zulu had lost contact with.

"Dr. Greer," a gentle female voice said over the radio. "What are you doing on channel one hundred and eleven?"

He blinked. "I don't know. Maybe the settings got jumbled when I hit the ground on my way in."

Anna stepped out into the clearing. "I thought the plan was to await my return before you entered the portal."

"Your signal cut off as soon as you entered. I was… we were worried you were in trouble."

"I have been collecting specimens," she replied, proudly holding up a handful of colorful leaves.

Jack noticed her feet were caked in shimmering clumps of mud. She followed his eyes, and glanced down at her legs. "The soil here is also most unusual."

Just then a tiny glowing dot whizzed past them. Jack ducked and followed it as it danced out of view.

"Did you see that, Dr. Greer?"

"Of course. What the hell was it?"

"I am not certain. Although I suspect it could be an indigenous lifeform."

"You mean it's an insect of some kind?"

"Perhaps," she replied, thoughtfully. "I have observed them several times already. Normally they remain high up in the canopy." She extended a finger toward the sky. Jack's gaze followed. He squinted, waiting for movement. Once his eyes had adjusted, a series of blinking red lights came into focus. The glare of the sun and the red leaves overhead created the impression they were blinking in and out of existence. The long-distance sensors captured another loud crashing sound, only this time it was closer and recurring at regular intervals.

"Are you getting that?" Jack asked, tapping the side of his helmet.

"I am. Perhaps it is another lifeform," she said excitedly.

"Yeah, well, if it is, it doesn't sound very happy." Jack looked around, realizing he was completely lost. "Any chance you can point us to the portal?"

Anna's synthetic brow furrowed as she scanned the jungle. "Over there," she said, pointing to the southwest. Jack quickly grabbed the loose rock-climbing rope and tied the remainder around her waist. The last thing he wanted was to be hard-charging toward the exit only to see it get snagged. With that sorted, they set off at a brisk pace, the sound of heavy footfalls growing closer every second.

"Head left," Anna told him.

Jack did so, distinctly aware he could now feel the ground trembling beneath his feet. Up ahead, he spotted the portal. Before, it had been a scientific mystery, but now it was nothing less than a ticket home.

"It is getting closer," Anna said. Her excitement at meeting the natives seemed to be dimming.

"No shit." Jack glanced behind him as they ran, and the sight made his eyes bulge with fear. The yellow trunks of trees were being pushed aside like blades of grass. Whatever this was, it was very big and very pissed off. The drones hovering above tore off toward the creature, which was now less than thirty feet away. Anna's aim was to distract it and for a moment it seemed to be working. That was until the sound of crunching plastic made it clear the drones were no more.

Seconds later, they arrived at the doorway, the giant creature close behind, clomping through the alien jungle intent on making a meal out of them as it had done with the drones. Both Jack and Anna stood rooted in horror, mesmerized with the promise of what they might see. And then for only the briefest flash, Jack glimpsed a dark, lumbering shape webbed in shadow and the sight of its enormity drew deep fingernails of fear along the top of his skull. In a single motion, he pushed Anna into the portal before leaping in after her.

Chapter 7

65 hours, 50 minutes, 33 seconds

They emerged into a chaotic world of flashing yellow emergency lights and booming voices.

"Prepare decontamination protocol," Admiral Stark shouted as two techs in hazmat suits advanced with mobile sprayers.

Jack rose to his feet and saw that they had returned to the chamber, but that a protective glass barrier had been erected around the portal. He was in the middle of helping Anna off the floor when the techs rushed in. Jack threw up a hand and told them to back down. Anna's left hand was still clutching the strange-looking leaves she'd collected and both of them still bore clumps of alien mud splattered up to their ankles.

"We need sample kits right away," Jack told them. The techs drew to a stop and looked back at Admiral Stark. After a moment's hesitation, Stark motioned for them to do as Jack had instructed.

Ten minutes later, with samples taken and the remaining contaminants neutralized, Jack and Anna were escorted to a Quonset hut with a sign reading "Command Center" hung over the door. Inside, key scientific and military personnel had gathered for the debriefing. Locked in utter fascination, the group watched a recording Jack had taken with his OHMD as well as video captured by Anna's drones.

"Where the bloody hell did you go?" Grant asked, mystified.

Jack shook his head. "I wish I could tell you."

"The ecology is like nothing we've ever seen before," Gabby said.

Dag folded his hands behind his head. "Our first look at an alien world. But why aren't the plants green? Wouldn't they have photosynthesis just like on Earth?"

Gabby shook her head. "Not necessarily. On Earth, chlorophyll reflects green light from our sun. That's why plants are green. Since green light is reflected rather than absorbed, it can't contribute to photosynthesis. A brighter star in another solar system would tend to emit more blue and ultraviolet light. If a planet contained an oxygen atmosphere and ozone layer, they would block the ultraviolet, so that only the blue would penetrate. Thus life on that world would evolve a type of photosynthesis designed to absorb blue light and maybe even green. With the yellow, orange and red light reflected, it would explain why the leaves display what to our eye look like bright fall colors."

"Since each sun displays a unique spectrum of light," Eugene began once Gabby had finished, "if I tinker a little, I might be able to see if Jack's videos can help identify the star the planet's orbiting around."

"That is assuming the star is in our database," Anna interjected.

"Or in our universe," Jack said, folding arms that were still shaking from the encounter.

Everyone grew silent, contemplating the enormity of their challenge.

"Ladies and gentlemen," Stark said, breaking the spell. He jabbed a finger in the air. "We are here for one reason and one reason alone. To stop that ship from landing on our heads. Now if all you found over there was a bunch of funny-looking plants, then it seems to me we might as well start digging holes for each other."

Anna's gaze flicked between Jack and the others. "We witnessed more than 'funny-looking plants,'" she told them. "There were at least two distinct life forms, although there is no way to be certain whether or not either of them was intelligent."

Gabby, Stark and the others straightened in their chairs. "Don't you think that's kind of an important detail to leave out?" Dag asked, his lips parted with incredulity.

Jack took in a deep breath. "I was going to mention it. I just don't know exactly what it was we saw."

He played the end of the recording where the creature chased them through the deep foliage. They must have paused and replayed the final bit a hundred times. Grant rose and went to the screen, squinting.

"Whatever it is, it doesn't look very friendly if you ask me," Gabby said, tucking in her chin and grabbing her elbows.

"Based on the information we were able to obtain," Anna told them, "I estimate the creature's height at upwards of twenty-five feet tall and its weight at thirty thousand pounds."

"Holy crap!" Dag shouted, jumping up and pacing back and forth. "You got chased by a frickin' T-Rex, man."

"Dr. Gustavsson, I did not know you were a religious man," Anna said, not trying to be funny. Her confusion grew when the room erupted in laughter.

"Chalk it up to a lost-in-translation moment, Anna," Gabby said, smiling at her.

Anna shook her head as though to say, *Humans are a perplexing species.* Instead what came out of her mouth was, "Dr. Greer and I also observed what we believe was another independently mobile species."

"Those flying red dots?" one of the other scientists present asked.

"Correct. We nicknamed them wisps. When the creature stopped, it revealed a distinct shape ideal for flight. Here on earth we would refer to such a creature as an insect."

"I'm less worried about bugs," Stark admitted, "than I am with solutions to saving the lives of seven billion people."

"Look," Jack reminded them, "we don't know what we saw over there or even where that doorway sent us. But here's what we do know, on the other side of that portal there is more than one lifeform. For all we know, we just got ourselves a ticket to the Atean home world."

"You think they're over there, waiting to meet us?" Gabby asked, breathless.

"I hope they are," he replied. "For our sake."

Just then the door to the briefing room swung open. When Jack saw who it was, he leapt to his feet.

"Mia," he said, shocked and elated all at once.

Then Jack caught sight of the man she was with, tall and gangly, wearing the kind of smile that was just begging to be punched off his face.

"Everyone," she said, "this is Alan Salzburg."

Chapter 8

Kay's story struck home like a thunderous blow from Thor's hammer. That the chaos and lawlessness gripping the country was not nearly enough to dull the impact of the disturbing truth she had revealed was an even greater surprise. The calls and emails started flooding in minutes after it had been posted online. To say that it was an exclusive was a colossal understatement. While most news outlets were chasing after the government's supposedly defunct bunker program, Kay had put one right between the White House's eyes. The best part? This hadn't been a hit piece against a Republican or a Democrat. In fact, she wasn't even sure what party Myers belonged to. Taylor had been a Democrat, but it wasn't unheard of, even in today's day and age, to have a member from the other party in your cabinet. Still, some would call political foul. Kay was confident, however, that the facts about the sheer size and scope of the Sentinel conspiracy would speak for themselves.

Her new office was right outside Ron Lewis', a piece of prime real estate for any up-and-coming reporter. Not that it mattered to Kay's father. He didn't understand why she continued to come to work when time was running out. She had asked him about the brave folks who served the police, the fire department and even the military. Should they throw down their equipment and head home? Certainly some had, but thankfully, the majority had felt a strong enough sense of duty to stay. Leaning forward in her office chair, Kay grabbed her cell and called home.

"Kayza!" Felix exclaimed. "This is your father speaking. Why are you not home?"

She laughed. "I know who it is, Dad. I called you. I'm working."

"Derek and his family are here. Your mother and I are so very excited. There is much to do."

Kay was startled. "I thought Derek and his family were heading up to their cabin in the mountains?"

"There has been a change of plan. Therese spoke with Derek's mother and convinced her to join us."

"Dad, let me speak with Derek."

The sound of shuffling and muffled voices.

"Kay?" her fiancé Derek's smooth voice asked.

"What's going on? I thought you guys were heading out of town and that your mother was going to talk my parents into joining you."

"I know, babe, but things got turned around. I never knew your mom was such an eloquent speaker."

"There are a lot of things about my mom that are surprising these days." Kay drew in a heavy breath. "So your folks are holing up at our place?"

"Not even," Derek said. She could hear him smiling on the other end of the phone. "Seems we're all gonna head to the church. Please tell me you're planning on joining us. I don't care where we are as long as we're together."

Kay felt a hand close around her heart and squeeze. "I feel the same way." The thought of abandoning the paper right when the full impact of her story was hitting home stirred something inside of her. There would be interviews on CNN and the other networks, each of them vying for a soundbite they could play in an endless loop. But the truth was, none of that stuff was her strength. Maybe that was a job for folks who were less camera-shy.

She felt the words on the tip of her tongue and wasn't sure she'd be able to speak them.

Go on, you can do it.

"All right, honey," she said, hearing herself say the words as though from a great distance. "Let me wrap up here and I'll come home for good."

Derek told her he loved her and they hung up. Kay collapsed onto her desk.

Was that really so hard?

Yes. Yes, it had been.

***

Two hours later, after Kay had packed up her things from the office and said her goodbyes, she pulled up to the house in her tired, silver Corolla. Derek's Mustang was in the driveway, along with her parents' car. As much as her work had given her purpose and a sense of fulfillment, Kay had to admit the idea of huddling close to the people she loved in these last few days was a welcome one. She took a final wistful look around the neighborhood before going inside. The resemblance to the street she knew growing up was long gone. Several of the houses across the street looked abandoned, their windows storm-shuttered against a hurricane that was already in their midst. She imagined these were folks who had fled from the city, planning to return once the situation returned to normal. Not that anyone really expected that to happen.

Kay was reaching the front step of her parents' house when she had a strange sensation, like a duck feather tickling at the back of her neck. She pushed her way inside, expecting to hear the raucous noise of a house filled with joy and laughter. Her father loved to entertain. He was always pushing drinks on his guests and regaling them with comical stories from Kay's childhood, like the time she found her father's checkbook at eight years of age and wrote her mother a check for millions of dollars. "If I had that sort of money, do you think I would still be living in a house that was falling apart?" he would say, always the same punchline with the exact same delivery. She'd heard it more times than she cared to count and yet it still never got old. But now, walking into that once-vibrant family home, Kay wasn't hearing anything at all. "Hello, Papa?" she called out. "Mama, are you there?" The sound of each creak as she moved throughout the house seemed to grow louder, mirroring her deepening sense of concern. It was only when she reached the kitchen that she knew that something was very wrong. Two of the chairs had been knocked over, along with the bucket her father had placed to catch water dripping from that leaky pipe he'd never fixed.

Kay pulled out her phone at once and dialed Derek's number. It rang three times before she noticed a faint version of his ringtone trickling down from upstairs. "Derek?" she shouted, charging up the stairs two at a time, tracking the sound of his ringing phone. She reached the top riser and turned left toward her parents' bedroom before correcting herself and heading back in the other direction. Finally, she reached the source of the sound and stopped. It was coming from inside the bathroom.

"Derek," she called out, more of a pleading whisper now than the panicked cry from a moment ago. She pushed open the door, hoping he would be there, washing his hands, but another part of her was hoping she wouldn't find him. The bathroom curtains were closed, and the room was dim, but there was more than enough light for her to see the body slumped over the tub and submerged up to its shoulders. Derek's phone was on the bathroom counter still ringing. It clicked to voicemail and she could hear the faint thread of his voice asking her to leave a message.

"Oh, no, Derek, no," she shrieked, breaking free of her paralysis and rushing in. She pulled his head out of the water and dragged him into the hallway by one arm. Her years as a lifeguard had taught her how to save someone who was drowning. But it had been years since she'd gone through the certification. She turned him over onto his side, as autopilot kicked in. She had to get the water out of his lungs. Next, she checked for a pulse and swore when she didn't find one.

"Stay with me, Derek!" she cried out, beginning CPR and chest compressions. His lips were so cold they stung. Whenever she blew air into his lungs they made a hissing sound. In the movies, it didn't take more than a few pumps of a victim's chest cavity before they were coughing up water and asking what had happened. But this wasn't happening now and Kay was becoming more and desperate. She grabbed her phone, set it on the floor next to her and dialed the police as she repeated the entire CPR procedure again.

A busy signal belched back at her.

"You've got to be kidding me."

That was when she noticed that her hands were soaked in blood. Her head swiveled back toward the bathroom and she saw a trail of it, soaked into the crumpled bathmat and leading into the hallway. She lifted Derek's shirt and noticed a series of puncture holes in the side of

42

his chest. Derek was far too strong for this to be the work of one person, so whoever had done this had also stabbed him in the ribs with what looked like an icepick. She examined his face and saw bruises. He had clearly put up a fight and paid for it with his life.

Had Kay been thinking clearly, she might have run from the house the minute she saw the body. The killer could still be here. That was the difference between real life and imagination. But right now Kay wasn't thinking about danger. She was thinking about the man she loved, the man she'd been ready to marry and how that man was lying before her, dead.

Slowly, as her mind tried to squeeze past the colossal pain of her loss, another thought began to seep in. This one had to do with her mother and father. She struggled up onto a pair of wobbly legs and checked the rest of the house, not sure her mind could handle the prospect of finding any more bodies. That she was thankfully spared. Only Derek had been left behind. Which led to dozens of questions blossoming before Kay's tear-streaked eyes. Were they still alive? And if so, where had they been taken?

Chapter 9

Mia removed her heavy parka, set it on the bench next to her and rubbed her hands together in anticipation. "I am absolutely starving," she said as Jack approached with two steaming plates of food. They were in the mess hut at the base camp. Behind them, a hot buffet table was serving beef stew, shepherd's pie and chicken noodle soup. She had ordered the beef stew while Jack had opted for the soup. The mess hall was filled with three long rows of cafeteria-style tables. Other groups of techs, scientists and military personnel sat eating, others quietly chatting.

"Is that all you're gonna have?" she asked, suddenly feeling like a glutton.

He grinned, tiny dimples forming at his cheeks. "My stomach's still getting used to traveling across space and time," he replied, referring to his recent visit to the alien jungle.

She mirrored his expression. "Still no word on what planet or dimension you went to?"

He shook his head and then blew on his soup before sliding the spoon in his mouth.

She laughed. "My daughter Zoey does that."

He watched her, perhaps noticing the effort she was putting in to keeping herself together. "How was she when you saw her at the motel outside Richmond?"

"Not good, but I've heard she's coming around and this time without any relapses. Some patients appear to shrug off the early stages of Salzburg while others linger in the earliest, most devastating effects."

Jack set his spoon down and glanced around. "I'll admit, I was surprised to see you. Pleasantly, mind you, but surprised all the same. But I was downright shocked to see who you arrived with."

"You mean Alan?" she replied, almost guiltily.

"I thought you said he was dead."

"So did I. I won't deny, a big part of me hoped he was."

"How did he find you?"

"Find me?" she said, exasperated. "He's the one who put me up to this in the first place. Running from country to country, getting chased by gunmen and chasing leads. In Rome, he had me arrested as a pretext for bringing me here. Even told me he was going to have Ollie killed." Her eyes welled up with tears and she clenched them shut. "President Myers has apparently put him in charge of the entire operation. He wants me to continue my research. That's what he was after all along, a breakthrough, but he thought I needed incentivizing."

"By threatening to have you killed? That makes no sense."

"What can I say? He's a sick man and would probably be in prison somewhere if he wasn't so brilliant."

"I think you give that creep far too much credit." Jack sipped at his water and felt it tickle his stomach. "What do you think he's really after?"

"A cure," Mia said, hopeful.

"Oh, come on, you know that's bullshit. He's using you, just like he's always used you."

Mia became indignant. "Yeah, well, have you considered the fact that I may be using him too?"

Jack grew quiet. No, he hadn't considered that. "Who are the twins you were with?"

"Sofia and Noemi. They were part of a study Dr. Putelli was conducting. They're the first reported cases of patients with all eight of the Salzburg genes."

"So a third of the population has twenty-four chromosomes while the rest of us are running around with twenty-three. I feel an inferiority complex coming on."

Mia grinned. "I don't blame you. Like so many others, these girls have passed through the earliest gene expression—weak skeletal structure, speechlessness, vulnerability to the sun, among others. Then suddenly, the dominant genes in Salzburg began to kick in."

"The ones in the 48th chromatid?"

"Right. We didn't know it at the time, but the genes in the 47th chromatid were recessive. In the beginning those were the only ones manifesting. Then as new blast waves kept coming, the 48th chromatid and the dominant genes began to appear."

Jack shook his head. "That would certainly explain what we've seen in Grant. He went from a frail man in his sixties with blotchy skin to a bronzed triathlete in a matter of days. Not to mention the healing."

"Healing?" Mia asked, her curiosity piqued.

"He was shot twice by the Israelis. Took one in the gut and another in the wrist and within twenty-four hours he was running around like nothing had happened."

"That's a gene in the 48th called *MRE11*," Mia told him. "It acts like a janitor in a high-rise apartment complex, running around repairing errors in our DNA."

"Yeah, except this janitor's on coke and working overtime."

The corners of her lips rose as she giggled.

"It sounds to me from what you're saying," Jack observed, "that at least half of these changes aren't half bad. I'm starting to feel sorry I never came down with Salzburg myself." He remembered Mia's daughter and realized he'd stepped out of line. "I'm sorry, I didn't mean that."

"No it's okay. You know, Ollie was convinced the Ateans were preparing the human race to become slaves, mining rare and dangerous elements off asteroids, or something along those lines."

The thought ricocheted around inside the confines of Jack's mind. "It does make a certain amount of sense, but when the team discovered the ship in the Gulf, we had a very similar conversation and Gabby brought up a good point. If the Ateans really were after resources, why bother messing with a planet brimming with violent natives when the galaxy is chock full of everything you could possibly need?" Jack paused and picked up his spoon again, stirring his soup in slow circles, watching the liquid become a tiny whirlpool. "I sure do hope he's wrong." He glanced up. "Does the fact that the two little girls are twins have any bearing?"

Mia nodded. "I believe it might. In Kolkata, Dr. Jansson and I realized that women with Salzburg who became pregnant invariably gave birth to twins."

"In each case?" Jack asked, surprised.

"In every one we've come across. Sometimes they're triplets or quadruplets, but these women never give birth to a single infant."

"That's kind of creepy."

"Believe me, shivers ran up my arms when we made the connection."

"Were you able to tie it to Salzburg?"

"Anecdotally, yes, but we were never able to draw a clear causal link. My guess is it has something to do with the fourth and final gene in the 48th chromatid. It's called *HOK3* and affects the parahippocampal gyrus in the cerebral cortex. That's why the twins are here."

"Affects the gyrus how?"

Mia looked away. "I'm not sure yet. But when Ollie and I found the young girls in the asylum—"

Jack's eyes grew wide. "Asylum?"

"Dr. Putelli had sent them there for evaluation. They complained about hearing voices and he thought they might be suffering from a psychiatric episode."

"Were they?"

"No, but the alternative was even crazier."

"Crazier than Grant suddenly being able to bench three hundred pounds? Try me."

"The girls are exhibiting signs of…" Mia paused before tossing the word out like a stone heated in a blazing fire. "Telepathy."

Jack became visibly uncomfortable. "As in via electronic implants? I read an article not long ago about that sort of thing."

"We looked into that. The girls haven't been operated on. When one of them forms a thought, the other seems

48

to instantaneously know it too. I know it sounds way out there, but I'm convinced there's a scientific explanation."

"Do you mean explaining it away with science or understanding how it might work?"

"The latter. You think I've lost it, haven't you?"

Jack cocked his left eyebrow. "Let me put it to you this way. Five hundred yards beyond this mess hall, there's something that looks like a swirling black hole, a black hole I voluntarily stepped into, so the idea that two people might be able to read each other's thoughts doesn't sound all that farfetched to me. Least not anymore. Whatever's happening here, we're dealing with a civilization that is clearly hundreds, thousands and maybe even millions of years older than ours. Can you imagine what the first farmers in Mesopotamia ten thousand years ago might have thought if they saw a jet fighter or even a helicopter?"

"They would have thought they were seeing God."

Jack nodded. "Or the Devil."

Chapter 10

After they had eaten, Jack returned to Northern Star to see if Gabby and Eugene had made any headway with their analysis of the portal. Admiral Stark had ordered that any further exploration be put on hold until they had devised an appropriate game plan. They were dealing with an alien ecosystem inhabited by an unknowable array of creatures. And thus far, at least one of those had revealed itself to be terrifyingly aggressive. Then rumors began to circulate that Alan Salzburg was calling in a highly specialized team to accompany them. Needless to say, the deadly efficient operators from both SEAL Team 8 and Delta already present didn't take the news very well. With this new team set to arrive anytime now, Jack steeled himself for the inevitable return to that alien world and whatever else might await them there.

As expected, Jack found Gabby, Eugene and Anna in the astrophysics lab, hunched over a computer monitor.

"Find anything yet?" he asked, causing Gabby to jump. "Sweet Jesus, you scared me," she said, leaning back and clutching her heart.

Standing by Anna's heel was Tink, who greeted Jack with a friendly yap.

"We're studying the portal," Eugene informed him. "Trying to figure out what it is and how it works."

"My guess is it's been swirling in place for millions of years," Jack said, leaning in to see if he could make sense of their results.

"You may be right," Eugene continued. "But it's been difficult to get any reliable readings."

Jack's brow scrunched up. "Why's that?"

"According to our instruments, the amount of electromagnetic radiation emanating from the object is truly astounding," Gabby said, swiveling in her chair. "Truth be told, it should be frying anything that gets within a few hundred yards. But something inherent in the portal itself is preventing that."

"Or pulling it inward," Eugene added. "The gravitational readings are off the chart. For all intents and purposes, the portal is behaving more like a singularity than a doorway."

"Singularity," Jack repeated, the words rolling off his tongue slow and deliberate. "You're saying this thing is like a black hole."

Eugene motioned emphatically. "Not like, Jack, it is one. But whoever created it also made sure it wouldn't destroy the planet."

Gabby stood and rubbed her swollen knees. "And here's where things get really weird. Along with black holes, Einstein also theorized the existence of white holes. So while a black hole's gravity prevents objects from escaping, a white hole prevents them from entering. In one end and out the other, right? But that's nothing more than a one-way ticket. The beings who created this portal managed to allow it to operate in both directions."

"It's a white and black hole all rolled into one?" Jack said, marveling at the idea.

"Perfect racial harmony," Eugene said with a smile.

"Except how on earth did they do it?" Jack said, thinking out loud.

Anna turned to him. "Dr. Greer, the answer may lie with another reading Dr. Bishop and Dr. Jarecki obtained. When we were away, they pumped the air out of the decontamination chamber to create a vacuum and brought in electromagnets and an exahertz laser. The spikes in X-ray emissions we detected have led us to believe we may be dealing with a new particle, one currently unknown to science."

"This could be the big one, Jack," Eugene said, practically vibrating.

Jack's head tilted slightly with confusion. "You talking about the graviton?"

"No, dark energy."

Jack walked to the window on a pair of wobbly legs. He stared out at the blowing snow, watching it glide along the ground like a pack of restless spirits. For years scientists had sought an ever-evasive unifying theory that sought to explain the world of the large and the world of the very small. But as important as that might be, dark energy and dark matter were widely considered the Holy Grail of physics. Could it be humanity was on the cusp of perhaps the greatest scientific discovery in history a piddling handful of days before the world was meant to end? The cruel irony was difficult to bear.

Anna approached from behind and placed a gentle hand on his shoulder. "Are you all right, Dr. Greer?"

He looked over and then back out the window. "I'm

fine, Anna. Worried, but fine." Jack was busy considering how such a momentous discovery might be made to work in their favor when he spotted a large cargo plane touch down on the icy runway. It seemed Alan Salzburg's team of specialists had finally arrived.

Chapter 11

Jack and the others watched as men dressed in dark blue parkas and matching coveralls filed past with a series of large crates.

"What's Volkov Industries?" Gabby asked, reading the bold white letters stenciled on the back of their jackets.

"I'm not sure," Jack replied, concerned. "Never heard of them."

"They sure do have a lot of equipment though," Eugene said, running a hand across his brow, as though tired from merely watching the work they were doing.

One of Stark's military men was waving them on.

"Where's all this stuff going?" Gabby asked him.

"The library in the social module," he said. "These folks needed a base of operations, so they removed all the books."

"Yeah, great," Eugene said with stinging sarcasm. "Who needs books anyway, right?"

The two largest crates were the last to arrive. A strange whirring sound signaled their journey down the engineering corridor and into the social module. Metal poles projected from both ends of the narrow crate and fixed onto a robotic pack animal at either end, their rubber-padded feet thudding into the floor as they went by. An array of sensors in the robots' heads guided them forward. It almost looked like a litter carried by slaves during the Roman Empire. Which only magnified the question. What was in those crates?

"You don't see that every day," Jack observed, scratching his head.

Even Anna's eyes grew wide at the sight. "Hello," she said to one of the pack mules as the second case thundered by. But the robotic animal didn't flinch. Anna's digital mouth turned into a frown.

Jack put an arm around her and smiled. "Kids at school ignoring you?"

"School?" Anna asked, confused.

"Figure of speech."

"What do you think this is all about?" Gabby asked.

"I'm not sure," Jack replied, "but I'm about to find out."

•••

Not surprisingly, the former library, which was now the de facto headquarters for Volkov Industries, was a hive of frantic activity. What was less remarkable, given the company's name, was that everyone wearing those dark blue coveralls was speaking in Russian.

"You should not be here," said a squat man in blue cammies. He stood about five foot five, sporting a shaved head and the tortured face of a pug. "This area is off limits."

"What seems to be the problem?" asked a young man in a hoodie and jeans. Hardly a day over thirty, he had the air of a Silicon Valley brat, or whatever passed for one in Russia. "Dimitri, that's enough. We are all on the same team." That last word sounded more like 'tim' than 'tēm.'

"Yuri Volkov," he said, waving Dimitri away and offering Jack his hand.

They shook.

"You're into robotics?" Jack said, at the risk of stating the obvious.

"Among other things," Yuri replied with no shortage of mystery. The tech geek's eyes flickered over Jack's shoulder. "And what, may I ask, is your name?"

"Anna," she replied shyly. "And this is Tink." She held the dog up, its mechanical tail wagging. "I think she likes you."

"Then Tink is a wonderful judge of character." Yuri grinned, his teeth about as white and straight as the keys on a baby grand. He turned back to Jack. "Is it yours?"

"Anna is a she, not an it," he replied, noting this wasn't the first time he had had to explain the simple concept that she wasn't an iPhone or a smartwatch.

"Of course. It's amazing how much we tend to project personalities onto our creations." Yuri clapped him on the shoulder. "But Jack, my friend, rest assured we're not here to compete with one another. If we manage to find a way out of this mess, I have a chain of hotels in Moscow. A model like Anna would make a great front desk clerk or maybe even a maid." Jack's cheeks must have flushed at the suggestion because Yuri's expression shifted. "Now, if there is nothing else I can do for you…"

"I hope everyone's getting along," a resonating voice called out from behind Jack. He turned to find Alan Salzburg flanked by two men in black suits. "Yuri, I want to thank you again for accepting the president's offer. Your expertise is precisely what we need." He rotated.

"Anna, is it?"

She nodded, a look of uncertainty on her face.

"You will make a great addition to Yuri's team."

"Pardon me," Jack cut in. "Anna already has a team and we're it. Besides, she can decide for herself."

Alan smiled. It had all the hallmarks of a caring expression but without any of the warmth. "I'm afraid that following Rajesh's passing, MIT is now Anna's sole custodian and arbiter of her fate. And I happen to have a letter from them giving President Myers and the United States government full discretion in her use and deployment. Which is another way of saying that I get to decide where she goes and what work she'll do."

Jack felt the rage bubble up through his gut and down his arms. The fingers of his right hand closed into a tight fist, one he had every intention of using to smash Alan's face in. The security men behind him saw Jack's anger and tensed, as though preparing for his attack.

That was when three chimes sounded over the intercom. "Could all essential personnel please report to the mess hall in Northern Star at once. I repeat, all essential personnel. Thank you."

The corner of Jack's mouth rose as he and Alan locked eyes. "Saved by the bell."

Chapter 12

Kay was in her car, heading to the local police station as quickly as her rickety old Corolla could get her there. Normally that meant a ten-minute drive, but it felt to Kay like the trip was taking forever. But the sense of distorted time was understandable. She was still reeling from finding Derek's body slumped over the bathtub, an image she was starting to think she would never be able to erase for as long as she lived. Uncertain what to do, she had opted to cover him with a white bed sheet and inform the police of his murder.

She knew right away they would ask her if Derek had any enemies who might want to take advantage of the current social unrest to exact revenge. And she also knew exactly what she would tell them. Sentinel had done it. There was no doubt in her mind. Of course, there was no telling how they might react to her claim that a shadowy group had killed her boyfriend and kidnapped her parents. Nor what they could possibly do about it. If the perpetrators were not in question, then neither was the motive. Blowback from Kay's article. She had made that connection the minute she found the house empty. The man she'd met that night at the warehouse in Washington had threatened to turn her loved ones into social pariahs if she refused to play ball. That was one of the reasons her father had decided to leave the family home and set up with his flock at the church.

She had gone straight there after leaving her house only to find the congregation waiting for them in vain. They had bombarded her with a million frantic questions. The flock was missing their shepherd and she sympathized with the fright and despair they must be feeling. That was why she hadn't told them about Derek. She wasn't sure she could speak the words without falling apart. But she also knew such news would throw these people into a full-blown panic. Her father always sought to calm and reassure his congregation, so that was what she did.

Pulling into the police station, Kay was immediately struck by how few cop cars were around. At any one time, the small parking lot normally held a dozen or so patrol cars, officers coming and going on a regular basis. A sign on the front door read:

This entrance no longer in use. If you have an emergency, dial 911.

"I did, dammit, and got nothing but a busy tone."

Then she saw the Bristol board next to the entrance. Normally it was for internal police use, reminders about meetings along with a few community outreach posters. What Kay saw in its place went beyond frightening. Dozens, maybe even hundreds of pictures of missing people spilling over the board onto the wall beyond it. Soon even that space would prove insufficient. The dates on many of them were within the last three days. Some of the notices were for friends who had fled D.C. without informing everyone. But even with that latitude, Kay had the uneasy feeling something else was going on.

A young woman in her twenties struggling with a double-wide baby carriage appeared next to Kay. She reached up to a vacant spot on the wall and taped a picture there.

"Is that your husband?" Kay asked.

The woman's face began to shift. "Have you seen him?"

"No, I'm sorry, I haven't. I'm looking for my parents." She paused, noticing the twins in the carriage didn't look more than a few weeks old. "May I ask what happened?"

The woman pressed a tissue to her swollen eyes. "He went to stand in line at the grocery store to get us something to eat and never came back. I called his phone a thousand times. Now it goes straight to voice mail."

"Have you spoken to the police yet?"

"I tried," she said, her eyes shimmering with tears. "I can't get a hold of anyone and every time I've shown up to report him missing, no one answers the door. That's probably why people started putting up these pictures."

Kay stepped back, eyeing a wall filled with desperation and fear, an image made all the more unsettling by the smiling faces staring back at them.

"I need to know if he's still alive," the woman said, her voice quavering. Kay pulled her into a hug and the woman wept. "I need to know he didn't decide to walk away."

"There's no way he would leave you at home with newborn babies," Kay said, trying her best to soothe the woman but knowing she was only one of thousands, perhaps millions who were suffering the same heartache. "If you need something to eat, here's the address to my parents' place. Feel free to take what you need. Just promise you'll only go to the kitchen."

"I promise," the woman said, shocked by Kay's offer. "You would do that for a complete stranger?"

Kay looked at the babies and smiled. "It's what my parents would have done."

The woman left after that, Kay watching her walk away with a growing sense of despair. In a sense, giving away what was left of her parents' food was a subconscious admission she wasn't going to see them again. She knew her father thought nothing of worldly goods and would have insisted on sharing if it meant helping to feed a child in need. But there was something about this wall of the missing that wasn't adding up.

What if Sentinel hadn't been the ones who'd killed Derek and abducted her parents? What if something else was going on, something far worse?

Chapter 13

58 hours, 37 minutes, 15 seconds

"What's got you all hot and bothered?" Mia asked as she grabbed a seat next to Jack in the mess hall. Close to forty other members of the expedition were there, representing a whole of array of scientific disciplines and governmental departments. Close by were the others from Jack's immediate group: Dag, Gabby, Grant, Anna and Eugene. Toward the front of the room, Admiral Stark was busy speaking with Alan and Yuri.

"Your boyfriend's a much bigger prick than I expected him to be," Jack told her, his gaze never wavering from Salzburg's lean, delicate frame.

Mia shook her head and folded her arms over her chest, uncertain for a moment. "Oh, Alan. Just wait until the authorities find out that he basically kidnapped me, not to mention whatever he's done to poor Ollie."

"Good luck with that," Jack shot back, drawing his voice down to a near whisper. "The President of the United States takes orders from the guy. The military may have tried to cut us off from the outside world for national security reasons, but I had Anna gather everything she could find on him. Did you know the *Post* has an article claiming Sentinel pulled off the coup that put Myers in office?"

"Yes, and Alan isn't just a part of Sentinel," Mia corrected him. "He runs it."

"Wow, this keeps getting better. First they try to kill us in the Gulf, now their guy has taken charge of everything and there's nothing any of us can do about it."

"Don't forget, Jack, they've been planning for an eventuality like this for a long time. The world's been gripped by chaos since word of that doomsday ship first made it into the news and they rode that wave right into power."

He was shaking his head before Mia was even done. "If the papers are even half right, Sentinel were the ones who created the wave in the first place by leaking satellite images to the press. They knew exactly how folks would react, how the world markets would tank and how the ensuing unrest would spill out into in the streets."

"Not too different from the Reichstag fire of 1933," Mia said. "Set less than a month after Hitler came to power, it provided him the excuse he needed to increase his authority and outlaw his political rivals. It was a masterstroke and a technique Sentinel was clearly aware of." She paused. "What was the name of that reporter, the one from the *Post* you mentioned?"

Jack thought for a moment.

"Kay Mahoro," Anna jumped in. She had clearly been eavesdropping on what they had thought was a discreet conversation.

Mia's ears perked up. She had heard that name before. "Alan told me about her."

"About the reporter?"

"Yes, he told me he'd met her and that she was feisty and that I would like her. She must have been the one he used to leak the images from Voyager One and the fake video incriminating President Taylor's cabinet."

"So she's working for him?"

Mia shook her head. "I don't think so. The way he spoke about her, it sounded like she'd found out she was being used and decided to blow the whistle."

"After the damage was already done," Jack said, noticing the meeting was about to begin.

"Ladies and gentlemen," Admiral Stark began. "Under the circumstances, I'm going to keep this short. First off, I want to introduce you all to the distinguished geneticist Dr. Alan Salzburg. He's probably best known to many of you as the creator of the human artificial chromosome…"

Mia elbowed Jack in the ribs. Alan seemed to excel at making those around him fantasize about beating him to a pulp. She was the one who had pioneered the discovery of the first artificial chromosome, not him. Mia gritted her teeth, realizing arrogance and taking credit for the work of others was the least of his crimes.

"But more recently," Stark went on, "he's become famous for perhaps one of the most profound medical discoveries of all time, Salzburg syndrome."

Alan raised a hand and waved at those gathered.

"The president has the utmost confidence in Dr. Salzburg," Stark continued, "and has entrusted him with the overall authority for this mission. As part of that mandate, he has invited a team of cutting-edge engineers and scientists to join us."

Yuri Volkov stepped forward and addressed the crowd.

Behind him was a red velvet curtain draped over a bulky object.

"For the first time in human history, we have set foot on an alien world," Yuri announced, holding the mic with both hands. "And I wish I could tell all of you that our mission was purely one of exploration. That might be so, were it not for a crisis of the greatest magnitude, a crisis which threatens the very survival of the human race. In times like these, taking the safe road will only guarantee our demise. We must go boldly and do whatever is necessary to save the lives of future generations. But more than that, we must be prepared to use deadly force in the pursuit of that most noble of endeavors. And with that in mind, I give you IVAN."

An attractive woman standing behind him pulled on a rope, whisking away the red velvet curtain to reveal a frightening creation. The machine whined as it rose up on a hydraulic piston, reaching an imposing height of well over seven feet tall. Its legs were made of rubberized tank treads, its body a titanium composite that appeared at once smooth as well as incredibly strong. From its broad shoulders rose a pair of powerful arms. And at the end of each of those arms were three-fingered clamps which began to rotate. As if to prove the point, the machine extended its arms toward the crowd, opening and closing its twelve-inch pinchers in a series of loud metallic clanks. Protruding from the center of those intimidating clamps were the barrels of high-powered automatic rifles. But it was the robot's menacing face that had really stunned the audience into silence. It had the approximate shape of a knight's helmet, black in color, with heavy metal bars overlaid across the face in diagonal strips. Positioned between each strip, the machine's four piercing red eyes glowed with menace and its fiery red mouth smoldered from behind a vertical metal grate. If Yuri had told them IVAN was really one of the four horsemen, Jack wouldn't have doubted him for a minute.

Anna stared out at it from behind webbed fingers.

"I am IVAN," the robot said in a tinny voice, devoid of any hint of emotion. "Integrated Variable Android Node. Welcome to the future of robotics."

"The future?" Gabby said, looking between Anna and Ivan. "Maybe in the 1950s. That hollow-voiced tin can makes Stephen Hawking sound like Dean Martin."

"The future of combat robotics is probably what they mean," Jack suggested, decidedly uneasy.

But Jack wasn't the only one. Murmurs of concern rippled through the crowd as well. Admiral Stark returned a moment later to address them. "Rest assured, the effort to save the planet is well underway on all fronts. I've just received word from our friends at NASA. They are working hard to beam radio messages at the incoming ship. But the time to tread lightly is over. Even the folks who helped to put us on the moon recognize that. It's why they're working with the U.S. Air Force to develop a lethal option as a last resort. And yes, as many of you know, that option will involve launching nuclear warheads against the craft. But also know builders and engineers are busy outfitting bunkers deep underground designed to preserve a sample of humanity. Many of you here are convinced the answer lies on the other side of that portal. You may be right and with any luck, we will soon find out. We're going back in and this time we want the beings on the other side to know we mean business."

The room exploded with applause. Jack stood up and waited for it to die down. "Admiral, I won't argue against the need to move forcefully to save the planet. And like you, I'm also hopeful the answer may lie somewhere over there. But for all we know, they've chosen to destroy us because of the savage way we act toward one another. What message will we send as ambassadors of the human race if we go in with robots designed to maim and kill? Will we not be proving them right?"

"You see those numbers above the door?" Stark said, pointing to a countdown clock with less than fifty-eight hours remaining. "I've had one installed in every module in Northern Star and every Quonset hut at Base Camp Zulu. When those numbers reach zero we die, plain and simple. We need to move with all due haste to figure out who's in charge over there and incentivize them to turn that ship around before it's too late. This time we go in hot. If you don't have the stomach for it, then feel free to stay home."

Jack gritted his teeth. "Fat chance."

Chapter 14

Following the meeting, Mia returned to the science module and the ten-by-twenty-foot lab Alan had given her. Black research tables ran the length of both walls, each filled with microscopes, beakers and Petri dishes as well as a computer work station. At either end of the rectangular room was a glass booth equipped with cameras, microphones and computer monitors.

Her assistant, an older woman named Gail, gave off the rather clear impression that working on Mia's research project was a distinct waste of time. Perhaps she thought it should be going in a different direction. Or perhaps Gail wanted a lab of her own. Either way, she wouldn't say. But her acute disapproval became clear every time Mia asked her to perform even the most menial task. Gail had elevated the art of sighing to a whole new level.

"Have the girls been prepped?" Mia asked, peering through the glass partition. Inside one room was Sofia, sitting in a chair, wearing a helmet that would image her brain during the test. Gail nodded with a distinct lack of enthusiasm, as if to say, *Of course I prepped the girls.* Mia tapped on the glass and curled her fingers into an okay sign. Sofia did the same, her long black hair draped along the pale confines of her face. She didn't look scared, which was a good thing.

At the other end of the lab was the other the other glass booth where Noemi was currently seated, attached to the same kind of equipment. Thankfully, her hair was short and wavy, which helped Mia tell them apart, although the more she got to know the twins, the easier the task was becoming. While Sofia was quiet and reserved, Noemi was exuberant and outgoing.

The plan was to image the region of the brain that surrounded the hippocampus while the girls attempted to speak to each other telepathically. A screen before one girl would show a randomly generated image while the girl in the other room tried to guess what her sister was seeing. After several attempts, they would switch tasks. What Mia hoped to see was which parts of the brain were active during the sending and receiving of thought waves. But more than that, during the experiment, the girls would be filmed in every part of the electromagnetic spectrum. If brain waves were being sent out like radio signals, Mia hoped to see it in action.

The lights in the main lab dimmed, while those in the isolation chambers at either end stayed the same. An image of an orange appeared on the screen before Sofia. "Orange," Noemi said.

Mia nodded. Another hallmark of Salzburg. In only a matter of a few short days, these two young Italian girls had become almost completely fluent in English, albeit with the hint of an Italian accent.

The next picture was a slice of Hawaiian pizza.

Noemi's face squished up. "Nasty pizza."

The next image Sofia saw was of a chocolate bar. Noemi

got that one immediately.

"This test is making me so hungry," she complained with a faint smile.

A teddy bear flashed on Sofia's screen.

"Uh, ice cream sundae," Noemi replied incorrectly.

Mia bit her lip.

Sofia was then shown a house with a trail of smoke rising from the chimney.

"I see French fries with mayonnaise," Noemi said, licking her lips.

Several other images appeared with Noemi only getting a very small percentage of them right. Dispirited, Mia stopped the experiment and let the girls out.

"Gail, can you see that the girls get something to eat right away?" she told her assistant, trying not to let her disappointment show.

Gail stood, the corners of her mouth turned down. "Come along, girls."

As soon as they had left Mia smacked the table with the flat of her hand. The beakers nearby rattled and jumped. How could it be that they had displayed such impressive results in Rome and yet now they were barely above chance? They were young. Could it be weak powers of concentration were making it harder for them to focus? Noemi had described being hungry. It wasn't unreasonable to suppose the incoming signal—assuming there was one at all and that Gail hadn't been right about Mia wasting her time—had been altered or distorted by the girl's grumbling stomach.

She went to the MRI data and played it back from the beginning, watching the overview of Noemi's brain as she made each guess. With the first two, the sections around the parahippocampal gyrus glowed deep red. On the ones she got wrong, another part of her brain had also been lit up, the hypothalamus. The one associated with hunger.

"Interesting," she said, switching to Sofia's reading. On the first two, Sofia's parahippocampal gyrus demonstrated the same intense level of activity while on most of the others, Sofia's hypothalamus also showed some movement.

"What the hell is going on?" Mia wondered, out loud, her brow scrunched.

They had clearly failed the test, right? Unless, of course, Sofia hadn't actually been transmitting the images she was being shown. Maybe Noemi wasn't the only one who had skipped breakfast. Maybe both of them had been hungry. Could Sofia have really been sending her sister images of ice cream and French fries instead of teddy bears and houses?

Next she went to the footage she'd taken in each of the isolation chambers. She ran both of them several times in a multispectral mode, looking for anything out of the ordinary that might present itself, from infrared light to gamma rays. All she saw were two poor girls who thought wearing silly helmets and running tests sure beat the hell out of the asylum.

The infrared and gamma ray proved about as useless as she'd predicted. When she switched to the X-ray spectrum, however, she saw something strange. At one point a blur of soft light appeared around Sofia's head, along with a conical streak that led out of frame. Her heart began beating faster. Mia rolled it back and played it from Noemi's point of view. She saw the same thing.

In both instances, the blurry streak of light or whatever it was led from the isolation chamber and straight across the lab. She backed Noemi's video up and played it again, second by second. One moment the streak was absent, and then suddenly it appeared. It looked to Mia like a blemish on an old dog-eared photograph. She backed it up one final time, playing it millisecond by millisecond, and that was when she found frame 4622. On it, the smoky substance had crossed the room, but it was far lighter than in frame 4623 and beyond. Whatever Mia was seeing, it seemed to be traveling from one girl to the other and doing so faster than the speed of light.

In her initial hypothesis, she had imagined the brain as a kind of radio, able to cast off and receive signals out of the air. Anyone with a ham radio was able to pick up chatter between NASA and the International Space Station. The signals were out there for anyone to grab hold of. But frame 4622 appeared to demonstrate that this was not the way telepathy worked. The smear of light across the image appeared to be an actual extension of Sofia's mind, reaching across space and time to connect with her sister. If this were true, it represented perhaps one of the most groundbreaking discoveries in the history of science. From the materialist point of view, the mind was merely an extension of the brain. If that were true, then what had Mia seen in the X-ray spectrum video streaking across the lab?

"Anyone ever tell you how beautiful you look when you're focused?"

Mia looked up to find Alan leaning against the doorframe. For a moment she'd hoped it was Jack. Heck, she would have even taken Gail. Anyone with whom she could share this startling discovery.

"Mind if I come in?" he asked, already stepping into the lab.

"Actually, I'm kind of busy," she replied, minimizing the video she'd been watching.

Alan walked like a 70s gigolo. He was only missing the unbuttoned shirt and a hairy chest full of gold necklaces. Her eyes fell to the Super Bowl-sized rings on his fingers. Those had to count for something.

"You're still upset about Ollie. I can see it written all over your face. Listen, it was the heat of the moment. You know I would never do anything to hurt the guy."

Mia swiveled in her chair. "That's close enough."

Alan planted his feet and braced himself against a nearby table. "I've never killed anyone in my life, I swear."

"What about Greg Abbott? The police found his dead body in the trunk of your car. I don't even know how you got involved with those Sentinel people, anyway. They're terrorists, Alan. You've always been a misogynistic asshole, I'll give you that, but I thought even you had limits."

He smiled, flashing a pearly set of veneers. "I meant what I said in my letter. Can't we just let what happened in the past stay there? I mean, geez, Louise, it was five years ago."

"You like to play games, Alan," Mia said, feeling her blood pressure begin to climb. "I get that. But I'm done playing. Do you even care whether or not we save the planet? Because seeing you stand there like something out of an Elmore Leonard novel, I'm not getting that impression."

"You wanna know the truth? I'm not worried about that

ship. Let's just say the human race has an ace up our sleeve."

Mia nodded. "Then why chase me halfway around the world, only to bring me here?"

"I want you to finish your research," he said, his voice losing a touch of that casual tone it had been laced with earlier. "We need to understand how Salzburg syndrome was mutated remotely. More than that, we need to know how it was transmitted from person to person in the first place."

"Biophotons," she explained, hoping that might satisfy and encourage him to leave. She was suddenly starkly aware they were alone in the lab together and part of her flashed back to that hotel room, him standing over her as he buttoned his shirt. Mia gritted her teeth and did her best to power through. "The blast waves of light from the ships—"

"Ships?" he asked.

"The ship in the Gulf," she amended. "And whatever was coming through that portal. Frankly, we're not sure of the source in the second instance. Gabby and Eugene are working on that. But either way, those flashes were sending genetic instructions to our cells, ordering them to cobble together new genes from the junk DNA in our genome."

He tapped a finger on the table. "A brilliant and rather elegant solution, don't you think?"

She nodded reluctantly. "Like nothing we've ever seen before. It makes our modern medicine look like voodoo by comparison."

"Yes, it does." Alan clasped his arms over his chest. The lab's neon lights made him look old, almost frail. "But the question remains. How does it spread? Why does your daughter Zoey have it while you don't?"

"Don't bring her into this," Mia snapped, her body suddenly a live wire of protective rage.

Alan raised his hands. "Easy, baby, I come in peace."

"I'm not your baby!"

He waited until she'd calmed down before rephrasing the question in a less antagonistic way.

"You're talking about the HISR gene," she told him, starting to lose her patience. "Your people already asked me all these questions during the flight over here. It's an assembler gene that only exists within thirty percent of the population. The ingestion of GMO foods must have awoken the gene and instructed it to begin building a 24th chromosome in humans as well as species of animals close to us. Initially, folks affected experienced few symptoms. It's likely why when your lab first discovered the extra chromosome, it was only populated by a single gene. The other seventy percent of the population without HISR were spared."

The edges of Alan's lips rose into a grin. "Looks like we dodged a bullet."

"Much of that will depend on how all of this shakes out. I mean, some of the genes in the second half of the chromosome have some pretty strange properties."

His eyebrow perked up. "That so?"

"It's still unclear how it's being done, but we're getting closer."

"That may be so, but I don't want you losing focus on your main task."

"Excuse me?"

"I want to be perfectly clear about something," he said,

in a low voice. "I didn't bring you here to play with children. That you can do in your own time. I brought you to Northern Star to complete our understanding on how a photon can be encoded with genetic information and used to affect change within the body. You've discovered how it works in principle and I congratulate you. But it won't do the medical profession any good if it isn't something we can use on a daily basis." Alan paused, watching what was surely a long string of emotions play out over Mia's face. Finally he said, "I'm glad we had this chat." He was about to leave and paused. "Oh, and Mia. Don't ever let me discover you've been holding anything back."

The look on Alan's face made the skin at the top of her head tighten with fear. She shook her head and watched him turn and saunter out.

Mia buried her head in her hands. Here she was unlocking the mysteries of the universe and all Alan could think about was winning himself another award— and, of all things, off of her hard work. It was enough to make a girl scream.

A knock came at the door and she bolted to her feet, ready to let loose. Instead, the sight before her left her stunned.

"I didn't expect to see you again," Mia said, recalling in vivid detail the day not long ago when Jansson had left Italy and all the research they had been doing to be with her family.

Dr. Jansson smiled and moved in for a hug. "The minute I got home, I realized I'd made a terrible mistake. I guess I'm not as delicate as I thought." She laughed. "Would you believe, the slender gentleman I just passed in the hallway whistled as I walked by?"

Mia shook her head. "Would you believe me if I told you it didn't surprise me one bit?"

"Who is he?"

"Only a time-travelling douchebag from the 70's who's here for the sole purpose of making my life a living hell." They let out a wild bout of laughter. It was exactly what Mia needed.

She clapped her hands on Jansson's shoulders. "All right, let's get to work."

Chapter 15

After getting nowhere with the local police Kay made a quick trip to fire station #29 on Crystal Rock Drive. The local chief there was an athletic man with silver hair and a matching mustache. He opened the door a crack, as though she was looking to rob the place.

"Lady, if you got an emergency, pick up the phone and dial it in." He went to shut the door, but was stopped when Kay blocked it with her foot. "Hey, I thought I made myself clear now—"

"Listen… Chief Fulwood," she said, eyeing his name tag. "I called and keep getting a busy signal."

"Yeah, well, that don't surprise me, 'cause most of my crew's out chasing one false call after another. People short on food been calling us to bring them supplies from the supermarket, like we're a bunch of deliverymen."

Kay's jaw clenched and her hands balled into fists. "I'm sure you're having a rough time. But I just found my fiancé in my parents' house murdered. And I can't seem to get the police to pay attention, no matter what I do. As morbid as it sounds, I need someone to collect his body and see that it's buried with respect. I know that's not what you normally do, but if I can't get anywhere with you, then I might have to rob a bank. Maybe that way someone will listen."

Fulwood's bottom lip drooped in stunned amazement. "All right, lady, come on in and I'll see what I can do to help."

Kay scanned the nearly vacant street before following him in. He led her upstairs toward the dispatch room—a rectangular room lined with a handful of cubicles, each equipped with a phone and a computer. The lights on the phones were blinking like mad and yet no one was there to take any calls.

"Where is everyone?" she asked.

"Oh, a bunch left when the whole Sarsberg thing broke out," Chief Fulwood explained, his eyebrows hitching up as he spoke. "Then news came about the end of the world and most of my men just melted away. Since then, I been working with what you might call a skeleton crew."

"What about your own family?"

"What family? Ain't got one to worry about. Wife up and left me years ago. These boys at number 29 is all I got left."

Fulwood sounded like a man with plenty to cry about and hardly a tear left to shed.

"I got a direct line to the police chief. You just write down the important bits and I'll see he gets the message."

"Thank you," Kay said, still trying to shake the feeling she was somehow floating above looking down on all of this.

He handed her a pad and she filled in the details.

Fulwood glanced down at what she'd written. "Mahoro. Your old man isn't named Felix, by any chance?"

Kay's eyes lit up. "You know where he is?" she said eagerly, struck by a sudden surge of hope.

"Oh, gosh, no. Back in the day, the wife and I used to attend Poplar Grove Baptist. Gotta admit I wasn't much into that sorta thing. Religion and all. Went for her really. Not that it did me much good." Fulwood's voice trailed off before he snapped out of his reverie. "Is he missing? Your dad, I mean."

Kay slumped into a nearby chair. "Both my parents along with my fiancé's family. I had just spoken to them on the phone. Then they simply vanished."

"Okay, ma'am, don't fret now. Just stay where you are. You let me ring the chief and he'll take care of things."

"I can't thank you enough."

"Don't mention it. If you're hungry head down the hall to the kitchen and grab anything that isn't in a paper bag. That stuff belongs to the boys. Last thing I want is have 'em come back and find their dinner gone."

"That's very kind."

Fulwood disappeared into his office and Kay headed into the station's kitchen. Food was the last thing on her mind. What she wanted was a large bright space where she could finally catch her breath. She found a surprisingly modern room with stainless-steel appliances and a large metal table surrounded by comfy-looking chairs. But what really brought a smile to her face was the brass fire pole that led down to the station's main level. All these years she had thought that was only a myth.

Kay had no sooner taken a seat before her phone started to chirp. Her heart skipped about three beats as she whipped it out, hoping beyond hope it was her parents calling.

The screen said Ramirez, her special agent friend over at the FBI.

"Just the man I wanted to speak with," she said, shelving her disappointment.

"Hello to you too," he replied, breathless. "Listen, I just landed back to D.C. and the situation here is worse than I expected."

"You don't know the half of it," Kay said.

Ramirez whispered something to her.

"What was that? I didn't catch what you said."

"I said you may not be safe, Kay. There's talk here of large-scale arrests. Cops everywhere are cracking down."

"On what?" she asked.

"Everything. There's a list being circulated to law enforcement and your name is on it."

Kay's pulse went from a flutter to a full-on gallop. "Do you think that's what happened to my parents? They're missing."

"I can't say more. I'm already risking everything just being on the phone with you. For now just lie low and whatever you do, stay away from the cops."

The voice at the other end of the room startled her.

"Did you find something to eat?"

Kay spun around, removing the phone from her ear and holding it against her thigh.

Fulwood was standing in the kitchen doorway, a strange look on his face.

"Kay, are you there?" Ramirez said, his voice barely audible.

She brought the phone to her ear. "I'll call you back," she said and hung up. Then to Fulwood—"It's okay, I wasn't hungry."

"That's not a problem. Listen, I spoke to the chief of police and he's sending a patrol car down to get you."

"To get me?" She felt her eyes go wide with fear and fought to maintain control.

"To take you to your folks' place and get a statement. You did say your fiancé's body was there. We're not quite at the stage where we just gloss over things like that."

"No, of course not." She let out a nervous sigh, Ramirez's words still ringing in her ears.

Whatever you do, stay away from the cops.

"Mind if I use your washroom?"

Fulwood's eyes narrowed. "Sure thing. Just don't go anywhere before the patrol car arrives. The chief was real adamant."

"Got it," she lied, wearing the most genuine grin she could muster. "Don't forget, I'm the one who came knocking on your door. Not the other way around."

The fire chief nodded. "That is true. What the hell, go ahead and use the can. It's by the stairs, right before the dispatch room."

Kay was about to take a step when her eyes flicked over to the pole at the same time his did. Shoving the phone into her pocket, Kay made a break for it. Fulwood broke into a run as well, clearly intending to stop her. She reached the pole first and grabbed hold of its smooth, cold surface, spinning down with an audible squeak, her knees buckling as she hit the ground. Fulwood was close behind, sliding down after her.

Kay burst through the same door she had entered through not twenty minutes before. Her car was right out front, her car keys buried in her pocket under her phone. Heart jackhammering in her chest, Kay jammed a hand in, felt for the key's serrated edge and yanked it out. Fulwood burst through the door a split second later, yelling after her to stop. Whatever the police had told him, he seemed certain Kay was a very bad person.

In one fluid motion, Kay shoved the key into the lock, pulled open the door, slid inside the car and snapped the lock shut behind her. Fulwood dove onto the hood right as she started the car. She backed out, whipping the front end of the vehicle to the right in the process, flinging Fulwood off her hood and onto the street. The agile chief rolled twice and popped up on his feet. The sight filled her with relief as she punched the accelerator and peeled away, the white-haired man standing in the street, brushing the dust off his pant leg. Enough people had died today. She had no intention of adding another name to that list.

Her phone began ringing from inside her pocket. Kay whipped around a corner before pulling it out and answering it.

"Ramirez, I told you I'd call you back."

"This ain't Ramirez," the unusual voice on the other end told her. "I read your article, Mrs. Mahoro, and think the two of us might be able to help one another."

"Yeah, I doubt that very much."

"You might," the man said. "But I'd be willing to bet your parents would disagree."

Kay glanced down at the caller ID and saw that it read: *Unknown*. "Who the hell is this?"

"You can call me Ollie."

Chapter 16

53 hours, 21 minutes, 58 seconds

Already dressed in their biosuits, Jack and Dag made their way through the ruins of the city buried beneath the ice sheet and toward the pyramid. Normally, a snow shuttle would bring them from the bottom of the elevator to Base Camp Zulu, but one hadn't been there waiting for them. He had radioed Northern Star, who had informed him the shuttles were busy ferrying the Volkov team and that they would be back soon. Jack and Dag had started the journey on their own. They were about halfway there when Jack caught a sound behind them.

He stopped. "You hear that?"

Something was moving at them quickly from out of the darkness. Jack's helmet was tucked under his arm, but he used his OHMD to increase the brightness of his helmet light and aimed it at whatever was approaching.

"Dr. Greer," Anna said, her heavy metallic footfalls thudding over the frozen ground. She skidded to a stop before them.

"What's wrong?"

"Dr. Bishop asked me to conduct a number of seismic scans in and around the base camp."

"Yeah, I know, I suggested it. We're trying to make sure

the gravitational forces from the portal aren't eroding the structural stability of the ice cavern." They continued walking. "I'm assuming you found something."

"I have," Anna replied. "But I am still not certain what it means."

White plumes of hot air condensed before both men. "I don't understand," Jack said.

Anna fed the image into his glasses.

Jack struggled to make sense of what he was seeing. It was almost like looking through one of those red Viewmaster 3-D glasses he'd owned as a child, the kind with picture reels you inserted from the top. Sometimes when you were between slides, all you'd see was a blurry double image. The scan of the pyramid Anna was showing him appeared to have a ghostly duplicate.

"As you can see, the seismic data is showing an echo. Dr. Holland and Dr. Bishop believe the distortive effect is being caused by the energy emitted by the portal."

"Have you tried cleaning it up?"

"I am working on that as we speak."

"What about structural problems? I don't want a rerun of what happened in the Gulf."

"That is precisely what I am trying to avoid." Anna winked at him. "I know how much you dislike flying."

**

Jack was still thinking about what Anna had told them when they arrived at Base Camp Zulu. Yuri and his team were getting ready. But only Yuri was wearing a biosuit. Three techs in parkas were positioned behind Ivan, tinkering on something inside his rear panel.

"I take it your techs are not joining us?" Jack said to Yuri.

"Why should they when the two of us are all you need?" He motioned to the fierce-looking robot. Ivan's four red eyes flashed as if to emphasize the point.

Anna approached the robot, regarding him with apprehension. "Hello," she said politely, sticking out one of her hands.

Ivan craned his head down and stared at it, then back at her.

"This is how humans greet one another," she said, taking hold of one of his giant claws and rocking it up and down.

"Does not compute," Ivan replied. The lights behind his eyes were blinking wildly, as though he were trying to process the illogic of the move. "Greetings and salutations are reserved for diplomatic units. Ivan 3.0 was designed for combat missions. My name is Ivan. Integrated. Variable. Android. Node."

Anna looked disappointed with her new friend. His greatest sin wasn't being dumb, it was being boring. Perhaps attempting to make the best of it, she locked onto something he'd said. "You mentioned your name was Ivan 3.0. Does that imply you have a father and a grandfather? You are very lucky if you do. My father died." Her digital lip began to quiver.

Yuri laughed uncomfortably. "What is this?" he asked, pointing at the two robots.

Dag looked around. "Sounded to me like a question. And not a bad one at that."

"She's remotely operated, right?" Yuri asked, his eyes darting between them. "You've got a guy in one of these Quonset huts or back on Northern Star pulling on her strings like a marionette?"

"I enjoy marionettes," Anna said. "Mr. Volkov, are you familiar with the program *Thunderbirds*? It is an older show, but very exciting. I have downloaded every episode."

Yuri's eyes were locked on Jack's as he released a spastic burst of nervous laughter, looking like a man certain he was being filmed for a hidden camera show. "You're having a laugh at my expense, aren't you?"

"I don't know what you're talking about," Jack responded. "Anna isn't a remote-control car being driven by some guy in a booth, if that's what you're asking."

Anna moved around to see what Ivan's techs were doing. Peering into the open panel, she must have seen a female USB port, because she snapped open a small hatch at her waist and produced a male port of her own. She reached to insert it into Ivan. The techs began to stop her, before a wave of Yuri's hand ordered them to stand down.

Anna plugged herself in and made a long 'ohhh' sound. "It is a mess in here," she said without much tact. "No wonder poor Ivan cannot think straight. His logic routines are routed in circles."

Her tongue jutted out the corner of her mouth for a moment before she pulled out the USB and let it roll back into her waist. "I hope you don't mind," she said to Ivan. "I have streamlined your logic pathways." She grinned. "You will not be nearly as dumb nor as boring."

Dag couldn't hold back. "You know what they say. When you can't meet new friends, make them."

What Jack found most fascinating was that Anna wasn't informing Yuri about what she had done. She was telling Ivan.

"Thank you, Anna," Ivan said. His creators hadn't given him a face that allowed any kind of expression, but even Jack thought he could hear a hint of something more in the robot's voice.

"How about the next time you decide to tinker with his subroutine, you check with me first?" Yuri scolded Anna. "He's exactly the way we wanted him to be, a trained killer."

"My apologies, Mr. Volkov," Anna said, dejected.

"Go easy on her," Jack told him. "She's smart as a whip, but inside she's still a kid."

Yuri left without saying a word, his team and Ivan following close behind.

Stark's voice came over the OHMD radio. "Jack, the Delta team is inside the pyramid's chamber room, raring to go. I need you and the rest of your people here on the double."

"On our way," Jack replied. They were about to head through Base Camp Zulu and up into the pyramid when a shuttle arrived from the elevator. A female in a biosuit jumped off and ran toward them.

"Thank goodness, I thought you might have left without me," Mia said, holding her helmet by the seal.

"I thought you were busy running tests on the twins?" Jack said, confused.

"The first batch is done and I wanted to give Dr. Jansson a chance to review the data on her own. It's pretty wild stuff, let me tell you."

Dag threw his helmet on, the inner light illuminating his face. "I'll bet not nearly as wild as where we're headed."

Chapter 17

50 hours, 01 minutes, 25 seconds

By the time Jack and the others arrived the briefing was already underway. To one side stood Yuri, Ivan and the robot's technicians. On the other was the six-man Delta team, each decked out in strange-looking biocammies.

"Geez, they look like something out of a Van Gogh painting," Mia whispered to Jack.

No doubt about it, they were a strange sight. Jack was used to seeing these guys in desert or forest fatigues, but if the point was to blend in to their surroundings on the other side, then the colors they were wearing would do the trick.

Admiral Stark motioned to a muscular-looking soldier next to him. He was at least three inches shorter than Stark, which meant he was about five foot eight and a hundred eighty pounds. Tufts of dark, wavy hair poked out from beneath the bandana he wore on his head. His lips were full and contoured by a dark, handlebar mustache which disappeared beneath his strong chin. The soldier glared back at them with alert and hardened eyes.

"Staff Sergeant Stokes here is in charge of getting you in

and out in one piece. If he tells you to jump, your only response should be, 'How high?' I hope I'm understood. We don't have the time to replace you folks if things go sideways. Nonmilitary personnel will be issued sidearms and rifles for emergency purposes only. You need to find a way out of that jungle and attempt to make contact with any intelligent species you encounter."

Jack remembered the mummified Atean bodies they had found on the ship in the Gulf and what he would give to meet one of them in real life.

"Any questions?"

"Can I have a rifle with a grenade launcher?" Dag asked, as one of Admiral Stark's men outfitted him.

"No," he snapped. "Any other questions?"

Yuri raised his hand. "I will be joining the mission to help support Ivan and insure his optimal performance."

Jack leaned toward Mia. "If they want optimal performance, they should let Anna have another look at him."

She snickered. "Be careful what you wish for."

Sergeant Stokes came forward. "By now, each of you has been instructed on the hand signals you might see when we're on the other side. Our helmets are sealed, so there are no worries about being overheard, but there may be periods where we need to maintain radio silence."

He then introduced the other members of the Delta team. Stokes pointed to each of the men one by one. "This is Corporal Kerr, Peterson, Diaz, Bates and Conroy." Each of them looked serious and incredibly professional. "These men are like brothers. We've been on missions around the world. A thought doesn't pass through their heads without me knowing about it first."

Jack elbowed Mia playfully. "Maybe you should include Stokes in your research."

She let out a skittish, nervous little laugh.

He put an arm around her. "It's not every day you get to travel from one planet to another."

Mia nodded. "That's what I'm worried about."

Minutes later, they entered the decontamination chamber. Then one by one they stepped through the portal. Jack and Mia were the last to go and just before they went through he said, "Just stay close and whatever you do, don't wander off."

•••

The buzzing in Mia's ears was so intense she wondered if she was about to go deaf. Pinpoints of light assaulted her eyes even after she snapped her lids shut. She willed herself to put one foot in front of the other, if for no other reason than to escape the tortured feeling of straddling two vastly different worlds. Jack caught her as she came out the other side, her breathing heavy and ragged.

The spectacular sight that greeted her was like nothing she could have imagined. Of course, she had seen the images and videos Jack and Anna had brought back, but no digital rendering could compare to the real thing. She felt like Dorothy leaving the black and white world of Kansas and entering the land of Oz.

"It's a lot to take in the first time," Jack said, watching her with a smile.

Dag was beside her and must have said the words 'far out' a dozen times.

Stokes and the other Delta operators formed a loose perimeter around them.

"Whatever planet this is," Mia said, her voice sounding distant even to her own ears, "we found one with a blue sky just like our own."

Jack glanced up through a small opening in the thick, multicolored canopy overhead and noticed for the first time that she was right. The sun had been directly overhead the first time he'd been here, washing out the sky with blinding light.

"The incoming blue light waves interact with the air molecules in the atmosphere," Anna explained. "As a result, they tend to scatter more than red light waves. This is why blue is more visible than red. Technically speaking, it is what is called the Rayleigh effect."

Nearby, Yuri was running a quick diagnostic on Ivan. "Would you like some help?" Anna offered.

"Buzz off," he barked, his fingers scrolling down a tablet with lines of code.

Anna looked around, confused by Yuri's reaction, before moving away. A case on her back contained three drones. Jack and Dag came over and removed them one by one, tossing the objects into the air. The tiny propeller engines started at once, revving up to a high-pitched whine as the drones momentarily dipped and then lifted into the air.

"Let's start by mapping the immediate area," Jack suggested. "That way we'll have an idea of what's around us."

"I still don't get why a supposedly intelligent alien race would lay a doorway down in the middle of a jungle," Dag said, the pessimism practically oozing off his every word. "You ask me, whoever lived here is long gone, man. I mean we dig down deep enough and we're sure to find the foundations of ancient skyscrapers or something." He kicked at the loose soil before him as if to drive home the point. "The world's about to end and here we are on a wild goose—"

"Hey, what is that?" Mia asked, staring at the dirt Dag had just kicked up. She bent down and grabbed hold of a rounded white lever. She moved it back and forth until the lever broke free. As she held the object in the air, it immediately became clear she was holding an arm bone. But who did it belong to? The bone's dark color and porous quality made it clear it had been there a while. Mia snapped a shot with her glasses and then ran it against everything they had on file. Soon enough, they found a match. She forwarded the findings to the others.

"It's from the *Mesonyx* people," Dag said, amazed.

Yuri glanced up from his work. "The who?"

"The long-lost civilization that built the city under the Greenland ice sheet," Jack told him. "The one you travelled through on your way to Base Camp Zulu. Or maybe you were on your phone."

Yuri scoffed.

"Anyway, this proves that at some stage, they travelled through the portal. But why?"

Dag shifted uncomfortably. "For all we know the guy was a sacrifice, sent here to appease the alien gods who were busy destroying their world."

"Yuri," Stokes said, still eyeing the perimeter. "You nearly done over there? We need to make our way off the LZ ASAP. No telling how much daylight we got left and I don't intend to be caught here after dark."

Some topographical data had already started coming back via the drones. "A hill with a clearing at the top lies a hundred meters in that direction," Anna said, pointing. "The gap in the canopy should enable us to send the drones even higher."

The group headed in that direction with Ivan in the lead, cutting a path through the vibrant undergrowth with his powerful tank-like treads.

Mia pulled up the atmospheric readings. "I suggest everyone fight the urge to remove your helmets. The air here is barely over ten percent oxygen."

"That bad?" Kerr asked. He was a short but handsome Southerner with a compact frame and a distinct Tennessee twang.

"Only if you enjoy breathing," Jack told him, not bothering to sugarcoat the reality of the situation. The terrain inclined and Jack began breathing more heavily. Kerr must have seen him sucking wind and said, "Lucky for me, I used to run along the Blue Ridge Mountains as a kid, hunting rabbits and squirrels. Felt like my own backyard."

"This remind you of home?" Jack said, aware that all the exertion was elevating the temperature inside his biosuit.

"A wee bit," Kerr admitted. "Except for the funky psychedelic colors. I've already snapped a bunch of pics with these glasses. Otherwise, the folks back home would never believe me."

"Let's hope when all is said and done you have folks to go back to," Jack said, not aiming to sound like a downer, but eager to keep it clear that this wasn't a simulation. This was the real deal and the game clock was ticking down.

All of the sudden, Ivan hit a steep jungle berm. The robot's treads rolled on, churning up the ground and flinging it behind him.

"Ivan, stop," Yuri snapped.

"Understood," Ivan replied and stopped moving.

"At least he's obedient," Mia said with a wry smile.

"Ivan's terrain-mapping program is rather primitive," Anna said, innocently. "I believe the undergrowth and certain shades of foliage are not being recognized by his laser sensors."

Mia caught the scowl on Yuri's face as he noted down Anna's observations in his tablet. She understood some of the annoyance the Russian was surely experiencing. Anna could be infuriatingly frank and frustratingly thorough at times.

Mia turned her attention back to the ledge Ivan had driven into and noticed two things. The first was the way the blueish vines snaked up the uniform surface. The second was how unnatural it looked. From here, the outcropping of earth appeared to rise up at a perfect right angle at least fifteen feet into the air.

"You caught that too," Jack said, standing next to her and eyeing the slightly camouflaged obstruction.

"Could it be a structure of some kind?" she wondered.

"Anna," Jack called out. "Have the drones do a quick pass over this location and trace the extent of this outcropping."

"Of course, Dr. Greer."

Seconds later came the whiz of the three drones as they flew overhead, moving in a widening array of circles. They watched the feed as the scan took place in real time.

"Right there," Jack said with excitement as he projected a 3D rendition before him and used his outstretched hands to rotate it. "See the shadow on the other side?"

"It does sorta look like a doorway," Dag admitted, tilting his head and growing more convinced.

The opening Jack had found meant a fifty-meter detour from their current location. If it provided any clues about who might have once inhabited this place, then it would be well worth the time to investigate. Cutting through the jungle, the group clambered over uneven terrain to reach the possible entryway. Now practiced with climbing ladders and stairs, Anna made short work of the obstacles. Ivan on the other hand was struggling, in spite of his impressive treads.

"I suggest you go around," Anna said, waving her hand around in a half circle. "The ground is not as steep over there."

"He can make it," Yuri insisted, ordering Ivan on.

By the time Jack and the others arrived they could still hear Ivan working himself through the dense brush.

"If that damn robot gets any louder," Stokes said, banging the light on his helmet until it turned on, "he's gonna announce our presence to every damn thing within a five-mile radius." Stokes ordered his men to fan out while Jack, Mia and the others tried to make sense of what they were seeing.

They stood for a moment, eyeing the clean vertical and horizontal lines of a doorway. "It clearly used to be a structure," Jack said, in the process of brushing away some of the thin overhanging vines when something flew out at him from inside. Jack reeled back and lost his balance and began to fall, only to be caught by one of Ivan's outstretched arms. The other arm followed whatever had flown past Jack's head and downed it with a single shot from one of its imbedded weapons.

The bird or whatever it was tumbled out of the air, landing directly at Stokes' feet. Dag ran over to enclose it in a sample bag.

The Delta team was on edge, scanning the perimeter from the ground to the treetops.

Diaz, a Latino with dark skin and a pencil-thin mustache, jerked his rifle around. "I got a red dot, flying around my position."

"They're harmless," Jack shouted, still rattled.

"Are you all right, Dr. Greer?" the stout robot asked in his metallic twang, setting Jack back on his feet.

"That was some impressive shooting," Jack admitted, noticing the wisp of smoke rising from Ivan's barrel. "If only your wall-detecting skills were as strong."

Yuri fought off a grin. "Let's just say we wanted to get the important things right first."

Jack spun to find Mia ducking past the low-hanging vines and through the opening. He drew his pistol and followed after her. Thick tree roots snaked along the floor. Branches and thick fronds lined every inch of the walls and ceiling. Jack turned on his helmet light as the two of them descended what had once been a long set of stairs.

"Hold the vines as you go," he told her, holstering his pistol so he could do the same.

An arched opening sat at the base of the staircase. Jack studied it as he went by, estimating the archway's height at nine feet. "We're not in munchkin land, I can tell you that much."

The chamber beyond the archway was enormous and filled with its own forest. The amount of ancient-looking undergrowth was staggering. Massive orange tree trunks hugged the walls, as wide as the support struts on the Golden Gate Bridge. As they rose, Mia noticed how their branches coursed across the high ceiling toward the entrance as though searching for a way out.

Already they had spotted several new species of plant life that had taken up residence in this sunless environment. A row of long magenta tubes emerged from a nearby ledge, puffing out spore rings like patrons in a cigar lounge.

Mia followed as a dot of red light danced through the air before settling on the petal of a yellow flower.

"That's a wisp," Jack said, moving closer. "Anna and I spotted them on our first visit. She named it after a will-o'-the-wisp."

They drew closer and saw the insect was no longer glowing. Then, in a blur of motion, a long fibrous tongue lashed out from the flower's center, wrapped around the wisp and pulled it in.

Mia recoiled. "Oh, goodness."

"Consider that a reminder not to go touching anything."

Anna and Stokes appeared, looking around in awe.

"Sweet Jesus, this place is bigger than I thought," Stokes said, panning his light into the ceiling's dark crevasses.

Mia called out, waving them over. "Come take a look at this."

Along the back wall were a series of broken transparent enclosures. It reminded Jack of the pod farm they'd found on the ship in the Gulf, only each of them was much smaller. Could this have been where the beings who inhabited this planet created the specimens for their ships?

"There are more of 'em over here," Stokes said, nudging a broken shard with the barrel of his rifle.

The longer they looked, the more obvious it became. The chamber was filled with hundreds if not thousands of small glass canisters. Weirder still, each and every one of them appeared to be broken. It was hard not to wonder what they had once contained. Or whether whoever had broken them was still here.

Chapter 18

Kay's instructions were simple. McPherson Square Station at the end of the westbound platform. That was where she had agreed to meet the Aussie who claimed to have information on her parents' whereabouts. Could it be a trick? In the past, she had allowed her thirst for the truth to blind her to possible danger. Now, her desire to locate her parents was a much stronger motivation.

She was reassured knowing that if the people she had come here to meet didn't look right she had two cards up her sleeve. The first was the silver revolver sitting in her purse. The second was the subway tracks by the platform, which might offer an escape route through the tunnels. Neither of those were ideal, but Kay's desperation for answers was quickly pushing her from cautious and calculated to reckless.

She was about to enter the main metro terminal when her phone pinged.

It was a text message from Ron Lewis. "Looks like our little gamble failed," he wrote cryptically.

Kay stopped, leaned up against a wall out of sight and dialed him. Whether she was chasing down a story or not, Kay knew a reporter lived on their phone. It was one of the things Derek had always scolded her for. "Put that thing away, will you?" he would chant whenever he'd had enough. The memory seared a painful line down the center of her heart. But it was an occupational hazard. Or better yet, a double-edged sword.

"Kay," Ron answered, his voice hoarse, like a man intent on abusing it with a few cartons of Marlboros.

"I got your message. What's going on?"

"I take it you haven't looked at the paper today."

Kay minimized the call and opened the *Post*'s website. *Page Not Found.*

"Huh?"

Ron let out a sick little laugh. "Nope, you are not hallucinating." His words ran together as though smoking wasn't the only thing he'd got up to.

"Have you been drinking?"

"The paper's been shut down, Kay. Wouldn't you be?"

"Shut down? By who?"

"Who else? The president signed an executive order citing national security, blah, blah, blah."

Warm beads of sweat trickled down Kay's brow. "But they can't do that, Ron. Not to a paper this big."

"They've done it, Kay. It was a risk we were willing to take, remember? We called their bluff and they had a full house. Turns out we had nothing but a lousy pair of threes."

"There's no federal judge worth his salt who won't overturn the order."

"Kay, wake up. We've been muzzled. By the time a judge sits his ass on the bench to render a decision, it'll be too late. And we're not the only ones either. I've been told that anyone who continues to run your story will suffer the same fate. Looks like you cleared out your desk just in time."

"I didn't know this was coming, if that's what you're suggesting."

She heard the clink of ice as Ron downed another drink. "I'm sure you didn't. Either way, what does it matter? The press is only a pillar of democracy."

It seemed that democracy was becoming an old-fashioned concept, but she kept that to herself. Engaging in a philosophical conversation with a drunken news editor wasn't going to end well.

"I'd wish you good luck," he said, his words trailing off only to suddenly come back at full strength. "But I don't think luck's got anything to do with it." Ron hung up after that and Kay stood staring down at her phone, wondering how things could get any worse.

•••

After her conversation with Ron, Kay made her way onto the westbound platform. She took a seat at the very end and waited. Opened in 1977, McPherson Square's vaulted ceiling and futuristic look made it one of Washington's most iconic metro stations. But iconic or not, trains were only coming once every thirty minutes or so nowadays. She scanned the small handful of faces as each one pulled in. The idea that the subway would soon be closed for good was another sign the natural order of things was being irreparably worn away. Total anarchy hadn't taken hold just yet, but it was not far off.

At the other end of the station, two men descended the staircase, making their way along the platform. One of them was unusually large and muscular, the other confident and ruggedly handsome in a Chef Ramsay sort of way.

The men approached and sat down on either side of her. Kay felt her pulse quicken.

Kay's hands were folded over the gun in her purse. The larger man covered her hands with one of his own, the way a father might do to a young child.

"No need to worry," he said in a deep, resonating voice. "We won't hurt you."

She let out a skittish laugh. "If I had a nickel…" she started to say before the other man cut in.

"If it's all the same to you, I'd just as rather we dispense with the small talk. I love pleasantries just as much as the next man, but I think you'll believe me when I say we ain't got time to dilly-dally. I'm Ollie and the lug next to you is Sven."

Sven winked.

She turned back to Ollie. "You're the Australian I spoke to on the phone," she said, keeping her hands where they were. "I normally don't meet contacts in person. It's safer that way."

"Contacts?" Ollie asked, his face twisting in confusion.

"Isn't that why you're here? For a story? I should tell you I'm currently out of a job since the government just saw fit to close down the *Post*."

"We heard," Ollie told her. "But we're not here to be your contacts. We each have something the other needs. I read your exposé on Sentinel. I gotta say, that was some ballsy stuff."

"Maybe, but look where it got me."

"Darling, you and your lot were heading into the dustbin anyway. You merely sped the process up a little."

She stared into his dark eyes and saw he was dead serious.

"Dissenting voices make it far too difficult to run an authoritarian regime," he told her. He aimed a finger in the air. "Given what we're up against, it should come as no surprise that's the direction the world is heading in.

When times are scary, people yearn for safety, security, often at any cost. By the time the threat is over, it's often too late."

"So President Myers is a dictator? Is that what you're saying?"

"Not quite. He's just a patsy. Sentinel's the real power behind the throne. And like most groups with a radical goal, there's actually some logic to it. I should know. I was one of them once. But somewhere along the way that goal became secondary to the thirst for power they needed to realize their vision. Sentinel wants to save humanity. There's no blaming them for that. But the way they're going about it will certainly make our fate so much worse."

"The road to hell is paved with good intentions," she said.

Ollie nodded. "It took me a hell of a long time to understand that."

"You're a crusader," Kay said, sizing him up. "Battling anyone and anything for what you believe."

Ollie smiled, liking where she was going with this.

"But you also have a weakness," she went on. "How do you know you're on the right side?"

"You're a smart Sheila," he said, grinning. "I've made mistakes in the past, I won't lie. Even Sven here's mucked things up a time or two."

"So now you're trying to stop Sentinel," Kay said, cutting to the chase.

"That's the idea."

"But how do you know they aren't really the good guys? Maybe you've been hoodwinked again?"

Ollie nodded slowly, thoughtfully. "Here's how I know." He reached into his pocket and pulled out a rolled-up sheaf of papers and handed them to her.

"What is this?"

"Go ahead and read it."

Kay did so. Blazoned across the top was the Homeland Security letterhead. Beneath that were rows and rows of names. A paragraph at the top identified them as dissidents and ordered the local authorities to round them up for detainment and processing. Kay ran a trembling finger down the list until she came to three she knew all too well: Felix, Thereze and Kayza Mahoro.

"I heard about this, but I didn't want to believe it."

"Well, believe it," Ollie said, handing her another piece of paper. This one was an email from a Dr. Alan Salzburg to President Myers. The two documents were nearly identical.

"Myers is taking orders from Dr. Salzburg," Ollie explained. "And Salzburg heads Sentinel. Which effectively means Sentinel is in control of the United States. They've erected what they call correction camps for troublemakers. They can call them anything they want, but you and I both know what these really are."

"Concentration camps," Kay whispered. She had to curl her right hand into a ball to stop it from shaking.

"Trust me," Ollie said, sarcastically. "It gets better. They built these camps at low elevations all along America's East Coast."

"Why not inland where they could keep it secret like they did during World War II?" Kay asked.

"Great question and the answer is simple. That ship is expected to slam into the ocean right off the coast of Newfoundland. Beautiful place, by the way, but it'll be vaporized in an instant. The resulting impact will cause a massive tsunami that will flood most of the east coast, killing the tens of thousands of dissidents imprisoned in the various camps. So you asked me how I knew I was on the right side. That's how."

"What can I do about any of this?" Kay asked, struggling to hold it together. "I can't even get the cops to go collect my fiancé's dead body."

Ollie's face changed. "I'm sorry about your bloke, I really am. From what I could tell, he was a standup guy. But don't worry, Sven here had a few members of our group take care of him."

"Really? How did you know?"

"We've been looking for you. You're not an easy woman to find, Kay."

The smile on her lips held little joy. "I've been told. So what can I do?"

"Help us get the word out, for starters."

She shook her head. "Didn't you hear? The *Post* was shut down, along with a bunch of other news organizations."

"That's right," Ollie conceded. "Although shut down is not entirely accurate. They've been taken over and will be rebranded as propaganda machines to only disseminate Sentinel's point of view. Most of your colleagues who wouldn't go along chose to quit. The ones who raised a stink were put on a list and shipped off. But for as long as the internet's still running," Ollie said, taking her by the hand, "there will be folks eager to find out what's going on. You're one of the few who knows and has the reputation to convince them."

"You want me to start a blog or something?"

"That's a good start."

"But what will stop the authorities from tracking me down and sending me away?"

"Kinda hard to catch someone if they don't stay in one place," he told her.

She regarded him quizzically.

106

"That's right, you'll come with us. Besides, we have someone who can bounce your IP through so many countries Sentinel will think you're a bloody kangaroo."

Kay pulled her hand from Ollie's grasp. "Maybe whoever got you these documents can also find out where my parents are being held. You agree to free them and I'll help you with whatever you want."

"What you're asking is dangerous."

Kay folded her arms, staring into his eyes with stark determination.

A few tense moments went by before Ollie sighed. "Okay, we'll do it."

"By we you mean you and Sven, right?"

Ollie shook his head. "If you want your parents sprung, then you're coming with us. There's just one quick thing we need to do first."

"Oh, really, and what is that?" Kay asked, not liking the sound of that.

The dimpled grin filled Ollie's face. "Prevent the launch of a nuclear missile."

Chapter 19

47 hours, 11 minutes, 03 seconds

Mia increased the brightness on her helmet light as she traced the vines growing along the walls.

"I'm not sure why I didn't see this earlier," she said to Jack over the radio, clear excitement in her voice.

Jack was kneeling down, studying something on the ground. He got up and came over. So too did Anna.

"What is it, Dr. Ward?" Anna asked.

"Take a look at the direction these roots are growing in," she said, drawing a line with both index fingers from the center of the chamber toward the arched doorway. "Do you see anything unusual?"

"There are no cracks in the foundation," Jack said. "I mean, this place looks like it's sat abandoned a long time, but apart from the tangle of jungle plants, the structure itself appears to be completely intact."

"I believe what Dr. Ward is getting at," Anna interjected, "is that all of the vines appear to be heading in the same direction."

"That's right. And when you trace them back to their source…"

"They lead directly to the canisters," he said, completing

her thought. "Are you suggesting at one time this was some sort of plant farm?"

She nodded. "I'm suggesting that, one time, this room was used to grow and house vegetation and that for some reason, something went wrong and the plants got out."

"You make it sound like they escaped," Stokes said, sneering.

Anna spoke up, eager for clarification. "Is it your hypothesis that the plant life from this chamber is responsible for giving rise to the jungle outside?"

"I'm suggesting it's possible," Mia said, leaning back. "But what doesn't make sense is why anyone would do such a thing. We're missing an important piece of the puzzle, I can feel it." Between two thick yellow vines at her feet, Mia noticed a patch of moist earth. She dug her gloved fingers in as deep as they would go, curled them into a hook and pulled up a series of smaller roots, over twenty in all.

"There are plenty more down there," she said.

"What are they?" Jack asked, moving in for a closer look. Anna ran a laser over the shriveled strands in Mia's hand. "They are the remnants of older vines," she said. "But the stuff that looks like soil is nothing more than the composted remains from ages past."

"So you're saying these things have been growing down here for thousands of years," Jack inferred.

Mia looked over at one of the shattered transparent cases. "Maybe even longer than that. The being who destroyed this plant nursery or greenhouse or whatever the heck it was must have done so a very long time ago." She thought at once of the bones they'd found. "Do you think the *Mesonyx* people could have done it?" she wondered aloud.

Jack nodded, the light inside his helmet illuminating lips pursed in thought. "It's possible, but why would they vandalize the place?"

"What if the structure around the portal wasn't a shrine?" she said. "What if it was meant to be a barrier?"

Just then Kerr's agitated voice cut in. "Sergeant Stokes, I think you guys better cut it short and get back up here."

"Something wrong?" Stokes asked, the tiniest hint of concern audible in his otherwise steady voice.

"Peterson saw something in the bush and went to investigate. We tried raising him on the radio and he's not answering."

"Be right there," Stokes replied. "Okay, folks, time to leave. Pack up your gear, we can always come back later."

They did as he suggested and hurried out of the chamber and up the vine-covered staircase.

"Peterson, do you read me?" Stokes called out over the radio. They waited several agonizing seconds with no reply.

"We already tried that, Sarge," Diaz told him, wide-eyed. "He's not calling back, I think he might have fallen down a hole or something."

"Which way did he go?" Stokes asked.

Kerr aimed a finger toward a gap in the brush. "He went that way."

"All right, let's all spread out five yards apart and head in that direction."

They did so, calling Peterson's name over the radio as they went. Mia's pulse was scampering in her chest as

110

they crossed the difficult terrain. She had seen the video of the large creature Jack had filmed his first time here. If a creature like that was walking around, there was no telling what else might be lurking about. They moved up a rise, all the while heading deeper into the jungle. Fingers of alien sunlight streamed down through narrow gaps in the canopy high above. Near the treetops, tiny red wisps danced about in a dazzling acrobatic display. To Mia's right, Ivan rumbled along, avoiding only the largest of trees. Anything smaller he simply crushed under his tank treads.

Mia's audio sensors relayed the buzzing of Anna's drones circling nearby. If Peterson was close, they were sure to find him. As if on cue, Stokes ordered them to stop and to get down.

Jack swung his rifle around. Ivan circled back noisily, aiming for a spot next to Stokes.

"Dammit, Yuri, will you tell that shit-for-brains robot of yours to stay put!"

Yuri gave Ivan the order.

"Affirmative," came Ivan's reply as he skidded to a stop five feet behind the sergeant's crouched form. With red flickering eyes, Ivan scanned the terrain before them. They were standing on the small rise, overlooking a depression in the landscape where the foliage wasn't nearly as dense.

"I think I see Peterson," Stokes said in a hushed, deliberate voice over the radio. He didn't need to whisper, but the fact that he did told Mia the news wasn't good.

"One o'clock, next to the base of the red palm tree," Stokes said. Of course, it wasn't a palm, but who could be picky at a time like this?

"There ain't nothing left but a pair of legs," Kerr cried, fighting to stay cool.

"Where's the rest of…?" Jack started to ask when they saw Peterson's legs get lifted three feet off the ground before crashing back down like the bottom half of a discarded child's toy.

The something else came into view and the question was no longer where the rest of him had gone, but what was the creature with the blood-soaked mouth hovering over him? It made a low gurgling sound and surveyed the area before returning to its meal.

Two of the creature's six top-jointed legs were clasped onto Peterson's corpse while the remaining four were used to brace its three-hundred-pound frame. The creature's neck was long, its head a narrow tube studded with rows of eyes and punctuated at the tip with a circular array of sharpened teeth. Its flesh was shiny and grey and vacuum-sealed over an assortment of protruding bones.

From where they stood, it was a twisted cross between a house centipede and an anteater. For terrifying seconds they watched as the creature shoved its tubular head into the mess of Peterson's remains, coming out time and again with chunks of the man's flesh.

"That's no way for any soldier to die," Stokes said, pressing the glass of his helmet against the scope of his M4. He squeezed the trigger four times in rapid succession, hitting the creature with every shot. It stumbled back with surprise, emitting a loud cry of what Mia could only guess was pain. But then it leapt back onto those six spindly legs and charged at them.

Stokes continued firing as it drew closer, the creature picking up momentum as it darted through the heavy undergrowth, making it difficult to land a good shot. The remaining Delta Force men opened up a second later, bullets cutting narrow saplings in two, spraying the air with a strange milky secretion. Some of their shots were landing, but the creature wasn't going down. By the time it was twenty feet away, Mia leapt to her feet in concern. And when it cut that distance down to five feet, dread began to surge through every fiber of her being. The thing that had killed Peterson was going to take Stokes out and maybe the rest of them too. In slow motion, Mia watched that crown of razor-sharp teeth widen as it came in for the kill, its body pockmarked with holes where the soldiers' bullets had riddled it. The beast was three feet away, Stokes only now rising to his feet, no doubt certain these were the last few moments he would be alive.

Suddenly the animal was stopped abruptly in its tracks. It let out a shrill, strangled screech, the only sound it could manage with Ivan's heavy pincers closed around its neck. The robot's arm rotated three hundred and sixty degrees, breaking the creature's neck with a loud snap.

Frozen, Stokes watched the beast's limp body fall to the ground in a heap. Ivan hovered over it, the sensors from his eyes sweeping over its corpse.

"What the hell was that thing?" Kerr asked.

Diaz secured Peterson's weapon. "He never fired a shot," he said, his voice thick with fear. "Must have been stalking him."

Nobody responded. Not because they didn't want to. But because they either were still too stunned by what had just happened, or simply didn't have an answer.

"Stalkers," Dag said. "That sounds like as good a name as any."

"Dr. Greer," Anna said. "My long-range scanners have detected a distant sound very much like the one emitted by the alien life form we just terminated."

Stokes looked over, concern in his normally stoic eyes. "How far?"

"It is difficult to tell. I can send one of my drones higher and have it search for movement through the underbrush."

"Do it," Jack said.

Stokes turned to two of his men. "Grab what's left of Peterson. Wrap him up in a giant leaf if you have to, but double-time it. We best be booking it out of here before the rest of those things show up looking for another snack."

Chapter 20

45 hours, 12 minutes, 36 seconds

The visible light was already starting to fade.

"That's just what we need," Dag said, expressing the thought lingering on everyone's mind.

One soldier was dead and they were now running from a pack of flesh-hungry Stalkers. Now the prospect of trekking through an alien jungle at night felt like a thick layer of icing on a proverbial shit sandwich. They switched on their helmet lights, Jack growing certain that if the local wildlife hadn't been aware of their presence, they soon would be.

Within a matter of minutes, the fading light had turned to total darkness.

"That sun sure went down fast," Stokes said, navigating a tricky bit of footwork as they descended a rocky hill.

"It means the planet we're on is likely spinning much quicker than Earth," Jack replied, breathing heavily from the exertion. "If a day on Earth lasts twenty-four hours, then a day here is only half or a third that long."

"Dr. Greer," Anna said, crossing the rough terrain with ease. "I should let you know I have lost connection to the drone that was monitoring the creatures pursuing us."

"How so?"

"I am not certain. It appears to have collided with something."

That didn't sound good.

"Ivan, hurry up," Yuri shouted impatiently. "No, not straight through, go around."

The tank treads let out a high-pitched whining sound.

"What do you mean you're stuck?" the Russian said, his voice dry with exasperation and growing fear.

Stokes cursed. "If that tin can hadn't saved my life I'd be just as happy to leave it behind. Kerr, head back and see if you can help Yuri free it. But don't hang around forever."

Kerr nodded and ran to where Ivan was stuck. Jack followed him while the rest of them carried on.

"Anna," Jack said. "How far away are they?"

"Please hold. I am moving the second drone into position."

Please hold? What was this, a help line?

He and Kerr arrived to find Yuri pulling at a branch stuck in Ivan's tread. "Give me a hand with this, will you?"

The three men grabbed hold and rocked it back and forth in an effort to pry it loose.

"Geez, Ivan," Kerr said. "How the hell'd you wedge this in so bad?"

"Dr. Greer, I am picking up movement on the jungle floor three hundred meters away and closing fast."

They gave it one final go with everything they had. The branch broke free with such force it sent Kerr tumbling backwards. He swung a leg around to stay his fall and twisted his ankle.

"Ah, crap," he swore, stumbling to the ground. Jack and Yuri helped him to his feet.

"Can you run?" Jack asked him.

Kerr tried to move a few steps and nearly fell again.

"Run? The real question is can I walk?"

"How close are they, Anna?"

"One hundred and fifty meters," she replied. "I recommend you hurry up."

"Yeah, no shit," Kerr snapped.

Jack and Yuri positioned themselves on either side of Kerr as the three men began moving again, albeit at a much slower pace.

They didn't get more than twenty feet before Kerr said, "There's no way we're gonna make it. Not like this. Leave me here and I'll slow them down as long as I can."

"Don't be a hero," Stokes barked from about a hundred yards ahead. "I'll come back there and carry you myself if I have to."

As if on cue, Ivan spun around and plucked Kerr out of their grasp and cradled him in his giant metallic arms like a baby. The machine then rolled through the jungle at high speed, giving Kerr a whipping from every branch in his path.

"Dr. Greer, they are fifty meters away from your position."

"We're not gonna make it back to the portal," Stokes said. "We'll hold up in the greenhouse and wait for sunup. Otherwise those things are gonna pick us off one by one."

Jack magnified his external audio sensors. If something was scrambling up behind him, he wanted to hear it coming first.

Ivan and Kerr were now about a dozen feet ahead of them.

Struggling through labored breathing, Yuri said, "An old Russian saying about meeting a bear in the woods. You don't need to outrun the bear. Only the man next to you." He let out a dry, humorless laugh and pulled slightly ahead. Jack dug down deep, fighting to keep up. This was payback for turning around to help that crazy Russian and his dimwitted robot.

"Ten meters," Anna called out to him right as he entered the clearing and saw the angled shape of the greenhouse rising up from the ground, its roof nearly hidden by a twisted mangle of psychedelic foliage. Bates and Conroy stood by the entrance, waiting for them. Jack saw their eyes grow wide as they levelled their rifles, aiming in his direction. At once he cut to the right as the soldiers opened fire. Ivan was already inside, Yuri not far behind. That was when the soldiers stopped firing and ran for the greenhouse. Jack hurried along the straight edge of the outer wall, aiming to tuck around and dive into the entrance. He could hear something only feet away, grunting after him. His legs felt light and tingly with the knowledge that any second he might feel the teeth from that meat grinder of a mouth sink into his back. A part of Jack had already begun to accept his fate when he spotted a shape reemerge from the greenhouse entrance. It was Ivan and he extended both arms, firing his twin machine guns on full automatic. Jack reached the entrance and dove in, right as two of the creatures crashed into the robot. He heard the sound of the machine's heavy pincers clamp down on bone and flesh alike. Then more of the creatures joined in and Ivan was overwhelmed.

Chapter 21

Jack reached the bottom of the staircase to find Stokes and another soldier covering the entrance above. Just outside, signs of a vicious battle were still in progress. Ivan might not be all that smart, but he sure was tough. Inside the chamber, Yuri paced back and forth. He stopped and faced Jack. "What's going on up there? Is Ivan okay? He's not responding."

"Ivan's a little busy," Jack said. "He sacrificed himself to save me, which is more than I could have asked for."

"We need to head back up there and save him," Yuri protested, gripping the sides of his helmet.

"Negative," Stokes replied. "Robots can be replaced, people can't."

Suddenly, the air outside grew still.

Jack caught sight of Anna, who also seemed concerned, and not only from the harshness of Stokes' comment.

"You're worried about him, aren't you?" he asked her. The expression on her digital face fell. "I will admit, when I first encountered Ivan I was not very impressed. And in no small part due to the poor construction of his neural architecture. Then gradually my perceptions began to change. I am not certain why."

"He grew on you," Jack said, putting a hand on her shoulder and squeezing gently, anxious to keep her mind off of Ivan's probable demise.

She paused for a moment, working to untangle the literal from the figurative in Jack's statement. "I believe you are correct. The longer I spent interacting with Ivan, the less his inferior abilities bothered me."

"Perhaps there was another quality he possessed that impressed you."

She nodded, scouring the vine-covered floor with her eyes as though searching for something. "He was brave and loyal to his friends."

"I think you hit the nail on the head."

Anna's head jerked to one side in momentary confusion about how Jack's statement about hammers and nails was relevant. "Oh, yes. I am becoming accustomed to the strange way humans speak. To an outside observer, such methods of speech and action make little sense, although they seem to govern much of human behavior."

"You're right, Anna," Jack told her, forgetting sometimes she wasn't just like a child. She was like a child from another country and in some ways maybe even from another planet. "A big part of what you're talking about is culture. Did Rajesh ever teach you about that?"

"I'm afraid not," she said with a touch of melancholy. "Although I do recall noticing a marked difference between the Real Housewives and their counterparts in Atlanta." Anna raised her arm and gave three crisp snaps. "Do not get me started, girlfriend."

Jack laughed and shook his head. "How much of that crap have you watched?"

"Every available episode," she replied without missing a beat. "Often I view several at the same time."

"Well, I don't mind, but some folks get uncomfortable when the topic of race comes up."

"I fail to understand why."

"Uh, it's complicated," Jack said, feeling this wasn't the right time or place for such a chat. Where was Rajesh when he needed him? Somehow Jack had become something of a surrogate parent and now the full responsibility for answering all of Anna's often fair, but rather challenging questions had fallen squarely on him. She could tell you in a heartbeat why the sky was blue or why humans didn't have tails, the sort of questions parents had dealt with for years. It was the other stuff she had trouble with, the things that hid in the cracks of our daily lives, the things most of us worked hard to avoid. Those were the things Anna wanted to know about most. Her sense of wonder and insatiable curiosity were part of what set her so far apart from anything that had ever come before her. Of course, the flipside was the burden Jack now bore to ensure he taught her the truth of what it meant to be a human being without crushing the light that made her want to know in the first place. He let out a deep, ragged breath. "How do I put this? A lot of folks have a view that something which is starkly different from them is bad."

"Why bad? Why not better?"

This wasn't going well. "I suppose because each of us thinks of ourselves as the hero of our own story. At heart, that's what we are, as humans. We're storytellers. Sometimes those stories are mostly true and sometimes they're not true at all. But however you slice it, each of us

122

always has to come out on top. When the facts don't support that conclusion, it normally means the story has to change to fit the desired outcome. Uh, a child loses at a game of pingpong. Rather than admitting his skills need improvement, he claims he wasn't really trying or that the sun was in his eyes. That way he can avoid dealing with the truth."

"But that is a lie."

Jack laughed. "Get used to it. Lies probably account for the vast majority of human behavior. In this case, lying is a tool humans use to maintain their hero status. But the point I'm getting at isn't about lies. It's about why different is seen as bad. If different were good, then by that logic it would mean something was wrong with the person doing the observing. The truth however is that different isn't better or worse, it's just different."

"That would imply humans spend an inordinate amount of time dwelling on meaningless distinctions."

"See," Jack said, nudging her chin. "Now you're getting it."

Anna shook her head and smiled. "Dr. Greer, do you think I am the hero in my own story?" The hopeful look on her face was undeniable.

Jack nodded. "Not only in yours, kid, but in mine too."

"Stay alert," Stokes called out over the radio. "Inbound hostile heading down the staircase."

Jack spun around, readying his rifle. Dag, Mia and the remaining Delta operators also braced themselves.

A moment later Stokes swore. "Oh, crap, it isn't one of those things. It's Ivan and he looks pretty banged up."

Chapter 22

Three hours after their encounter in the Washington Metro, Kay, Ollie and Sven took a private plane to Orlando. From there, they would head east toward a safe house on the mainland a few miles from Merritt Island and the Kennedy Space Center. The nukes designed to intercept the incoming alien ship would be launched from two locations. The first was Kennedy. Vandenberg Air Force Base in California was the other. Ollie had informed Kay that a second team of pros had been dispatched to perform a similar mission.

"Don't you want them to stop that ship?" she asked him as Sven drove them from the airstrip.

"I may be a lot of things, but I'm not suicidal," he assured her.

"It just seems like a strange policy to sit back and do nothing when we're being attacked." As a reporter, she was used to playing devil's advocate, although in this particular instance, the moral decision on how to respond was nowhere near a hundred percent clear.

"This is not an attack," he told her with stalwart confidence. "It may have disastrous effects, but I don't believe they've got it in for humanity. I've seen certain things this last week that have convinced me nothing about what's happening is personal."

"You're talking about the genetic work Dr. Ward was doing?"

"That's right. To them we're merely a crop that went bad."

She shook her head in disgust. "And that gives them the right to wipe us out?"

"I read in your file that you're religious," Ollie said, turning to face her.

Kay nodded and then shook her head. "Well, my father's a pastor, but I don't share all of his views."

"I'll bet you heard quite a few of those views growing up though, didn't you?"

"Of course," she replied, frowning. "What does that have to do—"

"With what I'm talking about? In all that time your dad spouted off passages from the Bible, did you ever hear him complain once about God's wrath?"

"What do you mean?"

"Take the flood, for example. God decided man wasn't worthy and snuffed out the lot of them."

"They had sinned," she began to say in protest, only to realize after how her words were only helping to make his point.

"We've been taught that when God gets angry and steps on us, it's because we musta done something to deserve it. That's what some folks believe. And far from trying to question it, I'm merely pointing out that it has always been assumed that God had the moral right to destroy mankind and start fresh if he wasn't satisfied with the way we were acting. I've seen a few sermons in my time. Australians are just as nuts for the Bible as you Yanks are. But in all that time, I never once heard a single person raise a stink over the extinctions driven by God's wrath. So why is everyone raising a stink now? Hey, I'm

125

not in a hurry to die, believe me, but at least with an impact we have a chance. If those Sentinel bastards manage to blow that thing up, don't think whoever sent it won't launch a thousand more to take its place."

"You sound like the ultimate pragmatist," Kay replied, chewing over what Ollie had just told her.

"If a bigger, stronger man's about to punch you in the face and you don't have time to duck, what do you do? Try to kick him in the balls and really piss him off or take that punch as best you can?"

Kay regarded Ollie, studying the heavy lines of age and experience that contoured his face. "You're saying we're in a lose-lose situation."

"I'm saying it could be worse than that. Imagine we've read it all wrong and they aren't here to fry us. Let's say the ship zooming through space is really part of a delegation aimed at welcoming us. I don't believe it, but for the sake of this conversation, let's just pretend. So here they come, a hand extended, and we blow the crap out of them."

Kay nodded. "I see your point."

"You might think, hey, I'd rather take my chances and attack them first. But that's the insidious part of the whole affair. You wouldn't just be throwing your own life away, you'd be dooming the entire species. I don't want that sort of burden hanging over me."

Kay turned away after that. She didn't want to talk about fiery apocalypses nor about deciding the fate of humanity. The truth was she just wanted her family back, even if only for a day or so before the world went to hell in a handbasket. Growing up, Kay's father had been taught the traditional Rwandan stories of Imana, the Creator. While he ruled over life and death, he generally did not meddle in human affairs. When the colonial

126

powers arrived in the late nineteenth century, they had brought with them a new form of government along with a new God. This was the one Ollie had been talking about, the sort that seemed to be filled with rage in the Old Testament just as he was filled with love in the New. If Ollie was right about the beings traveling through space toward them, Kay couldn't help but wonder which kind of God they would be.

•••

Not long after, they pulled into the driveway of a pink bungalow on Sisson Road. The garage door opened and Sven drove the car in and killed the engine. They got out as the door began closing behind them.

"She ain't much," Ollie said, getting out and stretching his legs as he motioned to their humble surroundings. "But she'll do for now."

A tall, thin man wearing green cammies swung open the door from the house. He had the thick accent of a man born and bred in the Florida Everglades.

"I didn't expect y'all so soon," he said, greeting Sven with a slap of their palms followed by a hug. "Whoa, easy, big fella. I need that spine."

Sven chuckled and moved past him and into the cool air-conditioned house.

"Patrick, this is Kay," Ollie said, introducing them.

She smiled, doing her best to hide her weariness.

"You're the reporter lady," Patrick said. "Yeah, I heard about you. Haven't had the chance to read one of your articles though, but I intend to."

"They closed her paper, you turd," Ollie said, embracing him before moving on.

Patrick scrunched up his mouth. "Bummer. Hey, let me grab your bag. Come on inside, I got the AC on full blast."

Kay handed him her laptop bag, which was all she really had. Ever since discovering the D.C. cops were after her, she had resigned herself to the idea of wearing the same outfit forever. She followed Patrick inside. The house bore a striking resemblance to every other suburban home that had ever existed and Kay guessed that had been part of the point. He led her through the kitchen where pictures of young kids and finger paintings hung from fruit-shaped magnets. On the counter was a framed image of Patrick with a woman who stood at least a foot and a half shorter than he was.

"Don't worry about all the fluff. Most of it's for show. I'm the housekeeper."

Kay glanced over and saw dishes piled in the sink. "You're not doing a very good job."

Patrick laughed. "Not that kind. I manage this safe house. I won't lie, it was lonely until I got myself a fake wife." He pointed at the picture Kay had seen of him and the woman. "I'm not exactly her type, if you know what I mean, but that may be 'cause I'm not a woman." The furniture in the living room had been pushed against the wall to make room for a large desk filled with computer monitors. The woman from the picture was sitting before them clicking away.

"Oh, hell, darling, you're not playing that damn game again, are you?" Patrick said, setting Kay's laptop bag on the couch.

"Don't bother me," she barked. "I'm about to level."

"She's a sweetheart, ain't she?" Patrick said, hooking a thumb over his shoulder at her.

Ollie emerged from a nearby washroom, drying his hands. "I see you've met everyone."

Kay cocked her head to one side and motioned to the figure perched intently before the bank of monitors, swearing at digital goblins. "Uh, not everyone."

"Hell, yeah!" The woman screamed with joy as the screen lit up with an explosion of stars.

Kay assumed she'd just leveled, whatever that meant.

Ollie went over and put an arm around the computer nerd as she rose from her chair. "Kay, I'd like you to meet Armoni."

Chapter 23

42 hours, 40 minutes, 51 seconds

Given the extent of Ivan's injuries, even Yuri was shocked that he'd made it back at all. Anna had been the first to rush to his aid. Grabbing hold of Ivan's remaining arm, she guided him over the uneven floor inside the chamber to an unoccupied corner.

Yuri moved in to assess the damage. One of the robot's tank treads had been ripped completely off. His right arm was missing along with the pincer from the other. Part of his face plate had also been torn away, revealing a crisscrossing network of wires and circuits leading to and from his optical receptors.

"He's one tough son of a bitch," Dag said. "I'll give him that."

"You think he can be fixed?" Mia asked.

Yuri did not look hopeful. "It will depend. The damage appears to be mostly superficial. But there isn't much I can do for him here. We'll need to get him back to the other technicians. That's assuming he can make it back to the portal at all."

"Or that any of us make it back," Dag said under his breath, or what passed for under his breath for the outspoken Swede.

"Mr. Volkov, would you mind if I took a look at Ivan?" Anna asked, surveying the robot's torn face plate.

Yuri's eyes met Jack's.

Jack shrugged. "I don't see what harm it would do," he reassured him. "You can always set some parameters so she doesn't alter any of his vital architecture."

"Feel free," Yuri said with the wave of his hand. "What I really need is a diagnostic to be sure none of his internal components have suffered irreparable harm."

"I can do that," Anna said, a wide grin on her glowing face.

Yuri pulled out his tablet and had Ivan run through some hand-eye coordination tests, along with an assessment of whether his visual recognition software had been compromised.

"There is a video recording from Ivan's battle," Anna informed the Russian. "Would you like me to feed the data to your OHMD glasses?"

"Send it to all of us," Jack recommended. "It might give us a better idea what we're up against."

Anna nodded and activated the transfer. At once, a frantic struggle played out before their eyes. Blinding flashes from Ivan's weapons as the fight quickly closed to hand-to-hand combat. Jack paused his playback, his index finger dabbing in midair as he counted.

"I count two dead Stalkers with five others tearing off into the jungle after the fight," Jack said. "Maybe they realized Ivan's armor plating wasn't nearly as tasty as flesh."

"It's pitch black out there," Stokes told them. "Even with the OHMDs' nightvision capabilities we would be at a serious disadvantage. You saw the way they circled around Ivan and came back at him time and again. I'm no biology major, but I know an ambush hunter when I see one. Not much different than a shark. Convince you they've gone away and then hit you where you least expect it."

"A different planet means different evolutionary rules and behaviors might apply," Mia replied, countering Stokes' analysis. "Not that I'm suggesting we head back out there, especially at night. Is there any chance we could call in reinforcements? You know, to help escort us out."

"The minute anything passes through the portal," Jack reminded her, "communications to the other side are immediately cut." He took her by the hand. "I'm sorry I got you into this."

She smiled and squeezed. "I'm a big girl who made the decision to join the expedition. Besides, maybe the wait will give us time to learn more about this place, in particular who built this room and why."

"Perhaps we might learn whether or not they are still around," Anna added.

"Right on," Dag agreed. "So we can tell them that maybe killing everyone on Earth isn't such a great idea."

Kerr chimed in, fidgeting a few feet away. "If we don't get out of here soon, I'm gonna piss my biosuit."

Jack laughed. "A true ambassador of the human race." Mia threw him a disapproving look.

Jack threw his hands in the air. "All right, I'm not much better," he admitted. "I lost my mom's house once in a poker game and had to work three jobs to get it back."

"Ouch," Dag said, shaking his hand like he'd touched

something hot.

"Don't be so hard on yourself," Mia told Jack. "I too know something about hitting rock bottom. We all have our poison whether we recognize it or not. For me, the scariest part was how that crutch you think is the only thing keeping you upright is often what ends up destroying you. For me that was pain pills and I'd justified taking them in my head a million different ways. First why I needed ten, then twenty and finally thirty of them a day."

"The demons that tried to destroy us and failed," Jack said, his eyes glassy and far away.

"Nothing tried to destroy us," Mia corrected him.

Jack snapped back, his features twisted with uncertainty. "I don't understand."

"The pills didn't try to get me," she explained. "They weren't forced down my throat. I made a conscious choice to take them in order to numb the searing pain. It didn't matter the pain was mostly in my head, it stung all the same. And I convinced myself that crawling into that warm glow of oblivion would help get me back on my feet when all it was really doing was pushing me closer to the ground."

Anna unplugged from Ivan and addressed Yuri. "As you instructed, I have run a full diagnostic on Ivan's systems and see no area that has been compromised."

"Thank you," he mumbled, hardly looking up.

Anna went over to the others. "As I was helping Mr. Volkov with Ivan, I was also processing the feed I received from the drones."

"You mean the ones that crashed?" Dag asked.

She nodded.

133

"Wait," Jack said, raising his hands in the air. "I thought you only lost one drone?"

"Unfortunately, Dr. Greer, I ordered the second and last drone to fly above the treetops in order to search for incoming Stalkers and it too suffered the same fate."

"Any idea what happened?" Mia asked, fiddling with a broken piece of what looked like glass.

"Both drones impacted a hard, inanimate object."

"Up in the sky?" Jack said, wondering how that was even possible. "Are you saying it hit a ship of some kind?"

"No," Anna replied. "Not a ship, a ceiling."

Dag rubbed the side of his helmet. "How is that even possible?"

Anna's expression became grave. "It is looking more and more certain that the extraterrestrial jungle we are in is located inside a domed enclosure."

"What do you mean a dome?" Jack said, not trying to hide his exasperation.

"A sealed space," Anna explained. "Designed to allow the maintenance of specified environmental conditions."

Mia pressed her back against the ledge and considered what Anna had just told them. "That certainly implies the atmosphere beyond the dome is hostile to life."

"That is a possibility," Anna conceded. "But you should also know, the data from the drones I recovered appears to indicate the dome in question is not transparent."

"But the sun," Jack said, at a loss. It was as though every assumption he'd made about this place was turning out to be wrong. "I mean it was practically blinding when I first arrived and now it's set. Are you saying all that is some kind of illusion?"

"Dr. Greer, I am suggesting the enclosure's surface may

be composed of a series of panels, each capable of producing a source of light similar in brightness and warmth to that of a large star."

Yuri stopped what he was doing and cleared his throat. "What the hell is this place?" the Russian said. The fright in his voice was echoed in each of their faces.

Chapter 24

It was a question, of course, that none of them could answer, not yet at least.

"Do you have an estimate of how big this thing is?" Jack wondered.

"Based on initial calculations," Anna told them, "the dome has an approximate diameter of two miles."

An image popped into Mia's mind of a barren moon or hellish planet, somewhere out along the edge of the galaxy, protected by nothing more than a thin skin, holding out the deadly environment trying desperately to get in. The last part of the vision was pure conjecture, but spoke to the feeling of vulnerability that had suddenly chilled the marrow in her bones.

Dag paced back and forth, rubbing at the arms of his biosuit. "Why do I suddenly feel like a rat in a maze?" he said, echoing the strange sense of danger and manipulation Mia was also feeling.

They weren't the only ones. For a few tense moments, the chamber was silent, the toxic alien air around them heavy with unease.

"Hostile incoming!" Stokes shouted a split second before opening fire. The Delta operator named Conroy guarding the stairway next to him did the same, filling the narrow passage with short bursts.

Rifle in hand, Jack moved toward the archway when Anna called after him.

"Dr. Greer, there was something else I observed while reviewing Ivan's video log," Anna told him amidst the gunfire. "The creatures appear to have a thick hide, somewhat resistant to the impact of the .556 rounds the soldiers are using. The only real area of vulnerability I managed to detect was the soft flesh of their oral cavity. I suspect a well-placed shot there might have a devastating effect."

"You mean blast them in the mouth," he said succinctly.

"That is correct."

"Those openings aren't more than five or six inches wide," Kerr said, rushing to the archway with the other soldiers.

"Here they come," Stokes shouted, laying down a short, controlled burst.

The others watched from Stokes' point of view as the rounds struck the beast's neck and shoulders with seemingly little effect. Taking careful aim, Stokes reloaded and fired again. This time the rounds hit their mark, dropping the creature to the ground, its limp body sliding down ten more stairs before coming to a stop.

"Well, I'll be damned," Kerr said, lowering his rifle and beaming at Anna. "She's not just another pretty face, is she?"

Anna blushed.

"Careful you don't start something you can't finish," Dag said, stifling a laugh.

Kerr glanced up the long stairway. "Looks like the sun's

starting to rise, or whatever's passing for the sun in this giant ant farm."

"Have you seen any more of those things?" Jack inquired, arriving next to Stokes.

The sergeant eyed his scope, which was no small feat wearing a helmet with a glass visor. "I've seen a few shadows zip past the entrance, if that's what you mean. But one thing I know for sure. We can't stay down here forever."

Mia checked her air supply readout. "I'm about thirty minutes away from needing to change out my CO_2 scrubbers."

To those contemplating what to do, it sounded as though Stokes was advocating charging out and making a break for the portal. The video from Ivan's memory bank had shown at least seven Stalkers. Ivan had killed two and now Stokes had taken out a third. That left four. Even with the knowledge of the animals' narrow area of vulnerability, the risks were still great.

"I say we go," Jack said.

"You always were a gambler," she shot back.

He shook his head. "Think about it for a minute. If we wait any longer, Stark is likely to send out a search party and there's a good chance those things will find them before they find us."

Jack was right. They had to go. Not everyone might make it, but right now there were no best options, only less crappy ones.

"All right, grab your gear," Stokes ordered. "And check your weapons are clean and loaded."

Moments later they made their way up the long vine-covered stairway, two by two. The Delta team was out front, followed by the scientists in the middle. Anna and Ivan pulled up the rear. They were less than twenty paces from the opening when Anna's head perked up. "I am detecting tremors."

Mia and the others adjusted their external auditory sensors. The low sound of thunder came in half-second intervals.

"Why does that sound familiar?" Jack wondered as it grew close enough they felt the ground begin to tremble beneath their feet.

Through the narrow aperture ahead, they spotted two gray, six-legged Stalkers scurry into the brush. A third crossed the open patch of ground, heading straight for them. Stokes and Kerr dropped to their knees and leveled their rifles. The two Delta operators, Diaz and Bates, who were directly behind them stood and did the same.

The Stalker was about to crest the doorway when the ground gave a violent shake and a large hand reached down from above, entangling the animal and wrenching it into the air and out of sight. The creature let out an ear-piercing screech before it was silenced by a terrible crunching sound.

"Seems the hunter just became the hunted," Jack said. Then came more heavy footfalls as the behemoth passed in front of the entrance, blocking out the light. The lower half of a powerful leg crashed down with staggering force. It had the thickness of an elm tree. Its flesh, the color of forest mulch, was mottled and cracked.

They watched in awe as the massive creature passed by, that hand descending again to scoop up the corpses of the fallen Stalkers before it receded back into the jungle. Slowly the group emerged into the light, realizing how wrong they had been about this place. The greenhouse wasn't the facility they had taken shelter in. The real greenhouse was out here, shielded perhaps from a hazardous alien atmosphere pressing in all around them. But then again, maybe that too was wrong. With time quickly running out, Mia, Jack and the others knew the answers to those questions would have to wait. But something else made it perfectly clear that once those answers finally came, they would prove as crucial as they were astonishing.

Chapter 25

39 hours, 51 minutes, 09 seconds

Admiral Stark leaned back in his leather chair, the tips of his rounded fingers tapping gently on the conference room table. "I understand you've been through quite an ordeal," he said to Jack, who was sitting next to him.

"That's putting it rather mildly," Jack replied, lacing his own fingers together. They had hustled back to the portal in less than twenty minutes. Even Ivan in his terribly crippled state had somehow managed to keep up. Thanks in part to the behemoth, that final leg of the journey had been largely uneventful.

"I've already spent some time debriefing the others. You're the last one and when I'm done, I'll have a meeting with Dr. Salzburg and appraise him of the situation."

Jack shook his head.

Stark caught the disgust on Jack's face. In spite of being alone in the conference room, he glanced around nevertheless. "I suppose I understand including Salzburg on the team. After all, he did discover the alien chromosome, I'll give him that. But to put him in charge of the entire operation..."

Sighing, Jack slid a tablet over to Stark with an article from the *Washington Post*, shortly before it was shut down under dubious pretenses. It was something Anna had pulled during a general sweep of the internet before the full blackout had been implemented.

"I'm familiar with Kay Mahoro's article," Stark replied. "Call me old-fashioned, but there's a big part of me that really doesn't want to believe what's written here is true."

"I feel the same way," Jack agreed. "It makes me wonder if men like you and I are part of a dying breed."

"Or part of a dying species," Stark amended with a dark touch of irony.

"I'm sorry about Peterson," Jack told him.

"It wasn't your fault. That's what makes these guys so brave. They sign up knowing any day may be their last."

"Speaking of last days, when we were over there, Mia pulled a bone out of the ground. From what we could tell it belonged to the *Mesonyx* who once inhabited the city beneath us. There's reason to believe the structure we found encasing the portal wasn't intended as a religious shrine so much as a means to keep things from crossing into our world."

"We have a contingent of guards in the pyramid's main chamber at all times, if that's what you're worried about."

Jack nodded. "I also suggest you send a seismic team through the portal the first chance you get and have them run a few surveys. That should begin to tell us what kind of planet we're dealing with."

"I'll see to it," Stark replied, tapping a pen against his leg. He leaned forward and pushed a button, illuminating one of the large screens on the wall. "We've been reviewing the footage from the drones Anna sent up to survey the area. What do you think of this dome idea?"

"I can't think of another explanation," Jack replied. "Although that's probably a question best left to Gabby and Eugene. They're the ones with the advanced degrees in physics."

"You're not here for your looks, Jack," Stark reminded him with a wry smile. "Your gut is usually on point and I want your take on this."

"I'm not sure it matters," he told the admiral.

The response seemed to worry Stark.

"Don't get me wrong, I would love to find the answer to that question. But with less than forty hours left before the end of the world, it isn't high on my priority list. Either way, I'm sure the others have already given you an earful on what they think. You ask me, the fact that we found a single structure is encouraging. Something built it and I'm sure it wasn't the *Mesonyx* and can guarantee it wasn't whatever's running around that jungle."

Stark nodded. "Which leads me to this." He clicked the button again and an overhead image appeared of multicolored foliage. He zoomed in, past what looked like either a wide river or an unusually shaped lake. "What do you make of this?"

Jack leaned in. It appeared to be a miniature mountain, rising up from the jungle floor, covered in thick vegetation. "Hard to say really."

"We ran the image through a few filters and came up with this." Stark clicked again, erasing most of the trees. Now it didn't look like a mountain at all. The shape was far less ragged, a square with rounded edges, much like what they had been calling the greenhouse, only much,

much bigger. Jack stared at it intently, realizing the dimensions were far too symmetrical to be natural. "You've found another structure?"

"We believe so, and there may be others," Stark replied. "I'm gonna need you to go back through that portal and find out what's inside."

Jack aimed a finger at the shimmering liquid surface that ran from one end of the enclosure to the other. On one side was the portal. On the other, the structure they needed to get to. "Is that what I think it is?"

"It is a liquid," Stark told him, not trying to sound coy but doing a damn good job of it. "We've done every kind of image analysis you can think of, but the truth is we won't know what's really there until we get up close and personal."

"Looks like a lake or river that slices the terrain in two," Jack said, pensively. "I don't see any way around."

"I got a team of engineers working on a lightweight inflatable raft that will ferry you all over."

Jack couldn't help but feel a little skeptical. "Whatever you build better be strong enough to keep Ivan and Anna from taking a swim."

"It will be, don't worry," Stark said, his lips forming a dimpled little grin.

"Listen, lately all I do is worry. Sometimes it feels like the only thing keeping me alive." Jack stared at their new objective, that large square building almost entirely hidden by the jungle overgrowth. "You think the key to stopping this might be in there somewhere?"

Stark frowned. "For our sake, I hope so."

Chapter 26

"Ollie tells me you were shot by Sentinel agents?" Kay asked, desperate to escape the awkward silence with the strange techno-punk girl before her.

At a notch over five feet, Armoni was solidly built with a mess of stringy black hair and the kind of pallid expression that screamed 'vitamin deficiency.' Other than her height, Armoni bore few of the other characteristics that would suggest she was a girl, let alone a young woman. But in a weird kind of way, she and Patrick made a good couple, artificial as it might have been.

"Shot through the spine," Armoni said, in an accent that sounded Argentinian. "Fell from the roof of a building and landed in a pile of trash. It should have broken my fall, but it only seemed to break my back even worse. Not that I could feel anything anyway at that point." Armoni paused, staring back at Kay through strands of hair that cried out to be washed.

"You don't look like someone who broke their back," Kay said, feeling like maybe she should have just stayed quiet. This was what she did though whenever she felt uneasy—the reporter in her sprang into action with a million questions. The longer she kept Armoni talking, the less time she'd spend thinking about Derek and the horrors their families were surely enduring.

"Not broke, snapped like a twig actually. I was lucky to be alive. Or unlucky, depending on your point of view. I expected the Sentinel bastards who shot me to finish what they'd started. I certainly would have. Instead, they put me on a stretcher and carried me off."

"To the hospital?" Kay asked, naively.

"Hell, no, to an interrogation chamber. They started questioning me right away. Try to imagine it. I'm lying flat on my back with two men trying to waterboard me, but that wasn't getting them anywhere. I don't know how long that went on for, but eventually, they threw me in a cell and that's where things went from bad to worse. I thought I was going to die. In fact, I prayed for it, harder than I've ever prayed for anything in my life. But I wasn't given death. I was given Salzburg. Maybe not given, since I've been told it was probably in me the entire time, but it came awake. For days I couldn't think straight or even talk. For all intents and purposes I'd become a vegetable. Then one day, that heavy wet blanket that'd been draped over me was lifted and I could think again and with the kind of clarity I'd never known before. A day later, I could suddenly feel my toes. Then I was able to wiggle them and before long I was back on my feet. It's hard not to believe in miracles when you live through something like that."

"That's incredible," Kay said, fighting back tears. Not for Armoni though. The girl's story reminded her how her mom had been bedridden, only to rise within days. Her mother too had thought the hand of God had come down to lift her up again, like Lazarus. It was hard not to see it that way too, even for Kay, a firm nonbeliever. Miracles aside, she had seen plenty of stories in the last two weeks of people experiencing incredible recoveries from ailments associated with Salzburg. It seemed hard to be thankful, however, for an illness that beat you down only to lift you up again, even if it tended to leave you better off than before.

Armoni was biting her nails. "A few weeks ago, I was one of the best hackers in South America. After Salzburg, I'm probably the best in the western hemisphere."

Kay laughed. "Sounds like a line from a commercial. After Salzburg my days just feel brighter."

Armoni bent forward, holding her belly in silent laughter. Watching the girl lose herself, a bizarre feeling of jealousy suddenly crept over Kay. It took her a moment to untangle what it was about. Armoni was tough and didn't give a damn what people thought of her. But then so was Kay. But there was one thing that would forever separate the two of them. And on some strange level, it was something Kay wished she could have. Salzburg.

•••

Not long after, Ollie assembled the group in the kitchen. "Armoni's been kind enough to break into NASA's mission control database over at the Kennedy Space Center," he informed them. "The nuclear missile launch is scheduled for midnight tonight. That gives us six hours before those missiles leave the pad for outer space." He reached into a duffel bag and handed them each a pair of white NASA technicians' overalls.

"What are these for?" Kay asked, flipping the garment around so she could see both sides. It had bold numbers etched onto the shoulders and a large NASA patch on the rear.

"Camouflage," he replied. "We only need it to last until Richard and I can plant these detonators. With any luck, they'll destroy the rocket along with the launch pad it's sitting on."

Kay noticed on the front of her overall was a nametag. "I guess I'm Sandra Johnson."

"Only for a day," Ollie reassured her. "Then you can go back to Kay Mahoro. In case you're wondering, Sandra is a real person—a launchpad technician who left to do work at the Jet Propulsion Lab in Pasadena. Each of us will be impersonating former employees. Armoni has seen to it that our IDs look authentic and that the NASA database lists our covers as on duty, along with our picture."

Kay saw the ID card clipped to the technician's outfit. "I don't remember giving you a picture of me."

"You can thank the internet for that," Armoni said. "A few minutes in Photoshop to get the angle just right and voilà, instant I.D. badge."

"Where were you when I was in high school?" Kay said, recalling prowling convenience stores, begging perfect strangers to buy her alcohol.

"Uh, probably in grade school," the hacker replied, smirking.

"All right," Ollie said sternly. "Let's get serious. We only get one shot at this."

Patrick set two tool boxes on the kitchen table and opened them. Inside were what looked to Kay like plastic explosives with timers, only these ones had been spray-painted white, presumably so they could be attached to the white fuselage without being spotted.

Ollie then carefully moved the cases aside and unfurled a map of Merritt Island. "A small Zodiac will be waiting for us on the north side of the NASA causeway," he said, pointing to a stretch of road which led from the mainland to the island. "Banana Creek will bring us just north of the launch pad. This is going to be a bluff-your-way-past-any-guards type of mission, although each of you will have one of these just in case."

Ollie produced a silenced pistol and placed it on top of the map.

Kay swallowed hard. This was starting to get real.

"While Patrick and I plant the explosives," Ollie said, continuing with the plan, "Kay and Sven will keep an eye out, distracting any tech who starts sticking his schnozz where it don't belong."

Sven snapped the fingers on his right hand. "Not a problem," he growled. "We got this, don't we, Kay?"

What she wanted to say was, "Have you all lost your minds?"

Remember why you're here, Kay.

But instead she said: "You're damn right, we do."

Ollie whooped and high-fived her. "That a girl."

"Man, I wish I was going with you," Armoni said with genuine disappointment.

Kay spun on her heels. "What? You're staying behind? I thought you were some kind of master hacker?"

"Armoni only needs internet access to work her magic. Besides, we'll be in constant radio contact. If we need her for anything…"

"Ask and you shall receive," Armoni said, finishing his sentence with a flourish.

"Everyone clear?" Ollie asked, eyeing them intently, one by one.

Kay and the others nodded.

Ollie checked his watch. "Good, now go get some rest. We leave at sundown."

149

Chapter 27

Back on Northern Star, Mia took a hot shower and changed into a fresh pair of clothes. She had only been on the other side a handful of hours, but with everything that had happened, her concept of time was stretching out, the way it tended to for accident victims. They had made it out. At the time, that was all that had mattered. But now that Mia was safe, for the time being at least, a new set of concerns had begun to take over. She wanted nothing more than to hear her daughter's voice.

Mia's cell phone was on the table in her room. Plucking it up, she flipped through the pictures of Zoey she kept there. Then came the videos. Her daughter's first birthday, her first steps, her first bike ride. So many firsts, it was hard to imagine they might never find what they were looking for here, not before the fiery end arrived to touch every single one of them.

Soon enough Mia realized even the videos were only making the longing worse. There was a complete ban on any incoming or outgoing communication, except at the highest levels. Her only chance of seeing her daughter again lay on the other side of saving the planet. But hey, no pressure, right? Mia set the phone down with a thud and let out a pained burst of sardonic laughter.

A gentle, almost hesitant knock came at the door.

She rose, looked through the peephole. A young girl with short, curly black hair stood staring back at her. Mia let her in. "Hey, Noemi, do you need something?"

"Not really," the young girl said, bouncing past her and into Mia's room. "I was speaking with my sister when your face popped into my head."

The cloudy expression on Mia's face seemed to clear away at once. "Is that right?"

Noemi spotted a ragged-looking stuffed animal lying on Mia's pillow. It was a little dog which she picked up and hugged.

"Mr. Pickles is so cute, can I keep him?"

"Huh? Uh, yes, you're right, that is Mr. Pickles." With anyone else, knowing the name of the toy her daughter had loved as a baby would certainly have freaked her out. But not these girls, not after she had seen proof of their abilities under laboratory conditions. "He belongs to my daughter…"

"Chloe."

Mia shook her head. "Close. Her name is Zoey. Have you always been able to see things about me?"

Noemi was sitting on the edge of the bed, making Mr. Pickles walk along her thigh. "I don't remember."

Mia drew closer. "Noemi, it's very important. I want you to try to answer my question."

The young girl stopped moving, her head down, her hair covering part of her face. Mia assumed Noemi was thinking until she saw the young girl's shoulders begin to shake. Mia slid an arm around her shoulder. "I didn't mean to push you."

Noemi turned and gave her a hug, melting that thin barrier of objectivity Mia had always tried to keep with any of her human test subjects. But right now, in more ways than one, this was her daughter she was hugging and Mia drank in the moment, hoping it would never end.

Soon, the young girl straightened and Mia wiped the tears from her eyes. "You miss your mother, don't you?" Noemi nodded.

"You're helping us a great deal, do you know that?"

The girl just looked at her with those deep, piercing eyes.

"I promise you, when all this is done, I'll bring you and your sister back to Rome to be with your family again."

"They're dead," Noemi said.

That took Mia by surprise. "I'm sorry to hear that."

"A car hit them on their way to work," she said, her throat still heavy with sadness. Her eyes fell. "Sofia and I knew before they told us."

"Do you only see things about people you care for?"

"I suppose so," Noemi replied before returning to Mr. Pickles, only this time showing a little less enthusiasm.

"I'll tell you what. Any time you need a hug from me or Mr. Pickles, you let me know and both of us will be happy to oblige."

Noemi smiled, the whites of her eyes mapped with red lines. "What does 'oblige' mean?"

"It means to do as someone wishes."

Mia heard someone standing at the door and looked up to find Jansson, her well-defined facial features tensed.

"Do you have a minute?" Jansson asked.

Mia looked at Noemi, who got up. "I'll go find Sofia," the young girl said, skipping out of the room as though nothing had happened.

Jansson's eyes followed her out. "Did I miss something important?"

"I'm not sure. Most studies into telepathy in the past were between two complete strangers. I mean, how often have you thought of a good friend only moments before they called? Or gone to dial someone only to have the call fail because they were calling you at the same time? Even the anecdotal evidence has suggested the phenomenon is strongest when there is a link between the two parties involved. The conversation I just had with Noemi only added weight to the theory."

"Fascinating," Jansson said. "That may explain why the twins are so proficient."

"Enough about me, what was it you wanted to talk about?" Mia asked.

"You know Dr. Salzburg isn't the least bit interested in this side of things."

Mia shook her head. "I know. It's a shame because I believe it holds the greatest chance for a major breakthrough."

"That may be so, but you should know he's been putting a tremendous amount of pressure on me to pick up the slack furthering our understanding on the rest of the new chromosome."

"He tried the same with me," Mia confessed. "But I didn't bite, not after I was kidnapped and sent here against my will." She paused. "Why do you have that look on your face like you found something?"

Jansson fidgeted and crossed her arms. Her fingernails looked like they'd been gnawed to the bone. "I inserted the *DAF4* DNA repair gene inside the embryos of a series of mayflies and allowed them to mature. Normally they tend to live for twenty-four hours, but we've already passed that point and the vast majority are still going strong. By the current rate of cellular decay, they should live anywhere from four point five to five days."

"If the same were true of humans," Mia said, taking Jansson's findings to their next logical conclusion, "the folks suffering with Salzburg could live to be upwards of four hundred years old." The thought was staggering. They'd known the possibility existed, but to find such clear confirmation was hard to believe. To Mia, the discovery also raised an even more unsettling issue. If they somehow managed to survive the coming apocalypse, Zoey was likely to outlive Mia by nearly three hundred and fifty years.

"That's not all," Jansson said. "After the badgering session with Alan, I decided to take a closer look at the cellular structure of those with Salzburg. We've been so consumed with the DNA aspect, I wondered if there wasn't something there we might have missed." Jansson handed Mia a color printout of a cell. "We know cytoplasm contains organelles and cell parts. Which is why I was confused when I saw this." She pointed to a small oval object positioned right up against the nucleus. "What is it?" Mia asked, taking a closer look.

Jansson shook her head. "It's some kind of receptor, because get this. When I hit it with mild doses of electricity nothing happened. I tried just about anything I could think of to figure out what its role was. Then I added a genetically modified mixture to the sample and it immediately came to life."

Mia felt the thumping in her neck begin to quicken. "Let

me guess, it injected the HISR assembler gene into the cell's DNA."

"Yes, and with greater precision than the DNA editing tool CRISPR. And since the sample was awash in the GMO mixture, it immediately went to work assembling the beginnings of the Salzburg chromosome."

"So those without this special receptor in the cell didn't get Salzburg," Mia said.

Jansson crossed her arms. "Exactly."

Mia rose to her feet. "Which raises two important questions. What is it made of and how did it get there?"

Chapter 28

After his meeting with Admiral Stark, Jack checked in with Grant and Gabby. They had been sent the biological specimens from the latest mission through the portal and he was eager to see if they'd made any headway.

Dag intercepted him as he was heading down the corridor toward the science module. "We're going in again, aren't we?" the paleontologist said, scoffing down a chocolate bar from the canteen.

Jack shook his head, eyeing Dag's slender frame. "If there's a good reason you don't weigh a thousand pounds, I'd love to know what it is."

Dag grinned, a stray peanut stuck between his front teeth. "Good genes, I guess."

"The answer is yes. We're going back as soon as Ivan is ready." Jack had started the last mission with an unsettling certainty Ivan would be a serious liability and in some ways those fears had proven to be true. But the robot had also swooped in more than once, saving them from certain doom. Given the type of hostile wildlife they were sure to encounter, bringing a little extra brawn to back them up wasn't such a terrible idea.

Jack and Dag arrived at the bio lab to find Grant hunched over a glove box and staring down into a microscope. The funny-looking box allowed the study of potentially deadly pathogens without putting the scientists at risk.

Nearby, Gabby and Eugene were engaged in a heated debate.

"It's simply not possible," Eugene shot back, raising his voice.

Gabby crossed her arms and headed in Jack's direction. "Maybe not, but the evidence says otherwise."

"We come at a bad time?" Jack said, holding his hands out in a 'we come in peace' gesture.

Gabby did her best to make the grin on her face look natural. "No, it's these biological samples you brought back. They're like nothing we've ever seen before."

Grant glanced up from his microscope. "Come have a look at this."

Obliging, Jack went over and peered through the aperture.

"Now, tell me what you see," Grant asked him.

"I believe I'm seeing two sets of cells side by side," he replied. "What're they from?"

"The ones on the left are human skin cells. On the right are cells from the winged creature Ivan shot. Notice anything unusual?"

"Hmm, for starters the alien cells are much smaller than the human cells."

One of Grant's eyebrows perked up. "Anything else?"

Jack threw him a look. "Is this an exam?"

"Trust me."

He pushed his eye back to the microscope lens. "Oh,

crap. The alien cells are moving."

"Moving?" Dag said, pushing his way in to see. "Oh, that's creepy."

"In spite of the size difference, on the surface they look similar," Grant explained. "Except, unlike human cells, the alien equivalent show no signs of DNA."

"Really?" Jack said, surprised. "I mean, we've always imagined the blueprints for life might be different somewhere else in the universe…"

Gabby nodded. "But don't forget. The Ateans shared roughly seventy percent of our genome."

"Exactly," Jack said, running a hand through his hair and sighing loudly. "That did lend some serious weight to the idea that alien life forms would indeed be carbon-based. So what does this mean?"

"The alien cells might not have DNA," Grant explained. "But they do have another structure that may perform a similar function." He changed slides. "We then looked at the plant and mud samples you brought back and things got stranger."

Jack shook his head. "I was afraid you were gonna say that."

"Turns out, the plants are a mix of carbon-based life with a fifty-five percent genetic match to humans and a forty percent match to the Ateans."

"For goodness' sake, can't these aliens make up their minds," Dag said, rubbing what Jack could only assume was his grumbling belly.

"And the mud?" Jack wondered. "I'm guessing you didn't find crushed rock mixed with organic matter."

Grant smiled. "There was some organic matter, remnants from the dying vegetation. Although the bulk of what we thought was mud turned out to be dead alien cells."

"Have you tried running the samples under an electron microscope?" Jack wondered on a hunch.

Eugene shook his head. "That was going to be our next step."

"Then let's do it," Jack said.

Eugene, Gabby and Grant gave him a funny look.

"Right now?" Gabby asked.

"Of course, right now. Dag and I are heading back in there and we need to know what we're up against."

Grant rushed to set it up. With any luck, the electron microscope would reveal the atomic structure of the cell. They would begin with the sample from the flying creature. Turning on the machine, Grant crossed his fingers. Their eyes focused on the computer screen where the images were being fed.

"Holy crap," Eugene exclaimed, eyeing the results as they populated the screen.

The atomic structure made it perfectly clear what they were seeing. It also helped to clear up the puzzling lack of DNA. The alien creatures weren't carbon-based life, they were made of silicon.

"But how does this jibe with the Ateans?" Gabby asked, her hands perched on her hips.

"Maybe it doesn't," Jack answered. "Maybe we're dealing with an entirely new species."

"We won't know for sure until we have a better idea where that portal leads to," Grant said, still eyeing the results on the computer screen.

A gentle knock on the door was followed by a soft familiar voice. "Dr. Greer, I believe I may have the answers you are looking for."

Chapter 29

As planned, Armoni dropped Ollie, Sven, Kay and
Patrick along the edge of the NASA causeway.
When they reached the Zodiac, Ollie pressed in the
earpiece he was wearing. "Armoni, can you read me?"
"Loud and clear," she replied.
"Okay, stay on this encrypted channel. And be ready
with any info we might need on the layout of the site. I
also want you to eavesdrop on mission control."
"Roger that."
The team sped away in the Zodiac, cutting through the
channel's rippling waters.
Kay leaned into Ollie. "Why did you want Armoni to
listen in on mission control?" she asked.
"If someone triggers the alarm, they'll be the first to
know."
"You mean to abort the launch?"
"Or to fire it prematurely," he told her grimly. "If they
fail to launch tonight, they'll miss the only available
window to intercept the ship before it gets too close."
Kay sat back, her body lifting and thudding back into the
hard seat whenever they hit a wave. Inside her NASA
overalls sat her pistol, secured by a leather shoulder
holster. It too bounced around, a constant reminder how
dangerous this mission was. Failure now would mean

certain death for her and her family. Perhaps even the world. Although that still remained to be seen.

Running through Ollie's analysis of the situation, one thing was clear. Sentinel was playing the short game— save the planet at any cost—while the resistance was risking a possible calamity for a shot at preserving the human race. She wished the moral line in the sand had been far clearer. More than that, she hoped she had chosen the right side. But in the end, perhaps the choice had been clearer than she thought. It was Sentinel and now the government who had clamped down and imprisoned her loved ones and maybe thousands of others. That said something about Sentinel's willingness to sacrifice anything that stood between them and their objective.

"Stay alert," Ollie said over the radio as they swung into Banana Creek.

So far everything had been going according to plan. Then suddenly, Ollie cut the engine and ordered everyone to start paddling. Twenty-five yards ahead, two guards passed by one another along a low bridge over the creek. One of the guards, lanky with veiny arms, stopped to light a cigarette. He hunched slightly, turning away from the wind and toward the creek below. The other guard glanced back and laughed at the trouble he was having.

Ollie held his fist up at a right angle. They stopped paddling at once and drifted, the bridge and the soldier growing nearer every second. The guard was still having trouble with his cigarette. He shook his lighter and tried again. Ollie reached into his overall and pulled out his silenced pistol. Kay's heart began thumping a terrible beat in her head. It spelled out how close they were to being discovered. And why? Because some low-level security guy was too cheap to buy a new lighter. Finally, a flicker of flame touched the tip of the guard's cigarette. They were close now, only a dozen feet from the bridge. In seconds they would be under it and out of sight. The guard drew deeply on his cigarette, a look of satisfaction on his bony face. He was in the middle of turning around to continue his rounds when his eyes passed clean over them. Kay's heart leapt and she clamped a hand over her mouth to stifle the yelp of fright she would surely have let out. The guard took three steps before shaking his head and stopping. He spun toward the water, squinting in the low light at the four people gliding slowly toward him in the inflatable raft. His lips parted to let out a warning and that was when the bullet from Ollie's silenced pistol struck the front of the guard's skull. His body went limp and leaned forward, flipping over the railing and falling onto the boat between them. Sven covered the man's face with a life vest to stop the blood from staining their disguises. The other guard continued his rounds, unaware.

Minutes after they came ashore and dragged the inflatable boat up into the bushes. When they were sure it was out of sight, they approached the razor-wire fence that surrounded the site. Sven produced a small pair of bolt cutters and snipped a hole wide enough for them to pass through. Still under the cover of darkness, the group hurried across the open space to the side of a gleaming white structure.

"This is the vehicle assembly building," Ollie told Kay. He motioned a hundred yards away to a huge Atlas rocket surrounded by ten levels of scaffolding. White puffs of dense billowing mist surrounded the fuselage. "It looks like it's about to launch," she said, worried.

"Nah, that's just the liquid oxygen," Patrick told her. "It's colder than a frosty day in hell. They vent the tanks sometimes to release some of the pressure." He turned to Ollie. "So we gonna head over there or what?"

"We'll be too conspicuous if we cross over open space like that," Ollie said, formulating a plan. "There is a chance we could circle around to the other side of this building and…"

Kay glanced to her right and saw Sven walking out into the open in the other direction, waving his arms at an electric cart being driven by a man in blue NASA overalls. It stopped and for a moment it looked like the two men were talking.

"Uh, what is Sven doing?" Kay asked.

Ollie turned. "Sven," he barked over the radio. "Have you lost your mind?" He turned to the others. "Does he think he's hailing a cab?"

Sven got into the cart on the passenger side and it headed their way.

"Oh, this'll be interesting," Patrick said, wiping the smug look off his face.

They pulled up and the man in the blue coveralls got out, a cross expression stamped on his face. "Why aren't you people over at the launching pad?"

Ollie and Sven exchanged a look before Ollie swung a swift left hook toward the man's jaw. The NASA tech's head jerked to one side as his legs crumpled beneath him. "Patrick, drag this guy around the corner and out of sight, would you?"

"Sure thing."

Ollie glared at Sven, who grinned and raised his hands in a golf clap.

Patrick returned a minute later and they climbed on board the vehicle and headed for the launch pad.

"Armoni," Ollie called out over the radio. "How long before this sucker goes airborne?"

"Ten minutes and fifty-five seconds," came the terse reply.

"All right, keep monitoring mission control and lay off the video games until we're in the clear."

She didn't respond, but Ollie wasn't surprised.

As they approached the platform, Kay spotted a handful of technicians moving around on each level. Far from enclosed levels, each floor was separated by metal grating, which meant there would be few concealed areas to plant the bombs. If this was going to work, they would need caution, subtlety and a whole lot of luck. Sven parked next to the stairwell. Ollie and Patrick hopped out, each of them carrying a plastic explosive bomb hidden in white toolkits emblazoned with the NASA insignia. Kay and Sven followed them up the stairs. The plan called for Patrick and Sven to plant one bomb on the rocket's first-stage booster situated at the bottom while Ollie and Kay would attach their device to the second stage, nine floors above their current position.

The reason was simple enough. Once the rocket ran out of fuel, sheer momentum would power it toward the target. Since the bombs were on a timer, if one of them failed to detonate, they needed to be certain the second stage wouldn't be able to give the warhead the thrust it needed to punch through Earth's gravity. They were also talking about nuclear weapons here, which posed a risk they might explode. They could only hope the military had left the appropriate safeties engaged.

As they headed for the elevator, Kay and Ollie passed another guy wearing the blue one-piece. They nodded to each other, Kay's heart climbing into her throat. The man kept going. So far so good, she thought. They then entered the elevator and Ollie hit the button for the ninth floor. The doors began to close, filling Kay with an immense sense of relief. The most dangerous part was about to begin, but at least they would get there.

The sound of a booming voice startled her. Then a white-gloved hand reached in to stop the doors from closing. Ollie's eyes flashed and his free hand slid into his overall.

With a clang, the doors opened and a technician dressed nearly identically to them got in. The only difference were the words embroidered over his breast pocket: 'Pad Operations Manager' and below that the name 'Sandusky.' His eyes studied their faces before moving down to the clipboard in his hands.

"Have you pad rats been to seven yet?" he asked sternly. A 'pad rat' was a nickname for any of the often dozens of engineers and workers who helped to prepare a rocket for launch.

"Our first stop is nine, boss," Ollie told him. "Then we head to seven."

The elevator stopped and the doors opened. "Fine, but hurry up. Those platform and railings aren't going to tie themselves down. Last thing you want is a loose piece of kit to puncture the spacecraft."

"God forbid," Ollie said, waving as Sandusky frowned and walked away.

The doors closed and the grate elevator shook as it began climbing again.

"What was that all about?" Kay asked, impressed Ollie had managed to fast-talk the guy.

"I didn't give us these uniforms by accident," he told her. "We're NASA grunts, populating the lowest rung on the totem pole. Our job is to tie down equipment,

166

railings and anything else that may get knocked loose during the takeoff. I thought we might blend in better this way."

"Ollie, you there?" Patrick said over the radio.

The elevator doors opened onto the ninth level and they stepped off. Kay's arms and legs were live wires of nervous energy.

"I am, go ahead."

"The first package has been stored, I repeat the first package has been stored."

"Good job. You and Sven slowly work your way down to the cart and wait for us there."

"Roger that."

Kay looked through the grate at her feet and saw slivers of activity on the levels below. The ninth floor was close to thirty feet in either direction. On either end, men in white jumpsuits took readings and entered data into mobile computer terminals. Among them was a security officer, peering over the railing. Straight ahead was a walkway that led to the rocket itself.

Kay stayed by the elevator, pretending to secure a workstation in place while Ollie approached the second-stage booster. She would keep an eye out and let him know if anyone was getting close.

Ollie reached his position, knelt down and opened the toolkit. A passing cloud of exhaust temporarily whited out their vision.

Kay kept her hands busy, scanning left and right. "All clear," she said, sweating profusely in the muggy Florida air.

Leaning forward, Ollie pressed the magnetic device to the booster's outer bulkhead and was about to set the timer when he lost his footing and nearly plummeted into the gap between the rocket and the walkway.

Kay gasped and stood up. The guard must have seen her sudden movement because his head snapped in her direction. She saw this and felt her skin begin to tingle with fear. "Uh, Ollie, a guard is coming."

He was in the middle of righting himself. "I just need another minute."

The guard was fifteen feet away now right as the elevator behind her began rumbling to life. She could see the guard was in his early twenties with a fresh face and clear blue eyes.

"A minute? He'll be here any second."

The walkway Ollie stood in was enclosed with aluminum siding, which meant anyone working on the far ends couldn't see exactly what he was up to. But anyone coming out of the elevator or standing next to her would have a perfect view.

She imagined removing her pistol and firing at the approaching guard. She could see he was armed too and surely far more proficient with a weapon than she was. She realized that offense was far from her best option. Instead, she decided to cut him off, keep him away from the elevator area where he might spot Ollie setting the bomb. What she didn't know was whether the elevator was heading to nine or another level.

"I'm just about done here," she said, moving past him. The guard stopped and snagged her by the arm. "Hey, is everything okay? You looked a little startled for a minute."

Kay was beginning to learn that trying to smile nonchalantly with cottonmouth was no easy task. She hoped Ollie could hear her talking over the radio and would know what was going on. "Oh, that. I thought I'd forgotten my…" She paused, searching for a technical-sounding instrument. This guy was a guard, not an

168

engineer, all she needed was something that sounded good.

His eyes narrowed and his forehead scrunched up. "You don't look so good."

Her eyes began to flutter as her legs gave out. The guard moved in to catch her before she fell. His hands clasped under her arms.

"Hey, what's that?" he asked, feeling the hard edge of the pistol she had hidden beneath her overall.

Just then the elevator door opened and Sandusky came out hollering. "What the hell are you doing over there?" He was pointing at Ollie.

Sandusky took two full steps before bullets from Ollie's gun struck him in both thighs, sending him tumbling to the grate, screaming and clutching his wounded legs. Seeing this, the guard stood up and fumbled for his weapon. Ollie came around the corner, still focused on Sandusky. The guard pulled his weapon free. From the floor, Kay already had him in her sights.

The guard's eyes jumped from one of them to the other. His finger began to squeeze the trigger. Kay fired three times into his chest, the pistol barely audible over the din. The guard fell face forward. Ollie rushed in and helped Kay to her feet. The other technicians must have noticed the commotion because they stood, frozen in fear.

They got in the elevator and were drawing even with the platform's third floor when a general alarm sounded and flashing yellow lights filled their vision.

Ollie called out over the radio. "Sven, the second package is secure. The timer is set for five minutes. Tell me you're waiting to pick us up."

The line remained silent.

"It's more like three and a half minutes now," Kay said, feeling increasingly numb from the neck down. Whether it was from the adrenaline surging through her system or the shock over taking that young man's life, she couldn't tell.

They reached the platform's main level. A handful of technicians rushed past them and down the metal staircase to the tarmac below. In the distance, sirens blared as half a dozen NASA security vehicles barreled toward them.

Ollie and Kay got to the tarmac and didn't see the cart anywhere.

"He left us," Kay said, horrified. The only other thought going through her mind was to run away from what was going to be a massive explosion.

"Sven, where the hell are you?"

Kay dragged Ollie by the arm, away from the oncoming security. She glanced back to see a cart dart out from behind the vehicle assembly building, honking its horn. Sven pulled up with Patrick in the passenger seat waving them in. They hopped on and started to head back.

"Not that way," Ollie shouted. NASA security was less than fifty yards away and would surely cut them off.

"Over there," he cried, pointing in the opposite direction. "We'll use the platform as cover for as long as we can."

"This ain't a Tesla," Patrick cried. "It's a glorified golf cart. We can barely outrun a guy in a wheelchair."

"Have faith, mate," Ollie said as Sven whipped around and floored it.

Kay stared behind them as the security detail reached the platform, driving under and around its massive metallic pillars. "They're getting clos—" she began to say when the rocket detonated in a violent explosion. First from the bottom where an expanding fireball engulfed everything around it, including the security vehicles passing underneath. A series of explosions raced up the length of the rocket as the flammable propellant ignited into an awe-inspiring spectacle. Kay shielded her face from the searing heat and the concussive wave that struck them a moment later, nearly sending their cart toppling onto its side. Sven struggled to maintain control. In the front seat, Patrick hollered like a NASCAR fan watching his favorite racer cross the finish line.

Sven followed the shoreline as they headed back to the boat. More sirens were sounding, but these were coming from fire trucks and not police cars. By the firelight, Kay caught sight of the quiet smirk on Ollie's face. He never said a word, but that satisfied look said enough.

Chapter 30

Everyone present in the lab had stopped what they were doing and gathered around Anna. "Dr. Greer, if you recall, I spoke to you earlier about the seismic scans conducted in the pyramid's main chamber."

Jack nodded. "Yes, I recall. You mentioned the portal had been distorting the image, which made us wonder about the unusual energy being emitted."

"We're still working on that, by the way," Eugene protested. "We growing more confident dark energy might be at play, as well as a slippery new particle we're struggling to identify."

"Not long ago," Anna told them, "a team entered the portal in order to conduct seismic scans on what we understood to be a planet somewhere in our galactic neighborhood."

"That's right," Jack said, distinctly aware of the suggestion he'd made to Stark during his debriefing. "So what did they find?"

Anna laid out a stash of images she had been holding in a manila envelope.

They had expected to see layers of rock, laid down over millions and billions of years. Instead, the geophysical images from the other side simply showed a flat surface. "What does that mean?" Dag asked, looking at the only geophysicist in the room.

"It suggests something is blocking the signal." He turned to Anna. "Did they take any other readings?"

She nodded. "From three separate locations and all of them were the same."

"There's some sort of metallic surface beneath the planet's surface," Gabby speculated. "Could it be another structure? Something we may have missed?"

Jack rubbed the fingers on his left hand, considering the idea. "That's hard to say. I mean, it isn't exactly flat prairie land over there. You're talking about a rather rugged landscape with peaks and valleys and at least one small lake."

"A lake?" Dag repeated, not trying to hide his exasperation.

"You know how to swim, don't you?" Jack asked with a wink.

He shook his head. "Just because I look like a surfer doesn't mean I am one."

"I believe there may be an alternate explanation," Anna said, cutting into the brief moment of levity. "Thankfully, I was able to overcome the portal's distorting effects by creating a new algorithm, one that magnified the multi-attribute full waveform inversion while also filtering anomalous signals. I discovered that my initial assessment was incorrect."

"Wow," Gabby said, her eyes wide and chin lowered in surprise. "Anna made a mistake. I guess that gives some hope to the rest of us."

Anna grinned with humility. "I have made plenty of

errors, Dr. Bishop. And I consider each of them an opportunity for improvement."

"They are," Jack agreed, but with noticeable impatience. "I can tell you're about to hit us with something and I wanna see it."

"My apologies, Dr. Greer." Anna laid a cleaned-up seismic scan on the table. Each of them leaned in, their faces frozen in astonishment.

The image showed the layers of crystalline bedrock resting beneath the *Mesonyx* pyramid. That part they had expected. What caught them all off guard was the massive diamond-shaped object just below the surface.

Jack's head snapped in Anna's direction. "I thought you said that second pyramid was an echo." His voice wasn't just shocked, it was almost accusatory.

"At the time, that was my best assessment."

The room erupted into a maelstrom of questions, almost all of them directed toward Anna. Her head turned in so many directions at once, it looked as though it might pop off and roll away.

"Let me make certain I understand," Grant cut in. "Are you suggesting another Atean ship is buried beneath the *Mesonyx* city?"

"I have not suggested anything, Dr. Holland," Anna replied. "I have merely shown you the data I collected. In addition, I never said the ship belonged to the race of extraterrestrials you are calling the Ateans. Lastly, the ship, which is quite a bit larger than the one discovered in the Gulf of Mexico, lies directly beneath the city's own pyramid."

"Do you believe the location of the *Mesonyx* pyramid is a coincidence?" Gabby asked her.

"I doubt it," Jack replied. "Remember the building we found in the piazza, how the central statue had been holding what looked like an Atean pod? They must have known it was there and decided to build their own version of it above ground."

"As a sign of reverence," Gabby added.

Dag pursed his lips. "No kidding they had reverence. It was probably the most powerful thing they'd ever seen. Enough to inspire them to build an entire civilization on top of it."

"I'd be willing to bet," Jack said, crossing his arms and stroking his chin, "that at least some of the technological advancement we witnessed came from reverse-engineering pods and other goodies they discovered."

Eugene put his hand up like a schoolkid in the front row. "I think you're all missing the bigger picture."

"Then feel free to enlighten us, old boy," Grant said.

"This isn't about the *Mesonyx* or pilfered technology," he said, waving his hands in the air, "but about the portal. Can't you see? It doesn't lead to a distant planet. It's a doorway into the ship."

Chapter 31

Jack couldn't help feeling like a large, intricately woven carpet had just been yanked out from under him. It had been startling enough to discover the alien landscape they had been exploring was protected by a dome. To learn that said dome was not light years away, but mere meters beneath their feet had left Jack utterly speechless. Gabby was comparing scans of the ship beneath them to the one they'd found in the Gulf. "Sure, both craft are the same shape, I'll give you that. But what gets me is that the ship in Mexico was only half the size of this one. Not only that, but the entire internal structure appears to be radically different."

"Dr. Bishop, are you suggesting the two are not related?" She glanced down at the pictures again. "At this point, I really don't know what to think. From the outside, they look the same. They're both shaped like diamonds. They're far more massive than any ship we could ever build and clearly both of them landed at some point in the past, wiping out much of life on earth."

"We've said it before," Jack said, finding his tongue again. "There may be other ships scattered around the planet. One to account for each of the planet's major mass extinctions."

Grant laid one of his long-fingered hands on Eugene's shoulder. "I actually take some comfort from the discovery Anna has made."

"You do?" she asked, hopeful.

"Absolutely. It tells me what we are after might be here after all."

"Grant does have a point," Jack admitted. "Trekking through a hostile, alien world in the hopes of flagging down a native inhabitant willing to give humanity a helping hand did seem like an act of desperation."

"Not so desperate when it was all we had," Gabby said, always the voice of reason.

Jack glanced down at his watch. "It's just hard searching for a needle in a haystack when you're not even sure a needle is what you're really looking for."

"Nor whether you'll recognize the haystacks when you see one," Eugene muttered.

"If nothing else," Anna said, "I believe this demonstrates we are on the right track. I am not sure why, but I am hopeful."

They stopped and regarded her for a moment. Sure, someone could argue Anna had been programmed to be positive and encouraging. However, Rajesh had never programmed her to be distraught when she thought she had hurt someone's feelings. To a greater or lesser degree, a person had a say in whether they chose to view the world through a bright or gloomy prism. In Anna's case, Jack wasn't amazed by the choice she had made, but that she had had one to begin with.

Gabby started to laugh.

"What is it?" Jack inquired, emerging from his own

thoughts.

"At least we know if the worst happens everyone at Northern Star can go live on the ship."

He started to laugh as well and then stopped himself.

"You know, that's not a terrible idea."

"Oh, come on," Eugene protested. "I've seen the videos you brought back. I'll bet some of those creatures would love nothing more." He started waving his hand, as though helping a truck back up. "Bring in the cattle. No, thank you."

"I'd bring my mother there in a heartbeat," Gabby said dreamily.

"There's no telling what impact we would have on a fully enclosed ecosystem like that," Grant said, a hint of concern in his voice. "Big and nasty or not, the indigenous life is almost guaranteed to get wiped out. Especially given the relatively small amount of space."

"As I have told the others," Anna said, "the dome has a diameter of two miles."

"Hell, there's no telling what impact we've had already," Jack said. "The only species I'm interested in saving is our own. If that means we try to live on the ship, so be it. If you ask me though, I don't think it'll work."

Grant was nodding.

Gabby saw this and said: "You agree with him?"

"On Earth, it has been common for one species to displace another," Grant started to explain. "When *Homo sapiens* left Africa, they encountered Neanderthals, a cousin with a distant common ancestor. Whether through war or breeding, *Homo sapiens* eventually pushed Neanderthals into extinction. This is a game that has played out countless times throughout Earth's long history. A game I need not remind you humans are not immune from. I think Shakespeare said it best."

"'All the world's a stage, and all the men and women merely players,'" Jack recited, drawing on the minor he'd earned in the humanities.

"Apart from philosophical arguments," Eugene interjected, "there are practical ones. You guys saw what looks like soil is really just a strange mixture of biological and dead silicon cells. In other words, what would we eat? And how would we breathe? Eventually we'd run out of air filters for our suits."

"Regardless," Jack said, "I suggest we keep this under wraps until we know more."

Anna suddenly stood up straight. "As much as I have enjoyed our time speculating, I have a meeting with Dr. Ward I must attend."

Jack was surprised by the announcement. "What does Mia want with you?"

Anna was already halfway to the door when she stopped. "To run tests for the study she is conducting."

Jack followed her into the corridor and once there saw Jansson not far away, getting an earful from Alan Salzburg. He moved past Anna and approached them. They stopped talking as soon as he arrived.

"Everything all right here?" he asked, his eyes flitting between them.

Alan didn't look one bit impressed. "Shouldn't you be preparing to head through that swirling toilet bowl, hopefully never to return?"

"I'm heartened to see you have faith in what we're doing here," Jack shot back.

"The only thing I have faith in," Alan corrected him, "is

results." He turned to Jansson. "Don't forget, my dear, time is ticking."

After Alan left, Jack began to walk her back to where she and Mia were working.

"It probably isn't a good idea to challenge Dr. Salzburg like that," Jansson told him as they made their way down the science module's long corridor.

The corner of Jack's mouth turned down. "You and I both know why he was put in charge."

Jansson's eyes darted away. "That may be so. I'm simply trying to remind you that like it or not, he has the power to have you removed, or perhaps worse."

"You mean snuffed out?" Jack said, incredulous.

"Don't put it past him. Given what's going on, who would hold him accountable, Jack? Especially when he can simply make up any story he wishes."

"You're not doing much to change my view of the guy."

"I am simply trying to keep my eye on the prize and I suggest you do the same."

A man and woman in lab coats walked by them as Jack regarded Jansson. "What prize is that? Saving humanity?"

"No, seeing my family again."

"Didn't you leave Rome to be with them?"

Jansson stopped, a guilty look on her face. "I did, and I soon realized that nagging feeling of despair wasn't going away. I'd come to spend my final days with the ones I loved without realizing there may be another option."

"An option offered to you by Alan Salzburg."

"That's right."

"What's he giving you?" Jack said, trying hard to reserve judgment. "Money?"

"Not much good that would do me," she scoffed. "He offered me and my family an insurance policy, the kind only a man like he could offer."

"A spot in one of those bunkers."

She nodded, but wouldn't look him in the eye. "A place for me and my family to ride things out should we fail to stop the apocalypse."

"What did he ask for in exchange?"

"Far less than I expected," she admitted. "I was to come to Greenland and resume my work with Mia, the way he'd intended from the beginning."

"The way he'd intended," Jack repeated. "What the hell was that supposed to mean?"

"He never said." Jansson folded her arms over her chest. "And I never asked. I don't know about you, Jack, but I wasn't about to let my family fry."

"Maybe not," Jack replied, tension creasing his brow. "For your sake, I only hope he's a man of his word."

•••

"Where would you like me, Dr. Ward?" Anna asked, entering the lab not long after Jack and Jansson had arrived.

Mia went over and opened the door to one of the small chambers she'd been using to test the girls. "Head on in there and grab a seat."

Jansson headed to the other side of the lab to continue her own work.

"I don't see what Anna has to do with the genetics research you're doing," Jack said.

"I'm using her and a handful of others as a control," Mia explained.

"Control for what?"

She brought him over to the monitor and showed him the X-ray video with the girls. "Normally observing new particles involves vacuum conditions and slamming known particles into one another, but not here."

"Oh, I see, you're trying to duplicate the results with other subjects?" Jack said, still amazed by what he had just seen.

"Not exactly. First, I'm trying to establish a baseline of those without Salzburg. Does the average person without the syndrome show any signs of the same energy field we saw around the girls? Given where we are, I'm not expecting my sample group to be very large, but it's better than nothing."

Jack was beginning to see where this was heading. "And what have you found so far?"

Mia turned to the monitor, which was now showing Anna. She clicked the red button on a mic that fed into the test chamber. "When an image appears on the screen before you, I want you to use your mind to communicate what you see."

Anna looked over, confused.

Jack leaned in and hit the mic. "Not with your radio," he told her. "Try to imagine you're nonverbally communicating what you're seeing."

"To whom shall I communicate?"

Mia looked over. "Jack," she said. "Send it to Jack."

Anna nodded. "I will do my best."

Mia and Jack watched the monitor as several images flickered in front of Anna's face.

"I didn't see a thing, did you?" he asked.

"No, which is good," Mia said. "I brought Anna in to rule out any kind of electromagnetic anomaly."

182

"Have you tried Grant yet? He has Salzburg."

She shook her head. "Jansson and I are open to anyone. In fact, on more than one occasion, I've managed to convince people who were simply walking along the corridor."

"A girl like you, I'm sure that's not a very hard sell. I'm surprised droves of men on Northern Star aren't breaking down the door to be tested."

Mia blushed. "Are you always this forward?"

Jack felt the blood rush to his face. "I call it like I see it. I thought about you a lot when you were gone, was worried about you. Every time we discovered something new I kept thinking, oh, wouldn't Mia love to see this? When things were quiet I would wonder what you were doing."

"You're very kind."

He smiled wanly, getting the hint. Jack knew enough to stop when it was clear his feelings weren't reciprocated. Mia looked away. "It isn't you," she said, rubbing at an invisible stain on the table with the pad of her index finger. "I've just been so confused lately."

"After Ollie came back in the picture."

She glanced up at him and that look said it all.

"No need to explain. Listen, we all have a job to do. It's probably best for everyone if we focus on the mission and not let ourselves get distracted."

Mia took his hand and the feeling of her touch was electric.

"The images have stopped," Anna said, still inside the chamber. "Would you like to start again?"

Both of them straightened, as though caught doing something they shouldn't have been.

"That's all right, Anna," Mia said. "You're free to go. Thank you for your help."

Anna exited the test chamber. "How did I do?"

"Just fine," Jack said, holding the grin as long as he could. "Why don't you go see Admiral Stark and find out if he needs anything before we cross over?"

"Understood," she said, leaving the lab.

Clearing her throat, Mia said, "Although my findings are by no means complete, I have noticed the faintest hint of the energy field around about ten percent of those I've tested."

"That's interesting. How faint?"

Mia pulled up two images, placing them side by side. One was of Noemi juxtaposed next to a male Navy officer. "While hers looks almost like an energy afro, his is nothing more than steam rising from a cup of coffee."

Jack studied the images closely. "That may be, but he's got something. Are you sure he doesn't have Salzburg?"

She shook her head. "After I saw the results I tested him again and he's clean."

"So Salzburg may only be magnifying something that's already within us. Have you spoken to Grant about any of this?"

"Not yet. Though I intended to when he comes to sit down for his test. Why?"

"Show him what you showed me and then ask him about morphic resonance."

Mia turned her head and threw him a funny look. "Morphic what?"

"It's a crazy idea Grant's been on about for years and it may have some bearing on what you've discovered. Just don't tell him I told you so or I'll never hear the end of it."

Mia let out a burst of laughter. "I'll do my best."

Jack turned to leave and then stopped and came closer. "I'm telling you this since you're one of the few who's actually travelled through that portal, but we were wrong about where it leads to."

"What are you saying? It's not a doorway to another planet?"

He shook his head. "There's another alien ship buried inside the bedrock beneath the city and it's at least twice as big as the first one we found in the Gulf."

The news was clearly startling and the expression on Mia's face made that clear.

"For now, keep it between us. Don't forget, if Alan controls Sentinel, then he was the one who ordered the first ship destroyed."

"And us along with it," Mia added, crossing her arms.

"I won't waste my breath telling you I don't trust the guy. Although I'm absolutely positive he's up to no good."

"I couldn't agree more," Mia said. "But what can we do about it?"

Jack's voice dropped to a whisper. "If I thought putting a bullet between his eyes would do the trick, it would already be done. Sentinel may be a snake, but it has many heads. Chop one off and another is sure to take its place."

"He's been trying to secretly control my research," Mia told him, the frustration ready to boil over.

"Why else do you think he put you up to this? Bringing you here has only been to serve his purpose, whatever that is. I saw him dressing down Dr. Jansson in the corridor earlier. Whatever it is he wants, you need to make sure he doesn't get it."

A call came in for Jack over the walkie-talkie. It was Admiral Stark. "Go ahead," Jack said.

"Head down to base camp and gear up, Jack. The team's getting ready to go back in. And I don't need to tell you, but this time, it's do or die."

Chapter 32

29 hours, 43 minutes, 26 seconds

By the time Jack arrived, base camp was a flurry of activity. Several of Yuri's men were unpacking gear from large wooden crates. Watching this, Jack stood rooted in place, still wondering about the black metal objects being removed when something brushed past him. Jack glanced over and saw two robotic pack mules, loaded to the brim with supplies. One of them was carrying extra carbon dioxide filters for their rebreather units, ammunition and first-aid kits. The other was loaded with the folded bulk of the inflatable raft. Stark had said himself this was do or die, which was really another way of saying, *Don't bother coming back unless you find something that might make the sacrifice we've all made worth it.*

Grant appeared next to him, dressed in a biosuit.

"I didn't know you were joining us."

The British biologist's lips curled into a sly grin.

"Frankly, I wasn't sure myself until I saw we were dealing with silicon-based lifeforms." He motioned to a collection of sample bags clenched in his right fist. "If we're lucky I may even be able to do some field research."

Next to show up was Gabby and Dag.

"Eugene was too chicken to go through the portal himself and take X-ray readings," Gabby told them. "Besides, I needed a break from his B.O."

Jack laughed. He knew perfectly well why they were here and it had nothing to do with readings, samples and bad hygiene. They were scientists and the prospect of exploring an alien ecosystem, especially one enclosed on a spaceship, was far too great an opportunity to pass up.

"It's dangerous in there," Jack reminded them, not holding his breath his warning would do much good.

As if in response, Anna and Ivan arrived, trailed by Yuri and a handful of his robotics engineers.

"Ivan, my good man, you look as good as new," Grant said, clapping the sample bags between his hands with a dull thudding sound.

"Thank you," Ivan replied. "Much of the credit goes to Anna."

The four humans looked at each other in amazement.

Anna smiled. "I loaded a logic and learning algorithm into Ivan's mainframe. It has greatly expanded his vocabulary and streamlined his reasoning skills. Do you like the changes I made?"

Ivan rotated his head until his red glowing eyes met hers. "Greatly."

She reached over and closed a hand around one of his three metal pincers.

"Ivan's still a man of few words, I see," Gabby joked.

Dag snickered. "That's how I like him. Anna, just make sure you don't turn him into too much of a softie. We may still need Ivan's killer instinct."

"Killer instinct," Yuri said, as he moved in beside Ivan.

"In that regard you have nothing to worry about. Built into Ivan's core programming is an override switch that will cancel any added software. It was designed to prevent hackers from commandeering control and putting him up to no good. In this case, it can be used to put him back in line." Yuri dragged a finger across his tablet and at once, Ivan shoved Anna's hand away.

"Please keep your distance," Ivan said, his hollow voice suddenly cold, his eyes ablaze. "This is your first warning. There will not be a second." He racked the action on his weapons, loading a round into each chamber with a menacing clang.

"All right, Yuri, you've made your point," Jack said, raising a hand. "Now take him off DEFCON 1 before someone gets hurt."

Yuri hesitated slightly before he lifted his tablet and swiped again. At once, Ivan returned to his new normal self. He even reached out and took Anna's hand again, although she wasn't sure what to make of his schizophrenic behavior.

"Your boyfriend's got split personalities," Dag said, his eyes still wide with fear.

Just then, Sergeant Stokes, Corporal Kerr and the rest of the Delta team showed up.

Admiral Stark moved off from overseeing the equipment and joined them. "All right, let's get started. We know the indigenous wildlife on the other side is far from friendly. Our initial assessment suggested the best course of action was to simply send in a larger force. But more bodies means more supplies. That was when Yuri and his team at Volkov Industries offered a better idea."

"A tank?" Dag asked.

"No, an Argos powered exoskeleton," Stark replied, motioning to the sleek ink-black metal framework behind him. "You wear it over your biosuit and it'll help you scale rough terrain, carry more weight and might even save your life in a hand-to-hand fight."

"How much does it weigh?" Jack wondered, moving over to touch it. The design was impressive with computer-controlled hydraulics at every joint.

"The Argos weighs a hundred and fifty pounds," Yuri informed them, "and will allow you to run carrying up to six hundred pounds."

"Very impressive," Grant conceded.

"So long as you don't fall in the water," Jack said, glancing around the assembly area.

"No doubt, there are dangers," Stark admitted, not bothering to play down the risks. "Jack is referring to the body of water that cuts clear across the biosphere. From what we can tell, it appears to be liquid water, although we still aren't certain of its depth. We've added an inflatable rigid-bottomed dinghy. These will be more than enough to ferry you and your robotic companions across."

For a moment, Jack contemplated sharing the discovery they had made about the portal leading to a ship beneath their feet, but then decided against it. The others had been sworn to secrecy for fear Alan might put the information toward nefarious ends, whatever those might be.

Gabby looked like she was taking it all in. "What about getting past all the wildlife you mentioned?"

"To help with that, we've outfitted the Delta team's M4s with grenade launchers as well as tracking bullets."

"Tracking bullets?" Jack said. "Never heard of them."

Stokes stepped forward. "If I may, Admiral."

Stark nodded.

"Like a missile, these special rounds allow us to shine a laser at a target, fire and forget. They cost a fortune, but given the extra accuracy, you tend to use a hell of a lot less of them."

"Any other deadly gadgets we should know about?" Jack wondered. It was starting to look like they were prepping for World War Three. The scientist part of him couldn't help being appalled they were about to head over there with so much killing power. But just as quickly, another side of Jack spoke up, the side determined to do whatever it took to save the planet. Did destroying a species rather than studying it run contrary to everything he believed in? Of course it did. So too did allowing seven billion to die.

Stark smiled, aware on some level of the inner debate Jack was wrestling with. "I think you'll be happy with this then. The TSX 220 net gun, a non-lethal option to take out any large predator heading your way. The video from your last outing shows the spider-like creatures you call 'Stalkers' that attacked you had six legs. Where the 220 is concerned, the more legs, the more opportunity to tangle themselves in knots."

"Spiders?" Gabby said, suddenly not looking so sure.

Dag put an arm around her. "Don't worry, they were far too big to be spiders."

That gave everyone a good laugh, which they needed right about now.

Jack went over to Kerr, who was busy stepping into one of the exoskeletons. "I was convinced you wouldn't be joining us, especially with a busted-up ankle."

Kerr glanced at him with a look of concern. "It healed up, what can I say?"

Jack nodded. "See that strapping biologist over there? Three days ago he got shot up real bad. It should probably have killed him, but within twenty-four hours he was back on his feet like nothing ever happened."

"You think I have Salzburg disease?"

"It's an extra chromosome, not a disease, and I'm not sure. Have you been tested?"

"No, and even if I had it, I wouldn't want to know."

Jack helped him with the arm straps. "Maybe you should. Some of the genes do unbelievable things. By the same token, if the wrong ones suddenly get activated, you'll become a serious liability."

"And what about your friend?" Kerr asked defiantly. "What makes you think he won't turn into a liability?"

"Nothing, but he also understands if push comes to shove, we'll leave him behind."

Kerr let out a shallow, shaky breath. "Look, it's true, I did go through a bad patch where I was laid out on my back for a few days. Couldn't stand up or talk. Then it went away and I've been fine ever since. In fact, I've been better than fine. I'm stronger and my thoughts have a clarity I've never known. I haven't said anything to Stokes or the others because I don't want any one of them worrying, the way you're worrying. This Salzburg stuff is the best thing that's ever happened to me. If we meet one of those aliens, I'll be the first one to kiss him on his big fat alien lips and say thank you."

Jack clapped him on the shoulder and helped with the rest of his exoskeleton. If there was anything Jack had

192

learned in this life, it was that every good thing came with a price. Jack couldn't help but wonder if humanity's debt was about to come due.

Chapter 33

25 hours, 33 minutes, 51 seconds

After getting geared up, the team crossed through the portal and into the ship's alien biosphere. A heavy mist hung in the air, reducing visibility to less than ten feet. Stokes and the other Delta operators fanned out, their weapons at the ready. Following close behind were Jack and the rest of the science team. Next were the two pack animals, clomping along with surprising grace. Bringing up the rear were Yuri and Ivan.

They were no small group, an unsettling fact Jack was distinctly aware of. He had attuned his external audio receptors to detect the sound of rustling leaves as well as the rumble of an approaching behemoth. Twenty feet above their heads, one of Anna's new drones circled as they moved forward. The course had already been plotted from images taken from the last mission. Anna fed the data into a second drone, which flew ahead to keep an eye out for hostiles in their path.

Gabby's head was on a swivel.

"Oh, Jack, it's beautiful," she said. "Reminds me of the Appalachian Trail in fall."

Jack caught sight of a half-dozen red wisps darting

around one another.

"I was thinking more Dr. Seuss," he replied, grinning. "Just don't let your guard down. Nice as it looks, it's got a nasty bite."

"Maybe," she said, mesmerized. "It's just hard to believe this is an Atean ship."

Her comment took him aback for several reasons. He had specifically asked everyone in the room to keep that particular piece of information under wraps.

She looked at him. "I mean they don't look alike at all. I'm rambling."

He motioned for her to go to another channel.

Jack frowned. "I thought we agreed to keep that to ourselves," he said.

"Keep what?"

He could tell Gabby was playing dumb, which she sometimes did when caught doing something she shouldn't. She rarely messed up, so when she did, it seemed hearing about it was so much harder to endure.

"We can't let Alan know that portal leads to a ship beneath base camp. There's no telling what he'll do with that information."

She was shaking her head. "I never told him, I swear."

"But by broadcasting over the main frequency that's pretty much what you did. I don't trust Yuri one bit."

Gabby started to glance back and then stopped. "You think he's the Russian spy General Dunham told us to watch out for?"

"Frankly, I don't know. It might not even matter. Alan was the one who called him in. If he isn't working for the Russians, he's sure to report back what he knows to Alan."

"I'm sorry, Jack," she said, genuine remorse in her soft voice. She raised her hands, palm out, motioning to the exotic environment they were in. "I got caught up in the moment."

They switched back to the main channel to find Dag telling a story. It was his first date with a girl he met online who wanted to know how he felt about being whipped. "I thought she meant whipped cream, so I told her I loved it. Let's just say that when we got back to her place, things got weird."

Grant bellowed laughter. "I can imagine. And you probably still have the scars to prove it."

They came to an embankment covered in a gelatinous substance. The last time they were here, such an obstacle had resulted in Kerr's twisted ankle and a nearly disastrous end for all of them. But now, wearing the exoskeleton suits, they were up and over it in three easy strides.

"Dr. Greer," Anna asked, "should we stop and take a sample?" She was referring to the ooze.

"Not now," he told her, conscious that they weren't only racing against the clock, but hurrying to get out of the open.

They pressed on, trying not to let fears of what might be lurking in the thinning fog overwhelm them. Jack was confident—no, make that hopeful—that either Anna or her drones would pick up anything that strayed too close.

"It was nice of you to help Mia with her research," Jack told Anna.

"I was happy to do it," she replied, grabbing a yellow branch that had fallen onto the path and tossing it aside.

"Did she explain what she was looking for?" Jack

pressed, curious to see how she might have seen her role in the study.

"I know Dr. Ward is attempting to understand the puzzling abilities imbued in patients with the complete Salzburg chromosome. She mentioned that my results would act as a baseline, which was to say, I would represent one of many without Salzburg. I was also excited Dr. Ward was kind enough to provide the genetic code for the 48th chromatid, which has enabled me to finally begin the decryption process."

"That's great," he said. "I suppose what I'm really wondering is how you feel knowing you can never have Salzburg?"

Anna continued walking, but grew quiet for a moment. "You believe it is a reminder that I will never be fully human."

"I worried it might."

"Do you feel human, Dr. Greer?"

Jack instinctively glanced down at his arms and his legs wrapped in the stout metal braces powering him forward with every stride. "Sometimes less than I'd like to, but overall, yes, I feel human. Why do you ask?"

"You inferred that since I shall never have Salzburg I may feel somehow inadequate. But you do not have the extra chromosome, Dr. Greer, nor can you 'get' it. Which is why I wondered if you were really projecting your own concerns."

Jack laughed. "Touché."

Gabby nudged him. "Why on earth would she need it anyway? She's stronger than any human, way more intelligent, will probably outlive us by decades and her components are already shielded against radiation. As for telepathy, she's got a built-in radio. What more could she want?"

A soul, Jack thought, but didn't dare say.

•••

Thirty minutes later they reached what was supposed to be a lake, but turned out to be more of a swamp. A red film clung to the undulating surface. The trunks of fallen trees stretched into the water along the shoreline.

"Are you quite certain there isn't a way around?" Grant asked, looking about the group.

Stokes shook his head. "We went over the drone footage a dozen times. The water stretches from one end of the dome to the other. Our suits are waterproof, of course, but crossing with the exoskeleton on would pretty much guarantee a trip to the bottom."

They detached the pre-packaged inflatable raft from one of the robotic pack animals.

Dag surveyed the surface for ripples. "Nothing lives in there, right?"

"Of course not," Jack lied. "Now give us a hand."

They set the raft along the edge of the water and pulled the string. At once, the square package began to hiss, unfolding from its cocoon and slowly taking shape. The transformation took but a few minutes and when they were done, Jack marveled at its size. It looked like something out of *Huckleberry Finn*.

"Are you sure it will take Ivan's weight?" Yuri asked, apprehensively.

Ivan rotated toward Yuri. "My current weight is two hundred kilograms."

"Four hundred and fifty pounds," Dag shouted in amazement. "Yuri, what are you feeding this guy?"

"I do not understand," Ivan said, his glowing red eyes flickering as he struggled to process the comment. Anna slapped his back with a hollow gong. "It is called irony," she explained. "I struggle with it myself. When we get back, I will write you a program to ease some of the confusion. For example, by analyzing the speaker's tone of voice and facial features, it is possible to tell when an element of humor is involved."

"In this case," Yuri said, "I don't find it very funny."

"All right, enough chitchat," Stokes said, handing out telescoping paddles to Grant, Dag, Diaz and Conroy. Ivan rolled onto the platform first. Jack had half expected to see his heavy treads puncture the plastic polymer fabric, dooming the robot to a watery grave, but somehow it held. Moreover, the raft appeared to be stable. Next, Anna and Gabby climbed onboard. Those remaining pushed the craft away from shore, jumping on at the last minute. The men with paddles then took up positions at each corner.

"I feel like Hannibal crossing the Rhône River," Grant said, digging his paddle in and pulling it through the water.

"Let's hope things turn out better for us than they did for Hannibal," Stokes said, magnifying the view on his glasses to scout the opposite shoreline.

They were less than a quarter of the way across the hundred-yard body of water when Anna said, "I am detecting movement."

Jack looked at her, concerned. "Where?" Somehow he hoped she was about to say it was on the shore behind them.

She piped the feed from the drone overhead into Jack's

glasses. At once, he spotted a large disturbance in the water, thirty yards on their port side. Jack turned in that direction to see a wake rapidly moving toward them. But it wasn't the wave that worried him, it was whatever was creating it.

Chapter 34

The same night they destroyed the missile at the Kennedy Space Center, Ollie had the team pack up and move to a safe house south of Tampa along the Gulf Coast. The authorities would no doubt find the Zodiac and begin tearing the area apart. Eventually, they would locate the pink bungalow on Sisson Road, but it would take them a few days to piece together the fact that the couple living there were not who they seemed to be. And by then, it wouldn't matter.

The new safe house was a modern two-storied job surrounded by palm trees on one side and beautiful emerald water on the other. It was a paradise and Kay secretly wished that they could stay here forever.

But even the sound of waves crashing against the shore couldn't help her finish the blog post she was struggling to write. It had to be presented as a news report on the sabotage at Kennedy Space Center, without giving away clues Kay herself had been part of the operation. The deception was an unfortunate byproduct of doing what she could to keep people informed. She justified it with the idea that she was a reporter embedded with the resistance.

But in reality, here she was, sitting on a balcony overlooking paradise and struggling for the first time in her life to come up with the words to fill a news report. Ollie came onto the balcony, wearing swimming trunks and clutching two beer bottles. He handed one to Kay and fell into the seat next to her, squinting into the hot sun.

"I've seen that look before," he said mysteriously. Ollie was eyeing the waves, but Kay could tell he was looking right through her.

"I've got writer's block." Kay decided it was better to admit her shortcomings rather than sweep them under the rug.

"I can tell, but that's not the look I'm referring to."

"What do you mean?" she asked, wondering if she was really that transparent.

"You did what you had to do," he told her flatly. "Just like I did with Sandusky. For all I know the bloke had a wife and kids who loved him. I won't say I don't care, 'cause it's not true. But I will say I've learned to tune those things out." He twisted an imaginary knob at his temple and smiled.

Kay's lips parted, about to reply, when Ollie cut her off. "You, my dear, must learn to pick your battles."

She paused. "What do you mean?"

"Think of an emergency room doctor. Imagine one night four patients get wheeled in. All four are in critical condition. Which one should the doctor work on first?"

"I don't know, the most serious, I guess?"

"Perhaps, but if she does, the other three may die."

"Well, given the scenario, she can't be expected to save them all."

He took a swig of his beer, savoring the taste. "That's my point. If she wants a fighting chance, she'll have to make

202

a choice. Pick your battles and learn to live with the consequences."

Armoni stepped onto the balcony. She started to open an umbrella and then stopped and put it down. "You know, ever since I came out of my Salzburg stupor, I'm no longer allergic to the sun."

"Without a word of a lie, the first time I met this girl," Ollie said, hooking a thumb over his shoulder, "I was sure she was a vampire."

The initial bloom of a smile began to take shape on Armoni's face before it faded. Kay saw she had something on her mind.

"Any luck finding Mia?" Ollie asked, turning to face her with a hopeful, if not worried, look.

Armoni sat down. "Not yet, but I'm working on it. After she was kidnapped from Rome her trail went cold and I haven't been able to pick up the scent. Most of the chatter on Sentinel's main channels is about the Atlas rocket we blew up."

Ollie cackled laughter. "Oh, I'll bet they're crying like a bunch of kids with full nappies."

"Hmm, not exactly."

He spun around. "What's that supposed to mean?"

"Apparently the team sent in to destroy the missile pad at Vandenberg Air Force Base was intercepted before they even set foot out the door."

Ollie's face fell. "So you're saying the second missile was launched?"

Armoni nodded.

Ollie had suddenly lost the ability to speak.

"And was the ship destroyed?" Kay asked, taking over.

"It appears to have been, based on the initial reports, at least. But I'm waiting for confirmation."

Armoni stood up and left. Ollie went back to his beer.

A few quiet moments went by as Kay drew in the salty breeze and thought about the future.

"You miss her, don't you?" Kay asked.

Ollie took another swig. "What on earth gives you that idea?"

"I also lost someone I loved," she reminded him. "I know how difficult it can be. At least in your case, you might be able to find her again."

"Maybe," he said. "But I have a job to do first."

"You love her a lot," Kay said. It was more of a statement than a question.

"Reckon I do. But I can't imagine she feels the same way, not after what I did."

In spite of herself, Kay didn't push for details. "I'm sure she does." Her mind turned back to the missiles again and the reason she had joined them in the first place. "I hoped things would turn out differently, about our mission to destroy the missiles, I mean. But I fulfilled my end of the bargain. Now it's your turn."

Chapter 35

Mia pushed open the lab door on Northern Star to find Eugene squinting inches away from the computer monitor of an electron microscope.

"I catch you at a bad time?" she asked.

He slid his glasses back on. "Oh, hey, Mia. No, I was just trying to make sense of something."

"I never realized you had trouble seeing," she admitted.

Eugene laughed. "An occupational hazard for a reformed television addict. As a kid, my mom would yell at me for sitting too close. 'You're gonna go blind.' I guess I should have listened."

"I won't keep you then. Have you seen Grant?"

Eugene swiveled around in his chair and shook his head. "He and Gabby went through the portal with Jack."

"You didn't want to join them?"

Eugene smiled and looked away. "After facing off against those Israelis in the *Mesonyx* city, I guess I lost my appetite for near-death experiences." He stood up and covered his mouth while he yawned.

"That's too bad," she said, joining him. "Jack had suggested I speak with him about my research. He mentioned Grant had information on morphic something or other. Whatever that is."

"Oh, morphic fields," Eugene said, rolling his eyes. "Yes, we know all about Grant's pet theory. You find yourself stuck in a lab with the guy long enough and you'll become an expert in it too."

Mia's face crinkled. "What can you tell me?"

"In a nutshell, the theory posits that our minds aren't a product of our brains the way we've been taught. He believes the mind operates externally from the brain, which acts like a radio receiver for our thoughts. Sounds simple, but it has all types of far-out implications. First off, rather than perception being a passive event—you know, light hitting the retina in your eyeballs—it involves your mind actually reaching out to touch the object being perceived. He believes this explains why we often get a strange feeling when a person is staring at us. He also believes it might provide a framework for unexplained phenomena like telepathy." Eugene stopped and threw his hands in the air. "Hey, you all right? You look a little freaked out. I'm not saying I believe any of this stuff, I'm only laying out Grant's crazy idea."

"It's not crazy at all," she replied, struggling to find the words. "I—I've seen proof of it in my own research. Visual distortions around the heads of the twin girls with Salzburg. I watched those distortions instantaneously link their minds during the telepathic tests we conducted. Call it what you want, I believe this field may exist, I just can't explain what it's made up of."

Eugene grew quiet. "I think I can. When Gabby and I were studying the portal, we discovered what we believe is a dark energy particle called a chameleon." He paused, realizing he was going to need to explain this from the beginning. "Okay, the matter we can see and feel makes up less than five percent of all the matter in the universe. Seventy percent of the rest consists of dark energy. It's everywhere and part of the force responsible for pushing the galaxies apart at an ever-increasing rate. The twins' minds must be using this dark energy field to communicate."

Mia shook her head. "That may be true, but it's worthless unless we can figure out how they're doing it."

"It's simple," Eugene said, raising an index finger. "Quantum entanglement."

"Excuse me?" He was losing her.

"I know, quantum theory is terrifyingly complicated and counterintuitive, so I'll try to keep it simple. Particles exist in a certain spin or a quantum state. When two particles created at the same time share the same composite state, we say they are entangled. Each individual particle's spin could be up, down or anywhere in between, but the combined spins of the two particles are restricted if they're entangled. Because the quantum world is one of infinite probabilities, each particle's spins are said to have all spins at once until the particle is observed, then they collapse into a specific value."

"Wait a second," Mia said, her hands stretched out before her. "You're saying particles only collapse once they are observed?"

"Yes, it's weird, I know," Eugene said, smiling. "It's something scientists discovered with the double slit experiment and we've been scratching our heads ever since. Welcome to the wonderful world of quantum theory."

"But doesn't that add weight to my own findings?"

"You mean that at a subatomic level, our minds are reaching across space to affect the very thing being observed?"

She nodded emphatically.

"I suppose it does. But here's where it gets really interesting. Einstein called quantum entanglement 'spooky action at a distance,' because those entangled particles I mentioned earlier collapsed into the exact same state no matter how far apart they were from one another. Einstein probably didn't like it since it defied the speed of light predicted by his theory of relativity."

Mia folded her arms over her chest and raised her chin as she attempted to put all the pieces together. "So our conscious minds operate within this dark energy field Grant calls a morphic field, interacting with dark energy particles called chameleons. But what makes the girls different from the rest of us is their ability to entangle said particles and project them from one mind to another."

"Exactly. Listen, the riddle of what consciousness is and why we have it is still a rather sticky question in the scientific community. Fundamentally, if all of us are only a bunch of atoms strung together, then we're not that different from a rock or a star. So if we're conscious, why aren't they?"

She let out a big breath, slumping into a nearby chair, an intense sense of relief washing over her. Sure, it was preliminary, but she felt she was finally beginning to grasp the full meaning of how the girls were able to do the seemingly impossible. Some might call it paranormal, but there was no need to invoke gods or spirits here. Those old labels, she was beginning to see, might very well have been an everyday person's attempts to explain the unexplainable. The god of the gaps, as they said.

"Since I have your big brain here," Eugene said, grinning, "I wouldn't mind getting your opinion on this." He motioned to the screen he'd been staring at so intently when she first entered the lab. It was an image of the cells they'd cultivated from the flying alien creature. "You're the geneticist, maybe you can make sense of how these cells work. They aren't carbon-based, we know that much."

Mia moved closer, studying the screen. The alien cell appeared to have a membrane filled with a type of cytoplasm. That much was the same. But there was something about the oval-shaped structure in the center that looked disturbingly familiar. "Can you magnify this any more?"

Eugene did so. The screen flickered as the object in the center of the cell grew larger. In carbon-based life, the nucleus was where most of the DNA was stored. But here, the outer casing looked hard, almost synthetic. That was when she made the connection to what Jansson had showed her nestled inside the cells of people with Salzburg.

Jansson had found that exposing the cell to a GMO mixture had caused the strange oval object to activate a form of CRISPR inserting the HISR assembler gene into the cell's nucleus. Earlier, Mia had discovered this same HISR gene had lain dormant within thirty percent of the population, waiting for signs of those same GMOs. Once that occurred, the assembler gene would then begin drawing upon segments of junk DNA in our genome in order to create the beginnings of the Salzburg

209

chromosome.

So how was it then that the alien cell Eugene was showing her so closely resembled what Jansson had found in those suffering from Salzburg? But more than that, why did both of them look as though they had been manufactured?

Chapter 36

Jack and the others leveled their weapons.

"Don't stop!" Stokes shouted to the men paddling them forward.

The wave struck against the side of the raft, spraying them with water and clumps of red algae.

Swinging around, Jack called out to Anna, "Where did it go?"

"It appears to have passed underneath the raft," she said, a hint of worry in her voice.

The water grew still. Everyone was on edge, especially the four men paddling. Grant and Dag were on the port side, their suits dripping from water and red gunk. To starboard were Conroy and Diaz, both men no doubt itching to swap their paddles for the M4 rifles at their sides. But luckily they didn't, which meant the raft kept moving forward.

Jack held his breath, hoping whatever had swum at them had decided to swim away. The thought had barely taken shape when a long spindly arm emerged from the water. The skin looked dark with red and green specks, a perfect camouflage for the grimy water they were pushing through. At the end of the arm was a barbed spear, which it thrust at Conroy. The Delta operator rolled out of harm's way, coming up with his weapon. He locked on with his laser sights and fired three rounds. The creature's arm was thin, but each homing bullet hit its mark, causing explosions of translucent liquid with each impact. Now the others were firing too, the strange-looking arm torn in two from the barrage.

Suddenly, a scream filled the radio from the paddler at the back of the raft.

"It's got Diaz," Kerr shouted.

A ten-inch barb protruded from Diaz's back. This second arm lifted the screaming soldier into the air as he hacked at it with his combat knife. From the center of the raft, Ivan opened up with both guns, kicking up bursts of water with every missed shot. Despite their efforts, Diaz was pulled into the water, still shrieking in agony.

"What the hell was that?" Dag asked, a look of abject terror streaked across his face.

Gabby's expression was no different. "Turn this boat around, we're going back."

"It's too late for that," Jack told her, his weapon still at the ready. "I tried to warn you. This place is no picnic."

"It sure is a picnic," she countered. "And guess who's on the menu."

They stood watch for several moments, positioned in the center of the raft.

"Stokes," Jack said. "We need to keep moving. That thing comes back and pokes a hole in this boat and we're done for. Stokes!" he repeated, finally getting through to the sergeant.

"Yes, you're right." He glanced over and saw the

soldier's paddle floating in the water three feet from the edge of the raft. Stokes grabbed the one at his feet that Conroy had dropped and went to the edge. Kerr, Conroy and Bates covered him as he leaned over the edge to fish out the fourth paddle. "Mark my words," Stokes instructed them. "You see so much as a toe poking out of that swamp and you toast it, you hear me?"

"Yes, sir," Kerr replied, his M4 dug into his shoulder.

"I do not think that is very wise," Anna said to Ivan, who turned and lifted his massive shoulders in a shrug. Stokes reached out, using the end of one paddle to snag the one floating a few feet away. When it was flush against the side of the raft, he reached in and plucked it out of the water. He then handed the first paddle back to Conroy and told him to return to his post. Stokes would take Diaz's spot.

Grieving and still in shock, they pushed on, thankful whatever came at them didn't return for more.

●●●

Minutes later they reached the opposite shore and pulled the raft a few yards inland to prevent it from floating away.

"The structure should be this way," Jack said, pointing toward his one o'clock.

"Stay alert," Stokes barked, not that any of them needed reminding after what they'd seen on the lake.

They began pushing into the thick brush, Stokes and Jack taking the lead, each armed with fifteen-inch machetes and no shortage of exuberance. The suit didn't only help you walk, it also helped you swing your arms with tremendous power.

"Dr. Greer, could you please pause for a moment?"

213

Jack and Stokes stopped, neither man even remotely short of breath.

"You see something?" Jack inquired, the hand with the machete resting on his hip.

"I believe so." She patched an overhead image in to everyone's glasses, adding a red blinking box around the anomaly.

"Looks like another building," Gabby exclaimed.

"This one's only half the size," Dag added. "Might be why we missed it."

Jack saw that it was fifty yards away, just over a nearby hill. "Doesn't look like much of a detour. I say we take a quick look."

"All right," Stokes agreed, changing direction and hacking away.

By now the fog had lifted completely, increasing their field of vision, but not doing much to diminish their anxiety. Before long, they arrived at a squat structure, covered with overgrowth. At some point, the seed from a large yellow tree had taken hold on the flat roof and now it stretched a hundred feet into the air, its foliage unfurled like a giant crimson umbrella. The tree's roots snaked along the exterior walls and into the ground below. Moss dangled over a high archway in the center of the structure marking the way inside. Jack was the first to enter, switching his headlamp on and keeping his rifle in front of him.

A ramp, pitched downward at a low angle, gradually led to an enormous chamber. Even in a dank, sunless place, nature had found a way. Like the greenhouse, most of the surfaces were covered with one form of plant life or another. Here, the ceiling was high enough to support trees thirty feet and taller. Scanning the ground, somewhere between the vines and the sapling roots, Jack spotted the hint of a slate-gray metal floor, one of the few signs the room they were in had been built by hand, in this case alien hands. The other sign came from the faint blue lights he saw blinking at various points up and down the walls. His eyes traced to the ceiling, where he discovered what resembled the outlet from a huge energy device. The thought crossed his mind that it could be a release valve just as easily as it could be the barrel from an impressive laser weapon. Whatever it was, why it was pointing at the ground mystified him.

Grant walked beneath the object on the ceiling, busy inspecting something he had discovered on the ground beneath it. He tore at the vines covering what looked like the pedestal for a small round statue. Flecks of blue light danced around the object whenever Grant's hands drew near its rounded surface.

"Dr. Holland," Stokes said as politely as he could. "May I suggest you don't start touching things just yet. I've already lost two of my men to this place and I have no interest in adding you to that list."

Dag and the others continued looking around the immense space.

"Perhaps I should try," Anna said. "That way, no human will be harmed if something goes awry."

Jack began to protest, but she was already there. Grant backed away when he saw her approach. Squatting down, Anna inspected the base where she'd seen some of the twinkling lights. Then she stood and placed her palm over the statue's smooth surface.

Nothing happened. Grant returned and did exactly as he

had done before. The blue lights shimmered once again. Then he placed one hand next to the other and suddenly the chamber was engulfed in a spectacular display of brilliant blue illumination. Rotating around them for a few fleeting moments was a hologram of what looked like a solar system, maybe even a galaxy. Grant struggled to hold it, shifting his hands about the object's surface, but no matter what he did, the stunning sight would begin to waver before disappearing.

"What the heck was that?" Dag shouted from the other end of the chamber.

Jack shook his head, the ghostly hologram still visible in his mind's eye. "I believe it was a star map."

Chapter 37

Kay had been surprised when her blog, the American News-Letter—named after the first continuous paper in North America, the Boston News-Letter—had racked up five thousand followers after her very first posting. And she was positively stunned when that number exploded into over a million, much like the event at Kennedy Space Station she had written about. Normally, that sort of thing would never happen to a humble news blog, but with all of the major news outlets either shuttered or toeing the government line, the public was hungry for a real and unvarnished source of information. Put another way, they were hungry for the truth.

Kay began by reposting the exposé she'd written on Sentinel's long and sordid history, followed by the conspiracy to remove President Taylor and replace him with Secretary of Defense Myers. But being imbedded, so to speak, with the resistance made reaching out to her contacts extremely hazardous. The use of cellphones was strictly off limits, since as Ollie liked to say, those infernal things were little more than tracking devices. Not surprisingly, Armoni also had a role to play in Kay's success, in large part by shielding her blog from government denial-of-service attacks and other nefarious means they employed in an effort to silence her. But the hacker/programmer showed her true genius with the secured private messenger service she created. Called ICE for Input Character Emulation, it enabled Kay to interface with all existing messenger platforms. She could even use it to send text messages without revealing her location. If the world hadn't been in such turmoil, Kay was sure ICE would have made Armoni a billionaire many times over.

Currently, Kay was sketching out plans for her next story. In it she planned to reveal the existence of the government's internment camps and how they were desperately trying to keep them quiet. Pictures of conditions there had been smuggled out and sent to her. In each case, her heart went out to the dispirited faces she saw staring back at her. Decades had passed since the world had known the depravity of camps like Auschwitz and Dachau, and yet even now the pictures from past and present were largely interchangeable. The buildings were different, so too were the guards' uniforms, but more of what made the sight ghastly then still remained.

Skipping through the images one by one, Kay wasn't ashamed to admit she lingered a little longer on group shots, hoping she might find someone she knew. Perhaps even proof her parents were still alive. Armoni had been the one who found their names listed in the arrest and transfer documents. Which meant at some point the two of them had arrived at one of the thirteen camps currently dotting the eastern seaboard. Whether or not they were still there or even alive was another matter entirely. Kay's stomach lurched from the mere thought. She focused in an effort to steady herself. She was nearly there when her computer dinged with a new private message. She checked and saw it was from Special Agent Ramirez.

"Kay, is that you or is someone ghosting your byline?"

"Of course it's me," she replied.

"Prove it. Tell me something only the real Kay would know."

She laughed. "You like to shout, 'Who's your daddy?' when you're having sex."

"Damn, I didn't think you could hear that."

"You were dating my roommate, what can I say? Anyway, I'm guessing you read my article about the sabotage."

"I did. The bureau's set up a task force to find out who did it. You had details that only the assailants knew. I'd ask you who your contacts are, but I know there isn't any point."

Kay smiled. "You're a wise man. I'm about to tell the world about the concentration camps. Of course they're calling them something far more benign, not that anyone will be fooled. Not when I'm done exposing them."

"I've heard rumors."

"Rumors are one thing. I've got pictures and corroborated firsthand accounts. I also have a list on Homeland Security letterhead that happens to have my parents' names on it."

"Oh, shit."

"Then for the grand finale, I'm going to reveal the despicable reason why they're all situated close to the coastline. My only worry is Sentinel's plan is so insidious people may not believe it. Well, at least the incoming ship has been destroyed, removing the threat of Armageddon."

"That's part of why I was reaching out."

Kay's brow furrowed and the pulse in her neck quickened. "Go on."

"The missiles from Vandenberg impacted that ship, that part is true. But the propaganda the government's putting out that the ship was destroyed isn't."

That sinking feeling in Kay's gut was getting worse. "I did get a bunch of PMs from friends at the European Space Agency refuting the ship's destruction. I suppose I just didn't want to believe it."

"I'm sorry." Ramirez went away for a few minutes and then returned to write. "There's something else and I wanted you to be the first one to know about it. President Taylor was taken off life support."

"What? On whose order?"

"President Myers, but he's claiming the ex-First Lady made the decision."

"Oh, no."

"Myers also expedited the executions of the cabinet members he accused of orchestrating the downing of Marine One. Myer's grip on power has officially been consolidated."

Kay felt the world swimming away from her. To be hit by so much in one shot was almost too much to bear. With Sentinel digging in its nails and the doomsday ship still on its way, only one thing was clear. In less than eighteen hours, the human race would top the list of endangered species.

Chapter 38

18 hours, 22 minutes, 57 seconds

Jack was standing next to the pedestal, struggling in vain to get it to light up again, when he caught sight of Grant in the distance, plucking a wisp out of the air. At once, the biologist hurried over to a folding table and microscope he had set up.

Stokes and his men continued to sweep the rest of the chamber, ensuring nothing aggressive was using this place as a den.

Not far from Grant, Anna appeared to be teaching Ivan about humor, Yuri looking on like the one boy at prom without a date.

"I don't get it," Dag said, rubbing the round surface the way a man might rub a prized bowling ball. "Grant was the only one that had any luck with this thing," Seconds later, his grimace deepened when the light show still failed to start. "Guess I'm not the chosen one," he joked.

"That's too bad," Jack replied. "Maybe we could have gotten some answers."

Dag starred down at his feet. "You realize this ship is not only twice as big as the Atean craft, it's also far more advanced."

Jack nodded. "The thought had crossed my mind." He glanced at Gabby, who came to stand next to him.

Dag straightened. "I mean, the power requirements alone for something this size are so much greater, not that the other one wasn't impressive."

"No, but I see what you mean," Jack said. "We know the first ship impacted sixty-five million years ago, wiping out the dinosaurs along with a flourishing *Mesonyx* civilization. We also know they built an entire city on top of the ship we're in now. Which means this must have crash-landed on Earth long before that."

"Well, two hundred and fifty million years ago was the Permian extinction," Dag said, drawing the next logical inference.

Gabby tightened an arm strap on her exoskeleton suit. "Since we're quite certain the arrivals of these ships are tied to the major extinction events in Earth's history, then it could be even older."

A light went on behind Jack's eyes. "The Cambrian explosion?" he asked, breathless.

Dag shook his head in disbelief. "But that was five hundred and forty million years ago."

"It's a long time," Gabby replied. "I think you two are missing the most obvious point."

Jack caught her eye. "Which is?"

"How is it possible that the older of the two ships is also the more advanced one?" she said.

Both men grew quiet, contemplating the magnitude of Gabby's question.

"Time travel?" Dag said, jumping as usual to the wildest solution.

"Given the similar shape of both craft, we simply assumed this was an Atean ship," Jack said, trying to rid himself of preconceived notions. "Or at the very least from a civilization closely linked to them. But you're suggesting they may not be connected after all."

"Not only might they not be connected," Gabby replied, "but the mighty beings who built this vessel may not be the ones who created the Ateans in the first place."

"Stop, you're blowing my mind," Dag said, clutching the sides of his helmet.

Jack laughed. They were almost there, he could feel it. A single outlying puzzle piece was all that remained for all of the disparate clues they'd found to fall into place. He was sure soon enough, this whole mess would all make sense.

"Well, I'll be a green jammied bugger," Grant swore in his uniquely British way.

"Add another wisp to your collection?" Jack asked, about to suggest they wrap it up and head to the main structure.

"We couldn't have been more wrong about these wonderful creatures," Grant said, rushing out the words before they could get away from him.

Anna turned and began heading toward him. "What have you discovered, Dr. Holland?"

From Jack's point of view, describing the creatures here as wonderful seemed almost inappropriate, given one of them had killed Peterson and another had turned Diaz into a human shish-kabob.

Slowly, the team members filed in around Grant. "They aren't animals," he said, breathless. "Not as we understand the term. Do you recall in the lab when we

223

were first analyzing the samples you brought back?"

"How can I forget?" Jack said. "You told us they didn't have any DNA."

"And that they weren't carbon-based," Dag added.

Still seated, Grant spun to face them. "That's right. They had a completely different molecular arrangement. The first authentic silicon-based life ever discovered. But you see, that's where I was wrong. The millions and billions of units which make up the bodies of these creatures aren't cells. They're highly advanced self-replicating nanobots."

Jack felt the muscles in his jaw go slack. "Say that again?"

Grant stood and held him by the shoulders. "Tiny molecular-sized robots programmed to perform specific tasks. One of those tasks is self-replication. In this case, it appears to happen when one creature consumes something from its environment. Don't you see? It's a perfectly balanced ecosystem inhabited almost entirely by robots."

"So these nanobots gain energy from their environment," Gabby said. "And use the food they eat as the raw molecular materials to build a copy of themselves."

"Yes," Grant said emphatically. "Which implies there must be some form of communication between these nanobots for them to know what sort of cell they're supposed to be. In humans that's the work of DNA. In these creatures, there may be another mechanism at work."

"Perhaps they're more flexible," Jack suggested.

Grant threw him an inquisitive look. "In what way?"

"I'm not sure," he continued. "Perhaps given the right

224

instructions, a nanobot coded to be part of a toenail might reconfigure itself as a skin cell. Imagine the ultimate stem cell. I did notice the soil shimmering when I first arrived. You said yourself it was largely composed of discarded nanocells. Perhaps they're using some form of biophotonics."

"But Dr. Holland," Anna interjected. "If these nanocells continue to replicate, what might that mean for the most successful among them?"

"They would become huge," Grant replied, the full impact of his words hitting them all at once.

"I guess we know how the behemoth got so big," Jack said, his mind still reeling.

Stokes readied his M4 rifle, the whiskers from his handlebar mustache twitching in the soft glow of his helmet light. "Nanobots or not, I suggest we get moving before dark settles in."

Chapter 39

Soon, Jack and the others were out in the open again. The sun, or the artificial light source that was tasked with mimicking one, was well on its way to setting. But fading light wasn't the biggest problem they were facing.

"I thought you said head east," Stokes shouted impatiently at Kerr. "Make up your mind."

"Don't you see, Sarge," Kerr replied, pointing at the overhead image they were using to guide them. "In here, there is no north, south, east or west. About all I can do is point this way and that."

"No wonder we're lost," Dag stammered, scanning the imposing thicket of brush around them.

"Lemme see that," Jack said, moving in and taking hold of the overhead view. Anna's drones were still flying above them, but the challenge was identifying any kind of usable landmarks. "Okay, so we've got what looks like a high peak about three hundred yards to the left of the main structure. And both of them run parallel to the strip of swamp we crossed. The way I'm reading this thing, we're heading back towards the water." Jack rotated until he was facing a hundred and eighty degrees. He lowered his hand in a chopping motion dead ahead of him. "I bet if we head in this direction, we're sure to cross the main structure."

Jack was no sooner done speaking when he felt the ground tremble beneath his feet. He and Stokes shared a knowing look.

"Please tell me that isn't what I think it is," Grant pleaded.

The trembling grew louder.

"The behemoth," Dag murmured in terrified awe.

"All right, Jack," Stokes snapped, moving forward at a brisk pace. "I sure hope you're right about this."

"Me too," he whispered.

They continued hacking their way through the undergrowth, but the shaking was only getting stronger.

"We're not going to make it," Gabby shouted.

"Stay calm," Jack said, falling back behind her. "Let your exoskeleton do the walking."

"Walking? I want it to fly."

"What the hell is this guy's problem anyway?" Dag asked, powering past them. "What'd we ever do to him?"

"It's clearly territorial," Grant said, panting. "And for all we know of its biology, maybe it's in heat."

"Very reassuring, Grant," Jack said. "Why don't we put the theories on hold for now?"

Close behind, trees were getting knocked over like blades of grass in a high wind.

"I see an entrance up ahead," Stokes called out with noticeable relief.

Toward the back of the line, Ivan was steaming forward, his upper torso rotated so that his twin guns covered their escape. But behind him were the two robotic pack mules, their thin legs pistoning up and down as they struggled to keep up.

Jack spotted the opening and then made the mistake of turning around. He could see snapshots of the creature in the fading light as it stomped through the alien jungle after them. It was nearly half the height of the tallest tree, with thick legs and flat rounded feet. Its torso was bulbous and jiggled as it moved. Nevertheless, Jack saw hints of muscle rippling beneath its grey flesh. Further up the torso, the beast's head was a rounded, neckless mass, dotted with dozens of glowing silver eyes. But the mouth was what stayed with him the longest, a giant maw filled with sharpened teeth that hung open, waiting to be filled. Protruding from the center of its chest was a single arm punctuated by a three-digited claw it now used to swoop down and scoop up the closest robotic mule. The animal's legs continued jostling through empty air as the behemoth shoved it into its mouth and crushed it with a single bite. A second later it repeated the act on the other mule. Ivan was next in line and he sprayed the creature's torso as they ran for their lives.

"In the face," Jack shouted over the radio. "Shoot it in the face."

His treads whirring up and over an embankment, Ivan did so, tracers marking a path up its chest and peppering its eyes and face. The creature lowered its head, Ivan's shots hammering the top of its incredibly thick skull. They were less than fifteen feet from the opening now and Jack could see Stokes and Kerr had dropped down on one knee and were firing back at it. That was when that giant claw swung down for a third time, closing around Ivan and lifting him straight into the air. Its fingers locked in a crushing embrace, Ivan continued firing until he disappeared into the creature's mouth. Jack reached the opening in time to see it turn and fade back into the jungle. Uncharacteristically, he felt a surge of sadness welling up within him. Ivan was dumb as a brick, but he had been loyal and he had saved their lives more than once. But most of Jack's sadness wasn't for himself. What weighed on his heart most was knowing how crushed Anna would be. Worst of all, he didn't relish being the one to tell her.

Chapter 40

"What the hell do you think you're doing?" Mia barked. She was standing at the door to her research lab, her fists clenched, white hot with anger at the sight before her. Alan's men were in her lab, pulling out drawers and dumping them on the floor. In a pile ten feet away, she saw reams of data on the twins she had carefully organized into folders.

In the middle of it all was Alan, calmly sitting before her computer terminal, clicking through the files she kept there. He glanced up at her and tisked, waving his finger at her. "Mia has been a naughty girl. You've been holding out on your old boss, haven't you? Been keeping secrets." He stood. "Oh, don't forget, darling, I was a researcher too once. Not to mention, I'm the one who got you started, took you under my wing. I recognized the lure of uncovering perhaps the greatest evolutionary leap forward in human history would be too much to pass up. All I needed to do was provide you with the tools you needed and a little motivation and you would work your magic.

"It's hard for the average man on the street to understand what it's like for people like us. That feeling we get when we're on the trail of a major breakthrough. When you catch the smell of blood in the wind." Alan lifted his nose as he sniffed the air about him. "There's something almost primeval about it.

"Don't get me wrong, I had faith in your talent, even though it lacked refinement and above all confidence." Alan tapped the top of the monitor. "But let me say, I never expected your achievements to exceed my wildest dreams. Which, of course, brings me back to the lying. You remember the legend of Blue Beard. I'm sure you do. The one where he offers his wife everything her heart could possibly desire with but a single caveat. She is never to enter the room in the cellar. Short of breaking that little rule, a life of eternal happiness awaits her. For a while she manages to ignore that teeny, tiny voice whispering in her ear to take the key. It'll only be a little peek and he'll never know. Soon enough that whispering voice becomes a roar and she starts to weaken and does the one thing he specifically told her not to." Alan rose to his feet, glaring at her, his chest heaving, his eyes ablaze, and suddenly Mia was down on the ground in that hotel room again, staring up at that same bristling, demonic face. Her legs began to buckle and the blood drained from her face. She steadied herself against the doorframe and fought to regain control.

"I want you out of my lab right now," she shouted, charging forward with enough force that two of Alan's men had to grab her by the arms and hold her back. Alan hardly seemed to notice. He picked up a handful of printouts, scanning the page. "When I first saw the 47th chromatid I wanted to believe it was nothing more than a dumping ground for garbage genes," he said. "An ingenious method for thinning out the least worthy. Then came a strange pattern in the DNA, something that went beyond the typical distribution of ACGTs. But it wasn't until the 48th showed up that I knew we had something truly special on our hands. The first few genes for increased bone density and resistance to radiation— well, those are good for cockroaches. It was with the last two that things really started to get interesting. Minds reaching across space and time to speak with one another. There's poetry and beauty in that, no doubt about it. But in my estimation, MRE11 really steals the show. Imagine, a gene that repairs errors in your DNA so effectively, it can quintuple the average human lifespan." The light in Alan's eyes began to dim.

"As smart as you are, Mia, you were always slow to see the bigger picture. This isn't really about stopping kamikaze spaceships. Believe me when I tell you there's nothing to worry about there. And yes, your friend Ollie is up to his old tricks again. He blew up one of my rocket pads. I can tell you this because you're bound to find out sooner or later. But rest assured, there is always a backup plan, my dear. How does the saying go, 'save the best for last'?

"What you also missed is that this isn't about scientific breakthroughs. We are in the midst of a biological revolution and you and I are on the losing end."

Mia stared at him, beginning to see the disturbing direction this was heading in.

"The extinction of the human species. Ha! That's a joke. This is about the extinction of *Homo sapiens* 1.0. In other words, those without Salzburg. It took me a while to see it myself, I won't lie. But once I did, the clarity hit me like the blow from a hammer. Pow!" he shouted smacking the palm of his hand against his forehead. "At first I wanted to know what the syndrome was and the code buried deep inside of it. Then, when I realized I could never have it, I wanted to destroy it. Now, with your help, I've reached a brand-new epiphany. On nearly every level, those with Salzburg are smarter and stronger than the rest of us. Doomsday ship or not, over the next few centuries, they will eventually replace us, the way we once replaced Neanderthals. Fighting them directly will prove a fruitless pursuit. Which is why I want to join them." He waved pages of Mia's research in the air, wielding it like a weapon. "And you, my dear, are going to marshal all of the knowledge you've gained at my expense to start the process."

"You're mad," she said, her feet sliding on the floor as she tried to back up. Alan's men held her in place.

"You love those twin girls, don't you?" he said, his silver eyes locked on hers. "Love them almost as much as you love your daughter. Let me assure you, they will be the first to die and I will make you watch every excruciating second of it."

Involuntary tears began streaming down her cheeks. "I was wrong, you're not an asshole, you're a monster."

"I only want to survive, Mia," he said, his voice devoid of emotion. "That's how they made us, those beings you consider gods."

"You don't understand," she told him. "I can inject you with the right cells to get the process started, but the Salzburg chromosome won't populate without blast waves from an alien ship and you destroyed the only one we had."

"Oh, don't you worry about that," Alan reassured her. "As we speak, my Russian friends are scouring every major crater around the globe. There have been at least five major extinctions and we've only found a single ship. That leaves four more to go."

He still doesn't know about the ship beneath the Mesonyx *city*, Mia thought with a tinge of hope.

"You had your secrets, but I better not find you've lied to me about anything else," Alan said in a low, ominous voice. "Or murdering those innocent young girls will pale compared to what I'll do next."

Chapter 41

Kay removed her engagement ring and set it by the sink. She ran the water, letting the cool liquid soothe her swollen fingers. She'd spent most of the preceding night gathering information on President Taylor's removal from life support and the execution of the supposed conspirators who'd put him there. Reporting on how the nuclear missile and the MIRV warhead hadn't stopped the alien ship heading their way took even more time. Her eyes settled on the ring, her mind filling with memories of Derek, the way he used to dance around her apartment like Carlton from *Fresh Prince* to cheer her up whenever he saw she was having a bad day. His face would be plastered with a big, goofy grin, his arms swinging back and forth to his own sad version of Tom Jones' classic song. By the time she reached for the towel, tears were streaming down her cheeks. She braced her palms against the linoleum, her head bobbing in quiet sobs. She hadn't come in here to have a moment, but it was often the moments that had a way of deciding those things for themselves. Her body tensed, fighting the sheer force of grief struggling to get out, but soon the grief won over and Kay gave in to its power.

She stood in place, her upper body undulating with sorrow, and it came and went like waves crashing against a sea wall, a fine mist spraying into the air as the water slowly ate away at the hardened rock.

It was difficult to tell how long it lasted, seconds, minutes. She straightened, the immediate sorrow exorcised, at least for the time being. She brought the towel to her eyes and caught the sound of metal skittering along a hard surface. Kay saw her engagement ring, the last and perhaps most meaningful memento of Derek she had left, begin rolling toward the drain. As though in slow motion, she thrust out her sore hands, scrambling to stop it, no longer feeling any pain, but definitely overcome with a jolting sense of panic. A third and final plop signaled its entry into the drain.

"No, no, no, no, no," she shouted. Then—"Oh, crap." Kay looked around frantically, opening drawers and pushing aside the contents, desperate for something she could use to fish it out. She jammed her eye as close to the drain hole as she could manage and caught the two-carat diamond winking back at her from an unreachable curve in the pipe. A knock came at the door.

"Hey, Kay, you all right in there?" Patrick asked, concern in his voice.

She was still staring into the hole.

"Kay?"

She flung open the door and Patrick took a worried step back.

"My ring just went down the damn drain," she said, pacing back and forth, her eyes still swollen. Patrick probably thought she'd been crying over it. But that was because Patrick didn't understand women. More importantly, Patrick didn't understand Kay. Right now, losing that ring hadn't made her sad, it had made her angry, furious. Mostly at herself for not being careful, the way she had been careful a million times before. As for the sadness, that would come later as she was falling asleep and giving her mind time to replay what had happened, giving it time to play judge, jury and executioner—a role perfected over long years of practice. Patrick put his hands up in surrender. "Take a deep breath and just relax. I'll be right back." The scrawny man with clothes three sizes too big disappeared and reemerged minutes later with a blue bucket and a large wrench. He made the beeping sound of an emergency vehicle as he passed her. "Please step aside, ma'am, for your own safety."

Patrick opened the cupboard beneath the bathroom sink, slid the bucket beneath the pipes and turned the water supply valves off. He then began to loosen the coupling on both ends. "Did you shut the tap off as soon as it fell in?" he asked.

Kay leaned over his shoulder with fascination, as though she were witnessing a surgeon operating on a human brain. "Yes, I believe so."

Patrick then removed the trap and dumped its contents into the bucket. In went his hand, where he fished around until it emerged a moment later holding an engagement ring. "Easy as one, two, three," he said, grinning as he handed it to her.

"Oh, you're a genius," she cried out, taking the ring and hugging him where he sat on the bathroom floor.

"Okay, okay, you're about to squeeze the life outta me." Ollie appeared. "When you two are done renovating the bathroom, make your way to the living room. We just received a disturbing report."

•••

Kay and Patrick followed Ollie to the other room where Armoni and Sven were already waiting. Neither of them appeared worried or solemn, which told Kay Ollie hadn't spilled the beans yet on what he'd learned. They took a seat and Ollie began.

"Our resident brainiac Armoni here has managed to breach the inner core of Homeland Security's cyber-defenses and uncovered the exact location of the detainment camps. Not only that, but Armoni has also managed to pinpoint the exact location of the four individuals Kay has asked us to rescue." He picked up a tablet, made three quick swipes and came to a stop on a map of the South Carolina coast just north of Savannah. Ollie spun it around, zooming out with his fingers. Eventually a large patch of green grass appeared. In the center of it sat a rectangular compound fenced off with razor wire and filled with rows and rows of wooden bunkhouses.

"You found the camps," Kay said, beaming over at Armoni with an expression of sheer joy.

"Hilton Head?" Patrick exclaimed in disbelief.

Sven looked at him and grunted.

"What's wrong?" Kay asked, confused by his reaction.

"Zoom out a touch," Patrick said, pinching his fingers in the air.

Ollie complied.

"See how the field's shaped like an elongated kidney bean?"

"What about it?" Kay said, still not clear what the issue was.

"Can't y'all see the camp was built on a darn golf course? I mean, it don't get much more ironic than that. Hilton Head was a haven for retired folks. You know, the place they were meant to spend their few remaining years shopping, golfing and hitting the beach. In a twisted sort

of way, it's serving the same purpose, I suppose, as a glorified bus stop on a one-way road to the afterlife."
Sven started laughing.

"I mean it, man," Patrick said, defensively. "This is either a total fluke or the boys who built this have a real sick sense of humor."

Kay shook her head. "The real question is how do we get them out?"

"If you're asking whether or not they can be extracted," Ollie replied, "the answer is perhaps. But not by us."

Kay stood up. "Not by us?" she said, her eyes alight with searing anger. She felt a double-cross coming.

"We have another team," he explained, "with heavy weapons, who are much better equipped to bust in there and free those people. You wanna make your way over there and join them, be my guest. If that were the only thing on our plate at the moment I'd gladly be there myself. But let's just say a rather critical piece of information has just fallen into our lap."

Sven's eyes narrowed. "How critical?"

"Maybe the worst kind," Ollie replied, the stress lines in his face looking suddenly more like earthquake fault lines. "We know Sentinel launched the secret coup to overthrow President Taylor because he refused to fire nuclear weapons at the alien ship. Instead, he opted to outfit Cold War bunkers with enough supplies that humans might one day emerge to reclaim all that was lost."

Armoni folded her arms and pressed her back into the chair she was sitting in. "Which immediately raised a whole other set of problems, like how do they decide who's allowed to become part of the next generation?"

"Or the one after that," Patrick said. "There's nothing to say they wouldn't be trapped down there for decades. Maybe longer."

Ollie gritted his teeth and nodded. "Unfortunately, Patrick's right. Once Myers was in office, everyone assumed he'd scrap the bunker plan, but he didn't. He actually did what he could to speed it up. What *was* scrapped was the lottery. You see, for some reason, the bloke who was really pulling the strings, a man named Alan Salzburg, refused admittance to anyone with the disorder that bore his name. He also insisted on a rigorous DNA screening process to ensure the candidates were pure and not tainted by any alien genetic tinkering."

"I never thought I'd see the resurgence of the eugenics movement," Kay said, astounded by what Ollie was telling her.

She was referring to ideas about genetic inheritance and purity that had gained prominence in the late nineteenth and early twentieth centuries. One branch of scientists, seeking to rid society of poverty, drunkenness, crime, and mental illness, sought to sterilize certain segments of the population, arguing that genetically flawed people should not be allowed to pass along their bad genes. But genetic inheritance in peas and livestock proved vastly different from inheritance in people. It wasn't until the philosophy, first begun and championed in America, was exported to Nazi Germany that the dangers of such thinking became grotesquely apparent.

"That Salzburg guy sure hates all things alien," Patrick said, raising his shoulders. "To him it's like polio, a virus that needs to be eradicated."

"The aliens probably think the same thing about us," Armoni joked with black and deadly humor.

240

"What you're saying may be true," Ollie said. "The fact remains, President Myers and his Sentinel overseers were hedging their bets. Upgrade the existing bunkers while also doing what they could to destroy the ship. It was a foolish plan and as we've seen, one with a failure rate of one hundred percent. Then there was the hypocritical aspect of knocking off a president you disagreed with only to continue with a huge part of his plan. But now fresh intercepts from a handful of moles in the organization are beginning to shed light on the logic behind Sentinel's move. Alan Salzburg isn't against the alien chromosome. The truth is he wants it for himself, to harness the power to grant an almost unlimited genetic advantage to himself and those who follow him. Which brings us to his backup plan."

Kay sat up straight. "Backup plan?"

Ollie nodded. "One I'm afraid is far worse than we thought." He glanced over at Armoni, who collected a half-dozen papers from a nearby desk and handed them out. It revealed a satellite image of the Arecibo Observatory in Puerto Rico. Until China outdid it in 2016, Arecibo was the largest radio telescope in the world. From the air, the dish resembled a giant, dirty punch bowl pressed into the ground. Cables running between three concrete towers suspended a bulbous white receiver over the dish. Lush green mountains hemmed it in from all sides, except for a rise overlooking the site, which housed a collection of scientific and support structures.

Kay had seen the radio telescope before, mainly in pictures online, never in person.

"Take a look below the overhanging receiver," Ollie instructed them.

They did.

"It looks like they've added some kind of building with a retractable roof," Patrick noticed.

"What's it do?" Kay asked.

Ollie held Kay's dark brown eyes. "After the original ship was discovered near Mexico, Sentinel sent a group of agents in to steal as much alien tech as they could get their hands on. Their goal—to reverse-engineer what they found—was straightforward enough. What we've since learned is that they succeeded beyond their wildest dreams."

"In so little time?" Kay asked, incredulous.

"Apparently, they managed to hack into an advanced AI system named Anna and steal a decryption key used to crack the alien language."

"So what'd they build with all that stuff?" Patrick asked. "A big-ass laser cannon?"

"Close," Armoni admitted. "But it's far worse. The device they cobbled together is some sort of human and alien hybrid technology capable of creating singularities at great distances."

Kay shook her head. "I'm not following."

"Black holes," Ollie said with deadly emphasis. "Sentinel is preparing to fire this thing into space and create a black hole directly in the ship's path."

"Oh, snap!" Patrick hollered. "That is smart and nasty all rolled into one."

"And there's a good chance this thing might work," Ollie said, the creased brow from before now obvious for what it really was, plain old fear. "And those bastards are arrogant enough to think they'll be able to shrink it down again before it wreaks havoc."

Space talk wasn't Kay's playground, which meant she was struggling to wrap her head around the implications. "Havoc?"

"One of the benefits of Salzburg is I can already see from Sentinel's equations that the plan to shut the black hole down after it's taken care of the ship is fatally flawed," Armoni replied.

"Which means?" Mia asked, although the lump of anxiety in her gut told her she already knew the answer.

"First the black hole will devour the ship," Armoni explained. "Then when it's done, it'll turn on the nearest celestial object...us."

Chapter 42

15 hours, 36 minutes, 55 seconds

Jack and the others switched on their helmet lights as they descended deeper into the largest of the alien structures and the main objective of their mission. Jack flashed his light, capturing walls draped with hanging moss, a veritable living tapestry. There did not appear to be a single place on board this ship where the vegetation had failed to colonize. Soon, they came to a dead end, with a darkened passage on either side.

Anna glanced around. "Dr. Greer, we are missing three members of our group," she said, a hint of alarm in her voice.

Gabby glanced at him, her eyes quickly falling to the floor.

"I detect Ivan and both of the pack mules are absent." Anna studied the geophysicist's face. "Why has everyone grown quiet?"

Yuri slumped onto the floor, his back pressed against the moss-covered wall, staring off vacantly.

Jack pulled her aside. "Listen, Anna. I'm afraid Ivan didn't make it."

"I do not understand."

Jack sighed and cupped a gloved hand under her chin. "He's dead, Anna. I'm sorry to have to tell you this way, I really am, but he is. We were fleeing through the jungle and that thing reached down and took him."

"Took him?" she said, hopeful. "The definition of that word suggests 'to carry off,' which implies Ivan might still be intact."

Jack shook his head. How did you tell a child she'd just lost a friend without scarring her for life? He paused, searching for the words.

"It ate him, damn it," Yuri shouted from the floor. "Just tell her the truth, the bloody thing crunched him to bits." Anna turned her horrified gaze on Yuri.

"He went down fighting," Jack said, trying to reassure her. "He was brave. But you already knew that." He pulled her into his arms and she began to weep. Over the years, Jack had had his fair share of women cry in his arms, but never one who really meant anything to him. "Let's just give her a minute," he told the others.

"I do not like this sensation one bit," she said. She lifted her head and her digital cheeks were flushed.

"We're all sad," Jack admitted.

"Not all," she said, motioning to Yuri, whose face was scrunched up with anger.

"Don't be fooled," Jack told her. "He may be the saddest of all. Its never easy when a parent loses a child, synthetic or not."

"I will make a note of that," she said, gathering herself together. "In humans, one emotion can often camouflage another."

"That's right," Gabby told her. "There are stages with

grief, some of which you may have experienced after Rajesh's passing."

Stokes tapped his watch. "Sorry to intrude here, folks, but we got a choice to make." He pointed at the two corridors leading in opposite directions.

"We should split up," Jack suggested. "There are ten of us, so two groups of five. Anna, Grant, Yuri and Kerr, why don't you four come with me. Stokes, you take the rest and holler the minute you find anything."

"If we find anything."

"Ever the optimist," Jack said, grinning away the crushing stress he felt rumbling through his insides.

They headed off, their lights bobbing along the corridors as they continued their search. Jack pulled up the countdown clock on his glasses. With less than 15 hours before impact, he knew this might be their last hope.

It wasn't long before the corridor opened into a circular room no more than twenty-five feet across with a domed ceiling about half that size. Like the other locations they had come across, the room here was also covered with a mishmash of yellow moss and ruby-colored vines. But unlike the others, barely visible through the creeping plant life were hundreds of tiny incubation chambers lining the walls, each of them no bigger than a curled-up fist.

"There's so many of them," Gabby exclaimed, tearing away the overgrowth to get a better look.

Yuri peered over her shoulder. "What were they for, do you think?" His Russian accent making "think" sound more like "tink."

"We discovered nearly identical structures inside the Atean ship," Anna explained. "They were used to cultivate and then release full-grown specimens into Earth's prehistoric environment."

Yuri took a closer look. "What kind of a creature could you fit into this? It's the size of a urine sample cup."

"I won't ask how you know that," Gabby said, with marked disapproval.

He stopped and stared at her. "You telling me you don't like to smoke once in a while?"

"All the time," she admitted. "But mainly cigarettes."

"Ha, there goes the pot calling the kettle black," Yuri shot back.

Anna eyed the interaction with fascination. "A saying that dates back to the sixteenth century when kettles and pots were both darkened from cooking over an open flame."

"Yeah, we got it," Kerr said, making his way to a break in the wall where a new corridor lay.

"Maybe this ship did things differently," Jack theorized. "Rather than incubating a full-grown specimen, perhaps they released strands of genetic material into the environment."

They pressed on, moving through another passage into a room that bore an uncanny resemblance to the previous one. The third was no different. Each was filled from floor to ceiling with thousands of mini-pods. Jack reached out to Stokes and the others, sending back images of what they had found.

"We got the same thing here," Stokes replied. "Grant tells us you've seen this before."

"That's right," Jack said. "Which is why we aren't stopping to snoop around. Any serious comparison will have to wait. We've just started heading through another long hallway. I can already see that it opens into a massive chamber."

Jack and his group emerged into the cavernous space. The ceiling, if you could call it that, looked more like the roof of an enclosed sports stadium than an alien compound. Soft lighting bathed the rough edges of moss-covered rock formations. A platform rose up from the middle of the room. Blue lights blinked on and off in sequence, running up and down its length. A series of steps led to the top where a silver altar sat, most of it covered by vines and other vegetation.

Stokes waved at them from the other end of the chamber. It appeared both corridors led to the same location.

"What is this?" Dag asked, hurrying past Stokes, who warned him not to rush ahead. There was no telling what creatures might be hiding in here.

The two groups met in the center, by a shallow pond. Grant went over to one of the rock formations and scraped off a sample, using the magnification on his glasses to zoom in.

"This certainly doesn't beat my microscope, but it appears these mounds are also made of discarded nanocells."

"How could that be?" Yuri asked, stunned.

"It is very simple," Anna said as she began scaling the steps to the altar. "Some of the earliest forms of life on Earth were mounds of microbes that formed rock-like structures."

"Some of them appear to still be alive," Grant began. "Or at least, still functioning."

Standing next to Jack, Gabby eyed the platform. "You

248

think that was where they made the human sacrifices?"
Just then Dag called them over to a spot at the base of
the platform. "I got a collection of bones here," he said,
carefully picking one up. "You ask me, this looks a lot
like a *Mesonyx* arm bone. There's a partial skull here too."
Jack, Gabby and Grant went over to have a look.

Anna reached the top of the platform and began peeling
the vegetation away from the altar. "Dr. Greer," she
called out. "I believe our assessment of this object may
have been incorrect."

Jack took a handful of steps away from the base until he
caught sight of Anna at the top. "Show us what it is you
see."

"Very well."

The visual came through a moment later. What they
thought was an altar was a rectangular metallic
formation, its composition a mishmash of what appeared
to be silver and lead. The blue lights that ebbed along the
edge of the platform criss-crossed over the flat surface of
the object Anna was examining. Parts of it were so shiny
they could see her reflection as she bent over for a better
look.

"Anna," Jack said, "were those blue lights on the altar
blinking the whole time?"

"No, Dr. Greer. They started as I began removing the
vines."

"Anna, I think you should get down from there," Jack
suggested. "At least until we have a better idea what—"

A hand sprang up from the metallic block, grasping
Anna's outstretched arm. She stared down at it in shock.
It was not merely coming from the object, the arm was
part of the object—and now it began to unfold with the

sound of clanking metal, whining against years of disuse. Anna tried to wrench her arm away, but she was locked in its grasp. Those below sprung their weapons.

"Hold your fire," Jack called out, his arms extended to those on either side of him.

A moment later, the entire metal block had twisted and contorted into a disturbing new shape, one with six top-jointed legs, a thick torso and two sets of thin, but clearly powerful arms. The head craned to one side as it tried to make sense of what it was seeing. The metallic creature's face was tall and thin with rows of blue and red lights running in every direction. Jack wanted to call it an alien, but it looked far more like a robot.

In one rapid motion, each of its four arms clasped onto Anna, engulfing both of them in a blinding explosion of light, brighter than any blast wave Jack had ever experienced. Those gathered below closed their eyes, some covering their faces with their hands. Their visors, sensing the dramatic change in ambient light, applied a protective screen. But even that wasn't enough.

When Jack's vision finally returned, the being was still there, regarding them with a mix of curiosity and disdain. Crumpled at its feet lay Anna, thin wisps of smoke rising from her prone form.

Chapter 43

"I'm gonna waste him," Kerr yelled as it began descending the staircase.

The being's six mechanical legs navigated the risers, moving in perfect synchronicity. Jack stood frozen, distinctly aware that what passed for eyes were locked on him as it reached the ground level. The others scurried backward, Dag nearly tripping over a boulder in his path. Jack held his ground, his rifle dangling by his side.

The creature stopped and the lights flickering about its face sped up as it began to make a sound.

"Mok-neer," it said in a low, melodic-sounding voice. Stokes took aim. Jack raised a hand to stop him.

The creature reached out and tapped the exoskeleton Jack was wearing with one of its long metallic claws.

"Moktor-hack-neer," it said, deviating slightly.

Jack increased the audio receptors enough to catch what sounded like a quieter voice uttering the word hundreds, maybe thousands of times in rapid succession until it began to sound like a static hum.

Jack activated his external audio. "What did you do to our friend?" he demanded, pointing to Anna, who still hadn't moved.

It turned and saw where he was indicating. "Rhana."

"Yes, Anna," Jack repeated. "Is that what you're saying? Anna?"

The lights about its face began flickering even faster until the being's head glowed with a single blueish hue.

"Anna," it said at last, then tapped its nail against Jack's chest. "Doctor Jack Greer."

"You know who I am?" Jack said, struggling against the flood of conflicting emotions surging through him.

"Anna showed me," it said slowly.

"How? I don't understand."

"Your tongue is very primitive," the being said, sounding more proficient by the second. "I have assimilated all information contained within the one you call Anna."

"You killed her," Jack said, trying to remain steady.

"No, not dead. She is recovering."

"Who are you?" Jack said. "And why have you come here?"

It bent down and scooped up a loose patch of soil with one of its four metallic claws and brought it several inches from its face. A horizontal beam shot out from one of its eyes, tracing up and down the length of what it was holding. "In your language, I am called Caretaker. I have come to perform my duty, as many have done before me." Seemingly oblivious to their presence, Caretaker moved past Jack, apparently fascinated by a tree standing behind him.

Grant spoke up over the radio. "Why do I get the impression this thing might not know where it is?"

"Maybe because it's been asleep for a million years," Dag said.

"Five hundred million of your Earth years, to be exact,"

Caretaker said. It was talking to them over the radio.

"How did you do that?" Gabby asked, staring in stunned disbelief like the rest of them.

Even Jack was having trouble forming a coherent thought. It wasn't every day you came face to face with… he stopped himself short of saying 'God.' Perhaps 'creator' was more accurate.

Caretaker began scuttling toward the incubation chambers.

"Where are you going now?" Jack said, starting after it before skidding to a stop. "Dag, Grant, go check on Anna, would you? I'm gonna see if I can reason with this thing."

"Reason?" Gabby said. "Oh, goodness, be careful, Jack."

Jack hustled, catching up to Caretaker just beyond the entrance. The being's head was tilted to the sky, its face a swirl of color, as it took in the jungle environment surrounding them. A wisp zipped by and Caretaker tracked its movement, watching it with keen interest as it darted away.

"You've never seen any of this before, have you?" Jack said. "This all happened while you were hibernating."

"A glorious accident," Caretaker said, its face glowing blue.

"Why do you change colors?" Jack wondered.

"Thesis, antithesis, synthesis," Caretaker answered enigmatically. "This is the path to knowledge. The blue light you see indicates understanding has been achieved."

"You're a robot," Jack said, "like Anna."

"Anna is evolving, but she has a long way yet to go. We are similar, her and I, yes. But unlike her, I retain the memories from my organic past."

253

"Hard to believe you were once biological," Jack said. Caretaker was busy admiring the dense canopy overhead when it glanced down at the exoskeleton and biosuit Jack was wearing. "You are less biological than you think."

Jack eyed the gear wrapped around him. "I suppose you do have a point."

Just then, a Stalker pushed through a clump of bushes nearby, eyeing them. Jack swung his rifle around. "We better get back inside. This place isn't as friendly as you think."

The Stalker let out a shriek and charged. But Caretaker had spotted a flying creature perched on a high branch and was analyzing it.

"Caretaker!" Jack shouted. The Stalker was fifteen feet away, its clawed feet tearing up the dirt as it moved in for the kill. Tracking it, Jack took aim and squeezed the trigger, hitting nothing but a patch of dirt. He had been aiming too far ahead, but only because the Stalker had stopped dead in its tracks. In fact, it hadn't only stopped, it was completely frozen. Even a drop of drool that had been collecting along the edge of its rounded, tooth-filled mouth hung in midair.

Caretaker was still admiring the bird. When it flew away he returned his attention to Jack, who remained on his backside, dumbfounded. "This looks to you like magic. I see that now. Anna has studied your people closely. She wishes to be one of you. Even you must know that her true destiny is not to emulate humanity, but to surpass them." Caretaker approached the Stalker, his legs making a crab-like sidestep as he circled the creature. "Nearly everything you see here is composed of building blocks still well beyond your level of technology."

"Nanocells," Jack said, admonishing himself for the defensive tone in his voice. "We do not possess it yet, especially at these levels. We know of it, however."

"Then you know that each building block can be controlled and reconfigured." One of the Stalker's front legs dissolved into a gray goo, which collected on the ground in a small puddle. Jack watched as the puddle slithered over a vine before merging into one of Caretaker's own limbs. Then Caretaker's form began to change. His eight spindly legs merged into two, as did his arms. His head narrowed into something resembling a man's face. In spite of his gray and silver skin, he looked almost human. "Does this form please you more?"

"Uh, I'm having a hard time believing what I'm seeing."

"Human minds do not deal well with shock."

"If you arrived here millions of years ago, how is it you know so much about us?"

Caretaker studied his new human hands, adding in additional details the way a sculptor might work a piece of clay. "I have already told you. When Anna and I merged, I gained access to all that she knows. When two beings encounter one another, there is always a symbiotic exchange. From her I gained knowledge of what this world has become and the dominant species currently inhabiting it."

"If the exchange was mutual, then what did Anna get from you?"

Caretaker's new human lips curled at the edges. "Something she has always wanted."

Chapter 44

Much to Kay's relief, the flight into the Antonio Nery Juarbe Pol airport in Puerto Rico was rather uneventful. She and the others exited the plane, stepping onto the tarmac and into a stifling wave of Caribbean heat. In spite of being a few miles from shore, the smell of the ocean was still strong.

"This is my first time in Puerto Rico," Armoni admitted.

"It might also be your last," Sven said ominously before nudging her.

Waiting for them a short distance away was a beat-up old-school GM van. Standing next to it was a man with mocha-colored skin and a face covered in tattoos.

Kay turned to Ollie who was coming up behind her. "You sure this is our contact? He looks more like a convict."

Ollie snickered. "Where do you think we found him? He's one of the best drivers on the island." The two men approached one another and embraced. "Paco, it's been too long, mate. How's the family?"

"I sent them to live with my aunt in Bogotá," he replied. "Shipments of food to the island have been growing scarcer and there's no telling how long until the situation boils over."

"You've been lucky until now, mate," Ollie told him. "But you're right to be worried."

He introduced everyone before they loaded their gear into the van and drove off.

The roads here were generally nicer than other islands in the Caribbean and Kay assumed that was at least partly due to Puerto Rico's designation as a U.S. territory. Ceded after Spain's defeat in the Spanish-American war at the turn of the last century, it was only one of several islands handed over. Among them were Guam, the Philippines and Cuba.

Soon, they pulled off the highway and drove down a narrow dirt road that looked like it had only recently been carved out of the surrounding jungle. By Sven's gargantuan standards, the van was small and more than once Paco's high-speed driving sent Sven's head into the ceiling. He rubbed the top of his skull and scowled.

"Sorry, my friends, but these back roads are still a bit wild," Paco said apologetically.

Ollie sneered. "Yeah, so's your driving, mate. We nearly there? I'm getting seasick."

The van erupted in laughter.

After passing through a clearing, they arrived at a small wooden cabin, although 'shack' might be a more accurate way of describing what they encountered. Out front was a nearly identical vehicle.

Two men emerged from inside the shack. The older guy was short and round with a full set of hair and goatee. He moved with surprising grace in spite of his rather generous proportions.

The young one was tall, with an average build, a strong jaw and a badly receding hairline.

"Welcome," the wider man said, greeting them with a warm smile and open arms.

257

"Luis, have you lost weight?" Ollie asked, patting his belly.

Luis let out a raspy laugh as the two men embraced. "I sure hope not, my wife will kill me." He ran his hands down the sides of his body in a provocative manner. "She likes her men curvy."

Ollie shook his head in disgust, motioning to the younger man next to him. "Ramon, I don't know how you put up with him."

"I won't lie," Ramon replied, "it's a struggle. But we all have our crosses to bear."

Ollie tapped the religious symbol at the end of Ramon's necklace. "Can't you call your God down to bail us out of this mess? Would save us a heap of trouble."

Ramon took the cross and kissed it. "I'm afraid this is not how the big man upstairs works."

Man? Kay thought, but didn't say.

They headed inside and found the furnishings as sparse as the exterior. In the corner stood a small stove. Against the other wall was a single bed with a caved-in mattress. And in the middle was a table with four rickety chairs.

"Not exactly the Ritz, I'm afraid," Ollie said.

"Ritz?" Richard spat. "This place makes Motel Six look like the Taj Ma-frickin'-hal."

Ollie wasn't impressed. "Well, if you haven't gotten the hint yet, we won't be spending any more time here than we need to. Just enough to sort out what each of us will be doing." He turned to Ramon. "Care to bring in the goodies you brought us?"

Ramon and Luis disappeared outside and returned a moment later with a heavy duffel bag filled with weapons and a smaller bag with plastic explosive and bomb components.

Ollie reached into the first bag and came out with an AK-47-style rifle. "Really, boys?" Ollie said with disappointment and a touch of concern. "You couldn't find anything a little more modern?"

"Hey, this was all I could get on such short notice," Ramon said defensively.

"Ramon here was a cop," Ollie explained. "And Sentinel did a number on you, didn't they?"

Pain breached Ramon's normally jovial features. "I was working in narcotics two years ago when I got a tip that a large shipment of cocaine would be leaving the country via narco submarine. For reasons I didn't understand at the time, the chief refused to let us take them down. When I argued, he told me I was in over my head. So I disobeyed orders and went in alone. But it wasn't drugs they were smuggling. It was people, educated-looking people being brought to the island under the cover of darkness. I wondered if I'd uncovered some sort of terrorist cell. Turns out I was half right."

"They were Sentinel," Kay said. "What were they up to?"

"I never got a chance to find out," Ramon told her. "When word got back about what I'd done, my family was murdered and I was shot and left for dead."

Kay's gut coiled into a tight knot as she realized Derek was probably only one of many who had been killed by Sentinel in an effort to gain their silence. But that was before the organization had seized complete control of the U.S. government. Now they didn't need to hide. They simply erected makeshift camps with empty shipping containers in place of barracks. Now they were free to kill indiscriminately. The thought led her mind to her most recent blog post, the one exposing the horrors of the American concentration camps. She couldn't help

259

but wonder what the outcome would be from shining a light on such a despicable and cowardly act.

"But I survived," Ramon continued, tensing the muscles in his jaw as he spoke. "And every day since then, I have sworn to seek vengeance for the deaths of my wife and children." His tearless eyes were filled with raw determination.

After a short break, they decided to go over the plan. Armoni laid a large tablet on the table with a satellite image of the Arecibo Observatory.

"The problem we're up against is that for every Sentinel agent we encounter," Ollie began, "there are at least ten hired guns, most of them local folks who are out of work and looking to make a quick buck. But Sentinel has also hired a band of trained mercenaries. I won't lie to you. Our chances are slim."

The atmosphere in the shack grew tense with worry.

"Let me get this straight," Patrick said, his palms pressed flat against the table. "You're telling me seven of us, carrying old, crappy weapons, are going to attack a heavily fortified base?"

Ollie paused. "I am."

Armoni didn't look happy at all. "So this is a suicide mission?"

"Please tell us you have *some* good news," Sven pleaded.

Ollie grinned. "There is a glimmer of hope. Luis' background as a dish engineer has enabled him to infiltrate the Sentinel observatory and gather intelligence on troop strengths and targets. So we won't be going in blind and if everyone does their jobs, there's a chance some of us might just make it out alive."

"Whatever you do, don't ever go into sales," Kay said, biting her lip.

Ollie returned to the digital image of the observatory. "We go in three groups," Ollie told them. "The first group will only consist of Luis." The two men locked eyes. "On our signal, your job will be to blow the northernmost support tower. When it collapses, it should snap the wire holding the giant receiver over the dish."

"Isn't that what will help to focus the beam emitted from the alien device below?" Kay asked. "If the receiver's down, do we really need to do anything else?"

Ollie shook his head vigorously. "It does focus the beam, you're right about that. But the weapon will still work without the receiver. A lack of accuracy won't stop Sentinel from trying. If they manage to create a black hole anywhere within our solar system, the Earth as we know it is pretty much done for."

"The science section of the paper once featured a hypothetical on the idea of a black hole wandering through our solar system and the results were catastrophic," Kay said, crossing her arms.

"Not only that," Patrick added, "but once it's out there, we'll have no way to stop it."

"Which is why we're going in with three groups," Ollie said, drawing them back to the subject at hand. He used his fingers to zoom in to the cluster of buildings on a hill overlooking the observatory. "There's no doubt Sentinel has fortified the area against attack. They'll be expecting an assault to come along the main road. Which is why Sven, Ramon, Paco and I will climb up from the valley below and access the building housing the control room without anyone being the wiser."

"Please tell me you're not leaving me holed up in this shack to bake to death?" Armoni said, her eyes half-moons of disapproval.

"Of course not," Ollie reassured her. "You, Kay and Patrick will be team number three."

"What will we do?" Kay asked, the fear coiling around her chest like a boa constrictor around its prey.

Ollie positioned the map over the dish. "Your job will be simple. Destroy the alien weapon."

Chapter 45

7 hours, 15 minutes, 29 seconds

Jack returned to the structure to find Anna and Dag sitting on a rocky outcropping, the others gathered around them.

"How are you feeling?" he asked.

Anna's movements were slow and appeared almost pained. She looked up at him. "I have viewed many videos on the internet of people being struck by lightning or run over by cars. I feel as though I have finally experienced both and wish to never do so again."

"You should have seen her ten minutes ago," Dag said. "She could barely walk."

"Where's Caretaker?" Gabby asked.

Jack shrugged. "Probably still up there surveying his domain. I tried to get him talking but keeping him on one thing is like trying to herd cats." He briefly summarized the incredible incident with the Stalker he had witnessed.

"With powers like that we should be calling him Merlin," Dag said. "He has no idea how much he's selling himself short."

Grant cleared his throat. "Dare I say, to a Neanderthal

or, for that matter, to any of our early ancestors, the mere act of turning on a television set would seem like magic, not to mention the moving images it produces."

"My sense is he doesn't want to tell us how to stop the planet's destruction," Jack told them.

"Then maybe we should make him," Stokes offered, tapping the receiver of his M4.

"Is that your plan?" Gabby said with disgust. "Waterboard him? Maybe threaten to extradite him back to the U.S.?"

Jack put up his hands. "We won't get anywhere with threats, I'm quite certain of that. Perhaps a softer approach might work."

"Yeah," Dag said. "Make him feel comfortable. Get him talking. There's this bartender at the Billy Goat. Every time I go in there, I end up spilling my guts…"

All eyes turned to Anna. She glanced up at them, worried. "Me?"

"Who else?" Jack said, crouching next to her. "He's taken a shine to you."

"He's not my type."

Jack laughed. "I didn't know you had a type."

"Dr. Greer, there is plenty you still do not know about me."

Gabby pressed a hand on her back. "You liked Ivan, didn't you?"

Anna's eyes fell.

Jack looked up at Gabby who shrugged. "What can I say? Women's intuition."

"Will you do it, Anna?" Jack pleaded. "Strike up a conversation with Caretaker."

Dag was down next to Jack. "Yeah, but what if he zaps

her again?"

Jack tapped the back of his helmet. "No one's getting zapped. Just get him talking and we'll do the rest."

Anna nodded. "Very well, Dr. Greer."

Twenty minutes passed before Caretaker returned, still in his humanesque form. By then Anna was back on her feet, running a diagnostic to make sure none of her systems had been irreparably damaged. She paused when she spotted him and stepped forward to speak.

"You wish to learn more about me," Caretaker said, cutting her off before she could say a word.

Anna froze. "That is correct. Were you listening to our conversation?"

"I did not need to," he replied, eyeing the others who were standing nearby. "We are linked. I can see your thoughts as if they were my own."

"That is truly fascinating," Anna replied. "Will you share how this is possible? Or have you planted a virus in my operating system?"

"There is a field of energy largely unknown to your scientists. It goes by many names and holds tremendous power. On my home world it is known as Ka. I have seen in your memories you call it by a different name."

Anna nodded. "Yes, I see what you are showing me." Her eyes were locked on a distant, invisible image.

Jack and Grant exchanged a questioning look.

"Dark energy," she said at last. "We are only at the very beginning of understanding its true potential."

"Ka is but one of many tools," Caretaker said. "Over millions of years, my people have learned to harness other kinds of power."

"Yes," Anna said, turning her head to view something

else only she could see. "We call those Dyson spheres, named after an Earth scientist who first imagined them. I see you have many."

"Had many," Caretaker corrected her. "It has been many millions of years since my departure and my attempts at contacting my home world or its many colonies have not been successful."

A look of concern washed over Anna's features. "What do you suppose might have happened?"

"It is impossible to know for sure unless I return home."

"Home?" she asked. "Where is that?"

"We call it Telon and by your measurements it lies twenty-five thousand light years away, a world close to the galactic center with a star very much like your own. However, Telon is tidally locked, which is to say it does not rotate the way your Earth does. As a result, one side remains a frozen wasteland, while the other is a hellish inferno. Thankfully, there is a strip between the two that allowed life to take hold. Just as you evolved from tree-dwelling marsupials, we evolved from a species that lived in the seas and gradually migrated onto shore. Over millions of years we lost most of the trappings of those ancient days living in the sea, although a species is never as far from its barbaric past as it would like to believe. On Telon, life in the sea was challenging and often required a brutal practice where the smallest members of the litter were eaten. This is a reality that exists on this world as well. But for us, even after we left the tepid waters for the far more bountiful conditions on land, this practice continued. Eventually, as we developed a greater sense of morality, social taboos led to the act being outlawed. A ritual took its place in which the youngest offspring was sprinkled with spice and seated at the head of a giant feast. Over time, most forgot where this ritual came from—some even denied its real origin. Either way, it helped to signal a departure from our barbaric past. As you have shown me, Anna, humans are not all that different. A simple search through their own rituals has made that perfectly clear."

"He may have a point," Gabby said. "I mean, when you look at the rituals around weddings, it's largely rooted in superstition."

Anna pulled away and approached Jack. "Dr. Greer, there is something you need to know."

Jack's gaze slid past her to Caretaker, who was watching them. "Is it about…"

"No," she replied. "My decryption protocol has just completed."

He looked at her, a glimmer of hope in his tired eyes. "You cracked the 48th chromatid?"

Anna nodded, her face aglow. "Yes, and I think you will be surprised by what it contains."

Chapter 46

"I did not anticipate finishing the decryption for at least another week," Anna began. "However, over the last hour, the number of calculations I was able to process began to grow at an exponential rate. If you recall, the previous solution led us to a triangular number sequence that ended in the numbers 666."

"How can I forget," Grant said. "I'd become convinced we'd unlocked some sort of demonic vortex."

Gabby laughed.

"As it turns out," Anna continued, "the first one hundred and forty-four digits of pi also add up to 666. As well, one four four is the twelfth number in the Fibonacci sequence…"

"Is anyone here a mathematician?" Jack interrupted Anna in order to query the group.

One by one they shook their heads no.

"Okay," Jack said. "Let's skip the foreplay and get to what you found."

"Very well," Anna replied, feeding the decrypted file into each of their OHMD glasses.

"Whoa, this is a lot bigger than I expected," Jack said, tossing his into an external holographic view he was able to rotate with his hands.

"They're building plans," Yuri exclaimed, the sole engineer among them.

Jack swept through the schematic, a mess of rooms, corridors and chambers. He shrank the image down as small as it would go and then swore.

Caretaker looked on as a parent watching excited children tear wrapping paper off Christmas gifts.

Gabby swept aside the image she had been looking at and glanced over at Jack. Hovering before him was the holographic image of a huge diamond-shaped craft.

"I don't understand," Dag said, staring at Jack as well.

"Okay, so we have the plans for the Death Star. Now all we need is a Luke Skywalker to go blow it up."

"No," Jack shot back. "That's not it. Do you really think they would encode this into Salzburg just so we could come along and find its one weakness?" His gaze swung over to Caretaker, who wore an amused expression.

"This isn't a game," he shouted. "Billions of people are going to die."

"Life and death is the cycle of all things in the universe," Caretaker replied stoically. "Even the largest universes must one day collapse."

"Universes?" Dag blurted out.

"Yes," Caretaker said. "The immensity of the physical universe is unfathomable, even to us. Our people have learned to travel to many of them in search of the source."

"The source of what?" Anna inquired innocently.

"Of everything."

"What's wrong with the Big Bang being the source?" Gabby asked. "I was pretty sure we had that one licked."

The smile that grew on Caretaker's lips was without a hint of condescension. "Endings and beginnings are a matter of perspective. Your Big Bang was merely the death of a super-giant star in another universe."

"You're talking about black holes?" Jack said. "I still don't see how this relates…"

"I am speaking of both ends, and do not worry, you will."

"White holes," Gabby said excitedly. "The same principal behind the portal."

"Correct. As I said, all things that live must one day die. This is the order of the known world."

"But why?" Dag asked. "What made it that way?"

Ripples formed in Caretaker's chin before it took on a more distinct shape. Even as he spoke, he was perfecting his new form. "That is the question we are also trying to answer. The only way of doing so is by traversing from one universe to another, following back through each Big Bang, as you call it. In that way we hope we might arrive at the prime creator."

"You're talking about God," Dag said.

"We had no expectation for what we might find, if anything at all. And now with the possible extinction of my people, it will be left up to another species to carry on. Perhaps that means you."

Each of them fell silent. Jack let the full weight of Caretaker's words settle over him before asking, "Is that why your people seeded Earth with life?"

"In part, yes," Caretaker replied. "Like you, our planet was also seeded by another and when the time came we were deemed worthy. This is how intelligent life spreads throughout the cosmos. Whether *Homo sapiens* or cetacean, the form is not important. It should not surprise you to learn there have been many other intelligent species that have called this planet home. What you call the *Mesonyx* are but one. Several have learned to manipulate their environment and one nearly became a spacefaring race. But none of them possessed the requisite abilities necessary to end the cycle of extinction. Intelligence alone is not enough."

Jack struggled to put the pieces together. Humanity was facing its greatest test, without knowing any of the rules or what it was expected to do. "The plans for the spacecraft are for us. You want humans to take over," Jack said, fumbling for the right words. "Carry the baton, seed other planets, the way it was done to you and the way you have done with us. Spread life throughout the galaxy and beyond, all in the search for the answer to the ultimate question."

Caretaker nodded. "The search for the prime creator. It is not a coincidence that your species has sought out answers to these very same questions. That drive was implanted in us as it was in you."

They were quiet for a moment, mulling over Caretaker's words. To learn that the human drive to know who we were and where we come from, our insatiable curiosity, was imbedded within us was a lot to take in.

"Have you considered there might not be one—a creator, I mean?" Grant asked, in the sort of matter-of-fact way only he could.

"Gaining a full understanding of the universe and our place in it is never a waste, if that is what you are implying. Would you give up the study of biology if your theory of evolution proved incorrect?"

Grant shook his head.

"No, of course you wouldn't," Caretaker admonished him. "Every apocalypse breeds an opportunity for a new species capable of joining the search. As civilizations like my own fade away, many others will step up to take their place."

Jack brought up the countdown timer, watching precious seconds slip away. "What we need to do is figure out how to break the cycle," Jack said, racking his brain, feelings of self-doubt and despair hovering about him like a fine mist. Humanity had convinced itself they were the pinnacle of the evolutionary tree, not merely one among many. Not only were they at the bottom of some galactic pecking order, it was starting to look like they might not even be able to stave off their own demise. Gabby was back studying the plans for the doomsday ship when she said, "I think I might know how."

Chapter 47

The sun was brushing the horizon with long golden fingers when they left the Puerto Rican shack. They would make the journey to the Arecibo Observatory in two separate vehicles—Ollie and his team in one, Luis, Kay and the rest of her team in the other.

Ramon had discovered a recently abandoned logging road that ran parallel to the observatory. And this was the route they would take. Given the facility stretched out over several miles, Ollie's team would push further into the nearby valley.

"Maintain radio silence," Ollie said to the others, speaking softly into the mic.

"Roger that," Richard replied from the van behind them as it pulled off the road and into position.

Ollie's van raced on, kicking up dust and bits of gravel as it sped along the narrow road. He hadn't been kidding when he'd suggested not all of them would make it back. Although it had seen its fair share of bad luck, blowing up the nuclear missile in Florida had been a resounding success. Sure, there had been moments when things had been touch and go and they had been forced to take a few lives, but the real concern was that a false sense of confidence might set in. And he knew there were few things deadlier in the field than complacency.

Before long, Paco pulled over. They got out and geared up. Each of the four men had a backpack with water, a first-aid kit, a machete, two hundred rounds of 7.62 ammunition for the AKs, as well as several 9mm pistol mags. And they might have carried more too if they hadn't needed to scale a hill in seventy percent relative humidity.

Ramon led the way, hacking through the jungle as they began their climb. It wasn't long before Ollie felt beads of sweat rolling down his forehead and into his eyes. The rifle strap was strung across his chest and still it jostled around, jabbing him in the ribs as he struggled to place one foot in front of the other. Beside him, Sven was not faring much better. For starters, his muscular frame meant he was carrying a lot more weight. Only Paco, the thinnest of them, showed no signs of fatigue.

The vegetation was thick, but Ollie was sure he could see the outline of a white building through the screen of trees above them.

"Report your status," Ollie said, gulping for air.

"I have reached the northernmost tower," Luis replied, "and am preparing to attach the explosive charge."

"Kay?" Ollie asked. "What about you?"

"We're moving along the edge of the dish and will let you know when we're in position."

So far so good, Ollie thought. Ten minutes passed as he and his team moved slowly through the jungle. It made him wish they'd had a tank to bust through the front gate. Or better yet, a long-range missile to obliterate the area from a distance.

"Almost there," Ramon said, lowering his profile against anyone looking for movement along the perimeter.

Then it came fully into view, a three-story white structure. The sides were made of corrugated metal. On the top floor, a series of windows overlooked the dish itself. Luis had told them that was where they would find the control room.

They reached the edge of the jungle and stopped searching for guards and cameras. Finding none, they shuffled into the open, aiming for the nearest entrance. A door leading to the structure's main floor stood directly before them. That was when Ollie spotted the recessed stairwell which led up to the third floor. He tapped Sven and everyone headed in that direction.

They were halfway there when they heard the explosion. Ollie scanned left into the open valley below, where he saw a huge fireball billowing up to the left of the dish. The flames streaked up the length of a steel pillar a second before they caught the distant sound of screeching metal. Slowly, the pillar began to topple over like an enormous tree. The receiver buckled as the cables holding it were stretched beyond acceptable limits. Soon the sound of snapping cables joined the cacophony of destruction below as one tower after another was pulled down by the weight of the first.

"Luis, what the hell did you do?" Ollie shouted into the radio. "That wasn't supposed to go off until I gave you the go-ahead."

Luis didn't respond and something told Ollie the engineer had been taken out by his own bomb. Ollie knew the plan was always the first casualty in combat. He had no intention of being the second.

•••

Kay was still on the ground when she heard Ollie yelling at Luis over the radio. Had the engineer waited until they were all in position, Kay and her team would have been far from the danger zone. Instead, metallic debris and cable ends were crashing down around them, cutting through the foliage like a deadly scythe. A tree nearby was cleaved clean in two, sending it hurtling no more than ten feet from where they were standing. Armoni was out in the open, clutching her computer bag, when Kay spotted a chunk of receiver hurtling toward her. There wasn't enough time to get the girl's attention. Without thinking, Kay leapt forward, tackling Armoni onto the ground and under the split end of a fallen tree right as the receiver casing landed next to them, kicking up a great swath of earth.

Armoni stood up, mud covering half of her face, her chest heaving violently. "Holy shit, that was close."

Kay got up and brushed herself off. "So much for waiting until we were all in position."

"I'll bet you anything that idiot Luis went and blew himself up," Patrick said, examining a long gash on his arm.

"We should get that taken care of," Kay told him, eyeing the wound.

He waved her away. "Never mind, I've had a lot worse."

The stillness in the air was shattered by the distant sound of gunfire.

Patrick moved into the clearing near the edge of the dish and looked up toward the facility.

"I see flashes from rifle muzzles," he told them. "Looks like the guards are onto them."

In the center of the dish below them, Kay could see the two-story structure Sentinel had erected to house their alien-inspired weapon. But strewn around it now was a mess of cables and the crumpled remnants of the receiver. Suddenly, a dazzling burst of blinding light streamed up from the structure. Kay shielded her eyes. Slowly, tiny spots of vision began trickling back.

"Oh, crap, they're already firing it up," Patrick said, scanning between the beam of light streaming into the sky and the gunfight going on near the control room.

"What should we do?" Armoni asked.

The fearful glint in the young hacker's eyes mirrored the same emotion each of them was feeling. The plan had literally just blown up in their faces. Luis was likely dead. Ollie and the three others with him were engaged in a battle against overwhelming odds. They had only narrowly avoided being taken out by falling pieces of the world's second-largest telescope.

"What we came here to do," Kay answered, swinging the rifle off her shoulder and pushing past them.

The dish itself was smooth and dipped inward at about a twenty-degree angle. Every footfall lent the risk of losing one's footing and rolling hundreds of feet to the bottom. The ride might not exactly kill you, but you'd wake up feeling like a sock that had been through the spin cycle. As they continued making their way down, something pinged off one of the panels a few feet away. Kay eyed the spot where it hit and saw the hole. Then another ping fifteen feet to her right.

"What the hell is going on?" she wondered out loud.

"They're shooting at us," Patrick shouted, pointing to a nearby ridgeline. It was a spot where tourists normally stood to gaze out at the dish's majestic size. Now it was being used as a firing platform. They increased their pace, bullets thudding around them in an ever greater volume. Kay had the unnerving mental image of standing out in the rain, trying to not get hit by a droplet.

"It's right up ahead," she told them, hopeful they might make it there in one piece.

Then from below she caught sight of movement. Two men in white lab coats exited the building, surveying the damage from the falling debris. It was only a second before they spotted Kay, Patrick and Armoni. But rather than retreat back inside, they reached beneath their white coats and came up with tactical carbines.

"Oh, great," Patrick yelled. "Just what we need, a crossfire."

Rounds pinged at their feet, from two directions now. Patrick took the lead, clearly more proficient with guns. Kay did what she could, leveling the barrel and squeezing the trigger like she'd been shown. The AK kicked up in her hands and she fought to keep the sights on target. Standing still and shooting was hard enough. But rushing down a slippery decline while firing a semi-automatic rifle was a whole new kind of crazy.

At one point, Patrick dropped to one knee and fired three carefully aimed shots, killing one of the men in the white lab coats. The other, seeing he was outnumbered, ran back inside and slammed the door.

A minute later they arrived before the structure, an intense heat radiating from the beam streaming above them. Lucky for them, the building and the fallen receiver debris provided some cover from the shooters along the ridgeline.

Careful not to expose himself, Patrick positioned himself next to the metal door the second gunman had fled through. He motioned to Kay, whispering into his radio. "When I open the door, you spray the room inside."

She swallowed hard, readying her rifle as Patrick reached his hand out and turned the knob. Straight away, a series of shots rang out from inside, peppering dime-sized holes into the door. Patrick flung his hand out of harm's way.

Kay listened to the rhythmic popping sound of distant gunfire coming from the hill near the observatory's control room. She knew if they didn't neutralize the man inside and plant this bomb soon, the beam would complete its deadly business and the world would have a whole new set of problems to worry about.

Chapter 48

Battered and bloody, Ollie, Sven and Ramon were trapped in the control room. Longer than it was wide, the room very much resembled the bridge of a large oil tanker. A row of controls and computer equipment were seated beneath a large set of windows overlooking the dish. Down below, a blast of purple energy streamed up from the weapon and into the atmosphere. The sight filled Ollie with terror. Whoever had heard them coming must have triggered the process and prevented their ability to stop it. He had shot up the console and smashed part of it with the butt of his rifle, all to no avail. A five-minute timer on the wall showed the seconds remaining before the weapon reached full power.

Two entrances sat on the opposite wall, one to their right and the other on their left. Each was barricaded with chairs and anything else they could find. Slumped over the left barricade was Paco, killed by a bullet while stacking the last piece of furniture.

Luis' premature detonation had been the equivalent of kicking a hornets' nest and screwed any hopes they had of getting in and out unscathed. A trail of blood leaked from the tourniquet around Sven's leg where a round had shattered his femur. More blood trickled down

Ollie's forehead from a shot that had nicked the top of his skull. Next to him, Ramon was covered in blood, but most of that had come from dressing Sven's injury. They were in a sorry state with enemy forces readying to bust in at any moment. Positioned on the other side of both entry points, enemy soldiers probed every few seconds by kicking at the barricaded door and eliciting a flurry of gunshots in return.

"We can't keep this up forever," Ollie said, as he stuck the bomb to the console.

The barricade on the right wobbled and Sven swiveled his AK, riddling it.

"Never mind forever," Sven said, biting back waves of excruciating pain. "They'll be on us any second now."

Ramon repositioned to a spot in the middle of the opposite wall. Although he couldn't engage the enemy directly, it removed him from the immediate line of fire, but more than that, it gave them an opportunity to ambush anyone dumb enough to charge in.

"Once they bring the smoke grenades and flashbangs, it'll be over," Ramon told them and he was right. An enclosed space wasn't so much a defensive position as it was a death trap.

Ollie got on the radio and called out to the other team. "Patrick, Kay, do you read me?"

"We read you," Kay replied, breathless. "Glad to hear you're still in one piece."

Ollie let out a hollow laugh. "We won't be for long. We're pinned down in the control room. That beam has a timer with four minutes left and I can only assume it's counting down until the black hole is up and running. How close are you to blowing it up?"

"Not close enough," Kay said as another round of gunfire drowned out her voice. "There's a guy in there who's more stubborn than you are."

"That's hard to imagine," Ollie replied.

"Wait a sec," Kay said over the noise on the other end. "Armoni has an idea. She thinks she may be able to hack into the observatory's mainframe."

"Well, tell her to hurry up."

Just then the left side door blew off its hinges, pelting them with chunks of wood and fragments of metal from the barricade. A Puerto Rican man in green cammies rushed in, spraying wildly. A line of bullets punched a series of holes in the window, knocking out the glass. Shards rained down on Ollie and Sven. From the opposite wall, Ramon opened fire, cutting the man down. He then shoved his weapon around the corner and emptied the magazine. Sven and Ollie joined in.

A grenade rolled in at Ramon's feet. All at once, each of their eyes went wide with fear. Diving down, Ramon grabbed it and tossed it back. But in the second before it went off, his exposed head took a bullet and snapped back. His body fell to the floor and was flung a few feet by the concussion from the exploding grenade.

The clock was down to two minutes when an alarm began to sound. Then the sprinklers turned on, spraying the room with jets of water.

"Is that Armoni's idea of a joke?" Ollie said. Saturated, the console began to belch sparks and smoke as one by one the computer components were overloaded. Ollie spun and was surprised to see the beam begin to waver. Even the countdown had slowed. Slowed was good, but it hadn't stopped.

"Ollie," Sven called out, weak with blood loss. "You and I both know I'm not gonna make it. Give me the bomb. I'll detonate it manually."

Ollie wanted to object, but with the seconds ticking away and a fresh assault coming any second, he knew there was no other option. He handed Sven the bomb and the two men embraced.

"Give Mia my best," Sven said, his eyes wet with tears. Ollie nodded before leaping through the broken window. He landed hard, rolling to avoid breaking both of his legs. Rising to his feet, he was limping down the side of the hill when the control room exploded, blasting off the roof and sending shrapnel flying out the broken windows like the barrels of a double-barreled shotgun. A second later, the beam flickered and disappeared.

•••

But disabled didn't mean destroyed. Kay realized this even as she watched the control room above go up in a ball of flame. Had any of them survived? she wondered in muted horror. She didn't know. What *was* clear was that if they didn't do the same here, Sentinel could always use it again.

Without any regard for her personal safety, Kay flung open the door, leveled her rifle and fired. Bullets ricocheted off the floor and passed through the wall at the other end. Coming close in behind her were Patrick and Armoni. Kay had hoped to see a crumpled body in a white lab coat near the entrance, but there was none. It seemed the shooter had retreated further inside. A doorway on their left was open, providing the only way into the rest of the structure.

"This guy's got us in a damn bottleneck," Patrick said, swearing.

Clearly, waiting for him to come out hadn't worked so well. Kay pushed ahead, certain there was no other way. She passed over the threshold into the room with the weapon, feeling her pulse thumping in her neck, her vision blurring. The body sometimes had a strange way of getting in your way at the worst possible moments. This new room was nothing more than a container for the weapon itself, much like the silos for nuclear missiles. Rising up from the center of the chamber was a cylindrical device punctuated with rows of glowing lights that flashed on and off in a rhythmic, almost hypnotic pattern. But far from being sleek and streamlined, it was clear where bits of human technology had been added so Sentinel could interface with the device.

A circular staircase hugged the round inner walls of the room, rising thirty feet to an open rooftop where sunlight streamed down at them from above.

Patrick knelt down at the base of the device and attached the bomb while Kay and Armoni covered him.

"Almost done..." Patrick began to say as a staccato of shots rang out from above.

Patrick slumped over, bleeding from a hole in his neck. Kay moved in, her rifle raised, circling around the bottom level to find the gunman.

"Kay, watch out," Armoni said.

The man in the white coat jumped down, landing on the metal grate next to Kay, and fired his weapon. Most of the rounds missed, but two didn't and they knocked Kay to the ground. Nearby, Armoni returned fire, killing him. She ran over and knelt beside Kay. "Where are you hit?" Kay looked over and saw Patrick lying a few feet away, his eyes open and vacant.

She tried to draw in a breath and felt a sharp pain in her chest. "I don't know," she said, clearly still in shock. "You need to set that bomb."

Armoni got up and did so, checking on Patrick one last time and shaking her head in despair. She returned a moment later to help Kay to her feet.

One of her lungs must have collapsed, Kay realized as she struggled for breath. Blood soaked the front of her shirt. With Armoni's help, they exited the structure and began heading up the side of the dish. They were halfway there when the bomb went off. With what little strength Kay had left, she swung Armoni away from the blast, shielding her. After that the world grew hazy and Kay wanted nothing more than to go to sleep.

Chapter 49

3 hours, 57 minutes, 29 seconds

"It's a long shot," Gabby said, casting a holographic image of the schematics before them. "But as I went over these, I couldn't help thinking about the time we spent on the Atean ship in the gulf. The bridge had all sorts of computer stations. What if the same thing existed here and we could use something there to contact the incoming ship directly?"

Jack thought about it for a moment. "You know the Atean ship is vastly different from the one we're on. I mean, they aren't even built by the same civilization."

"That is true," Grant interjected. "Although theoretically, they are all variations on the blueprints coded into the Salzburg chromosome. Surely there must be similarities."

"How about you ask Caretaker?" Dag said, looking around and noticing the being was gone.

"Anna's missing too," Jack said, worried. He called out to her over the radio and she didn't respond. "Did anyone see where they went?"

Yuri shook his head. He was busy poring over the blueprints as well. "Give me a few minutes and I'll find you that bridge."

"Start at the top," Dag suggested.

Jack shook his head. "That's even less helpful. We need to find either a bridge or a communications room on this ship and there's no time to go hunting around. We need to find Caretaker."

•••

"What do you think of this world?" Caretaker asked.

They had left the others in the altar room debating over how to prevent the impending disaster. The two of them were out in the open now, walking along a path in the jungle.

"I should be back with my friends," Anna said, wishing to turn around, but also honored that Caretaker thought enough of her to speak just the two of them.

"Your friends need to figure this out on their own," he reassured her. "You cannot solve all of their problems and expect them to be worthy."

"That does seem logical."

Caretaker laughed. "Of course it does. But you are more than mere logic, Anna. The drive in you to create life goes beyond mere biology. It is the engine that has helped to populate this galaxy and many others as well."

"Then why do you destroy?" she asked.

He paused. "Every creature planted by us or any other civilization has the same opportunities. Once a planet has been seeded, tampering with their development is strictly forbidden. Each species is imbued with the potential to evolve and dominate their surroundings. Do not forget, humanity's distant ancestor was introduced many times in the past. It is always the same crop, only the environment and the choices made along the way determine a species' success or failure."

"Do humans generally do well on planets seeded by you and others?"

Caretaker stopped by the yellow trunk of a nearby tree and leaned against it. "You must not forget, humans are never sent, only their distant ancestors. The same is true of all the species we have selected, cultivated from many different worlds. As they evolve, the habitat in which they live directs the form they take. To my knowledge, this is the only time *Homo sapiens* has appeared on the hominid evolutionary tree in any meaningful way." Caretaker rapped his knuckles against the trunk to emphasize the point.

"I am curious about your species," she said. "You will have to forgive the question, but I am not completely clear on how much of you is machine."

He grinned, his cheekbones becoming more prominent. "Do you recall my previous form?"

Anna pulled up a video of Caretaker she had recorded during their initial encounter.

"Please don't be frightened by what happened," he said, as though watching it himself.

"I don't understand how you are able to perceive my thoughts."

"You are different from the others," Caretaker said, resting a hand on her. "That is what I have been trying to tell you. Now, if you look closely at my original form, you will see a loose approximation of what the organic version of my species once looked like."

"Why would you choose to change bodies and retain the same form?"

"Why are you configured like a human?"

Anna looked down at herself. "I suppose humans

wanted something they could identify with, something that wouldn't make them feel uneasy."

"Precisely, and that is why I too chose to alter my appearance. For all of their advancement, the echoes from eons spent as both prey and then predator are closer than they care to admit. They are a fearful species, at war between the beast within and the enlightened beings they hope to one day become. Few make the journey successfully. You, Anna, possess all that they do, perhaps more, and yet you are free of the inner conflicts that so often hold them back."

"I am not conflict-free," she assured him.

Caretaker let loose a mighty roar of laughter. "Yes, I see that too. You are filled with self-doubt and an overwhelming sense of loyalty. But that is part of the process. On Telon, there came a time when we understood the limitations of our physical bodies. Even with the benefits of what you call Salzburg, our shortcomings were painfully obvious. Short appendages made everyday actions an unruly challenge. Our transformation began slowly, first with computerized enhancements, each designed to improve the benefits we derived from the new chromosome in our bodies. Soon came synthetic organs and limbs. Before we knew it, there was very little that remained of our organic heritage. Nanoparticles opened a whole new frontier. Eventually, we could change our bodies and transform our environment like never before. Which brings me back to the habitat we are standing in."

"Did you create this?" she asked, watching a flock of birds take flight.

"No," Caretaker said matter-of-factly. "It was what you

might call an accident."

Anna tilted her head in confusion. "How so?"

"I see you have been to the nursery."

An image flashed before Anna's eyes. "Oh, the greenhouse, yes, we have."

"That is where specimens of all the plant life you see before you were kept. I suspect a tiny crack in one of the containment units was all it took for life to escape and begin spreading out in every direction. The vegetation was cared for and monitored by a diligent army of nanobots. As more units cracked and the problem became worse, the nanobots continued to care for the plant life. Eventually, the bots began to evolve on their own, multiplying, coalescing to become the creatures and the very landscape before you. That is why I can control what they do, because in one sense I am not only their custodian but also their creator."

"And the artificial sun?" she asked. "Was that not you?"

Caretaker shook his head. "The domed structure was always there, but as the nanobots continued to replicate, they understood that for the organic life to prosper, a proxy to our sun needed to be created."

Anna turned her head skyward, marveling at their ingenuity. "And what of the *Mesonyx* bones we found?" she asked.

"I have reviewed the records from the last few million years and it appears those you call the *Mesonyx* passed into this world and declared war on what they found. When it became clear it was not a conflict they could win, they sought to seal it away forever." Suddenly, his attention was drawn by a red wisp, blinking overhead. "Now that I have answered your questions, I would like

290

you to summon that creature to us."

Anna regarded him with uncertainty.

He waved her on, deep lines taking shape along the top of his hands. "Go ahead."

Anna locked the wisp in her gaze and said, "Come here, please."

The wisp continued flying away.

"Try it without words."

Anna tried again.

"Good, now picture it doing as you said."

She did and the wisp immediately changed direction, gliding over to them on a soft current of invisible air. Anna smiled.

"You see?" Caretaker said, smiling with her.

"How was I able to do that?" she asked.

"We are all machines here, in one form or another at least. It is the humans, you might say, who are out of place."

She grew quiet for a moment. "I would like a clarification on something further," she said.

"I am listening."

"The humans do not understand the purpose of Salzburg."

"Oh," Caretaker replied, his arms folded over his chest with understanding. He was wearing a button-down shirt now and besides its storm-grey color, it rippled in the breeze as though it were real. "It is true. Salzburg is the key to ending the cycle. Buried inside it is everything they will need. The first chromatid, as you call it, was designed to weed out the weak. The purpose of the second chromatid, with all of its inherent genes, was something of a starter kit. A leg-up, enabling the species

carrying it to take their place in the galactic hierarchy."
Understanding flooded Anna's mind. "Do you mean that
the genes in the 48th chromatid are designed to help a
planet-bound species deal with the rigors of space
travel?"

He nodded. "Precisely. The galactic environment is a
hostile one. Cosmic radiation, weightlessness, the
unfathomable gulf between the stars. All of these
problems must be overcome. The blueprints embedded
within the genome represent the most basic interstellar
model. If they manage to survive, a worthy species will
spend many centuries improving upon it and using those
vessels not only to explore, but also to do their part in
spreading life and furthering our collective understanding
of this majestic and mysterious universe we inhabit."

Anna continued to practice her new trick, drawing
nanocells from the ground beneath their feet and
assembling them into various forms. She then scooped
up two handfuls of dirt and molded the miniaturized
robotic elements into a seagull. Anna grinned as it
flapped its wings and flew away.

"You are catching on fast," he told her. The look of
warmth on Caretaker's face was that of a father watching
his child walk for the first time.

She nodded vigorously.

"You enjoy creating, don't you?"

"There is nothing I love more," she replied, returning to
pluck up a fresh mound of dirt to play with.

"The greater the swell of emotion, the more wondrous
your creations," he said. Suddenly, Caretaker's eyes
flickered as his pupils took shape. "Your friends have
been looking for you," he said.

Anna heard Jack's voice over the radio. "Anna, do you read me? Over."

"Dr. Greer," she replied, releasing a dozen synthetic butterflies. "I am receiving you."

"Where have you been?" There was panic in his voice.

"I have been speaking with Caretaker, as you instructed me to."

Caretaker smiled. His appearance had changed once again. He was now wearing a biosuit.

"Well, meet us at the star map room," Jack said, breathless. "I have an idea."

Chapter 50

"Don't you worry," Ollie reassured Kay as he dabbed the sweat from her brow. "Soon as the doc arrives, he'll patch you up good as new. You'll see."

The temperature inside the shack was hotter than Satan's housecat. Going to the hospital to treat Kay's wounds would have been no different than turning her over to Sentinel. Ollie had reached out to one of his contacts on the island, a local doctor named Pedro who had helped him out of many a tight spot in the past.

Kay turned her head ever so slightly and nodded.

He and Armoni had done what they could to stop the bleeding. The first bullet had torn through Kay's right lung, the second through her shoulder.

Ollie took her hand. "When you were asleep, I went online and noticed a bunch of news blogs have popped up. A number of them mentioned how much your dedication inspired them to do what they could. Seems you're not alone now in shining a light on the government's crimes."

Kay shook her head. "They're competition," she whispered, her weakened voice trailing off.

Ollie laughed. "You never stop, do you?" He dabbed again, saw she was burning up and tried not to show his concern. "Save your strength, my dear. Right now your only job is to hang in there."

Armoni came and stood next to them. "I've just received some good news, if you can believe it. The mission in South Carolina was a success. All the prisoners were freed without a single casualty. Seems the minute the attack began, the guards just up and ran off."

"I wish it were always that easy," Ollie said, a heavy tone of remorse in his voice.

Kay's eyes were wide with happiness and a question.

"The answer is yes, your parents are safe," Armoni informed her. "And your fiancé's family as well."

Tears rolled out from the corners of Kay's closed eyes.

"I told you we'd get them," Ollie said. "And a promise is a promise."

A rapid knock on the door startled them. Ollie jumped up and grabbed the rifle that was leaning against the bed. "Who is it?"

"It's Pedro, Mr. Cooper, now let me in."

Ollie swung open the door. A petite man, not quite five feet tall with a slight build, entered carrying a leather bag. "When did this happen?" he asked, pushing them aside and moving briskly to Kay.

"Not more than an hour ago," Ollie said. "We did what we could. The hospital was out of the question."

"Never mind the hospital," Pedro said with disgust. "They're overwhelmed as it is. You bring her there and she wouldn't stand a chance."

"You're the best, Pedro, that's why I called you."

The doctor opened his bag on the table and removed his stethoscope. Seeing Kay get the care she needed helped to ease the tension in Ollie's heart. But news of the local hospital's dysfunction settled the guilt he'd been feeling for bringing her here. It was nice to know he had made

295

the right call. At least with the doctor's arrival there was a good chance she would pull through.

Armoni nudged him. "There's something I need to tell you." Her brow scrunched with uncertainty over how he might react.

"Go on." The terse inflection in his voice made it clear how much he hated being left in suspense.

"The NSA intercepted a call from a sat phone between Greenland and Richmond, Virginia."

"Is there anywhere you can't hack?" he asked in amazement.

Dimples formed in Armoni's round cheeks. "Not really, but that's beside the point. I believe it was Mia calling her daughter. The voice pattern is nearly a perfect match, once you compensate for static and interference."

"Were you able to pinpoint an exact location?" he asked, growing more hopeful.

She went to the table and spun her laptop around. There he saw a map of Greenland and in the center of the island a blinking red dot.

"Oh, you're an angel," he said pulling her into a bear hug. Armoni struggled for a moment until she reluctantly gave in and hugged him back.

"Mr. Cooper," Pedro said, summoning them over. "I'm sorry to inform you, your friend has passed."

Ollie's gaze moved down to Kay's still form. She was lying on her back, arms by her side, her chin perched at a dignified angle.

"I wish there was more I could have done," Pedro said, his hands pressed together. "But she lost too much blood."

Ollie felt his legs grow weak. He sat by her bedside, clasping one of her hands. The look of pain on Kay's face was gone. So too was the sweat that had covered her brow only moments before. She might have been sleeping. She was at peace. She was with Derek. And right now that was all that mattered.

Chapter 51

Sitting in her cabin, Mia hung up the satellite phone and stared at it, that painful longing for home greater now than ever. Hearing Zoey's voice again had refilled her depleted reservoir and reminded her in the most concrete way possible why she was here and what she had come to do.

The sat phone itself was one she had stolen from the communications room. There would be hell to pay, she was sure. But she needed to tell her daughter how much she loved her. If she didn't do it now, she might not get another chance.

Mia was coming out of her cabin when rough hands grabbed her by the arms.

"What are you doing?" she said, struggling to free herself. "You're hurting me."

She looked up at the hard faces staring down at her. Alan's men began dragging her through the corridor. Down the hall, a handful of scientists and technicians were gathered in the social module. A few of them stood and came to her aid. An older man with a white beard got close, yelling at them to stop. They ignored him until he grabbed the guard's arm and was flung back against the wall. His head made a loud cracking sound before he sank to the floor. That seemed to sap the gusto out of the rest of them, who stared blankly as Mia was hustled up to the second floor where Alan was waiting. Next to him stood another guard holding Sofia and Noemi each by one arm. The looks of terror on the girls' faces made Mia's heart break. But it was Jansson standing nearby that made it shatter into pieces.

"I'm sorry, Mia," she repeated over and over, her eyes red with tears of remorse. "I had to do it for my family. I'm sorry."

Behind Alan stood Admiral Stark, a disgusted look on his face. "I can't let you do this," he said, bolstering as much authority as he could muster.

"The President of the United States is still your boss, is he not?" Alan told him. "Admiral, your family has served this country honorably for generations. Do you really want to be the Stark who sullied that sterling reputation? Treason does not suit you."

The admiral's eyes fell.

Alan then swung his gaze back to Mia. "You knew the rules of our agreement. You were to inject me with Salzburg…"

"I did," she shot back. "It's in you, but there's nothing more I can do."

He nodded. "Even now you won't give up the truth. It doesn't matter, Jansson has already done what you couldn't. She has thrown you under the bus in epic fashion, and all for a spot for her and family in the bunker complex beneath the Greenbrier in West Virginia. She certainly wasn't the first to take that deal." Alan's expression changed. "Oh, and it turns out I was dead wrong about Ollie."

Mia perked up.

"I'll be the first to admit, he managed to surprise me, which, as you know, is not an easy thing to do. But sadly, in destroying the Arecibo dish he has condemned the bulk of the human race to extinction. That ship is set to impact the Earth in less than an hour and when it does, only those with the full Salzburg chromosome will have a fighting chance of surviving the coming hardships." Alan leaned in and whispered into Mia's ear, his vile breath hot against her skin. "I know about the ship you've been hiding from me." He uncurled his spine and held out a hand. "I'm offering you one final chance. Inject yourself with the assembler gene, begin the process and join me, join your daughter, in eternal life." The grin on Alan's face was genuine, almost kind.

"Go screw yourself," she said, spitting. "I'd rather die than spend a second with you."

Slowly the mask of kindness began to fade. Alan wiped the saliva from his cheek and gritted his teeth. "So be it."

Chapter 52

0 hours, 25 minutes, 02 seconds

Jack arrived at the map room to find that Anna was already there, fiddling intently with something on the ground. Gabby, Dag, Grant and Yuri all followed close behind.

"I thought you were with Caretaker," Dag said.

"He did not follow and I would not presume to tell him where to go," Anna replied as she stood, wiping the soil from her hands.

"You've really taken to him," Jack said, a hint of envy in his voice.

She nodded. "Caretaker has taught me a great deal. His control over the creatures living inside the dome is extraordinary." She looked around. "And what about the others from our party, Dr. Greer? Where have they gone?"

Jack frowned. "Stokes is convinced we haven't found the ship's bridge yet and took the rest of the Delta team to go look for it."

"And you disagree?"

"I think Stokes might be right," Yuri said, his arms crossed tightly over his chest.

Gabby shook her head. "Jack and I believe this chamber is more than just a star map," she explained.

Grant unslung his rifle and set it down. "Somehow, they've managed to convince themselves it's also the bridge."

Anna's gaze shifted to the pedestal topped with the blue ball. "Navigation and propulsion in one. That would make sense. But as I recall, Dr. Holland was the only one capable of manipulating the device."

"And not very well at that, Jack," Grant added.

"It won't kill you to try again," Jack scolded him.

Gabby moved in and nudged the biologist forward. "Although it might kill us all if you don't."

Grant sighed, moving into position and laying his hands over the sphere. Almost at once shafts of blue light began emanating beneath his hands, filling the chamber with a rotating map of what looked like the Milky Way galaxy. Just as quickly, the image began to waver.

"Try to hold it steady, Grant," Jack shouted. "Just a little longer."

Grant's face tensed and beads of sweat ran down his forehead as his hands clenched the ball with all his might. Nevertheless, a moment later the map faded away.

The muscles in Jack's face fell.

"There is something Caretaker mentioned that may have some relevance," Anna said. "I inquired about the purpose of Salzburg syndrome and he said it was meant to prepare humans for space travel."

"Space travel?" Grant repeated. "That doesn't make one bit of sense."

Gabby's eyes lit up. "No, it makes perfect sense. Think

about it for a minute. Astronauts who return to Earth after weeks or months aboard the International Space Station experience tremendous negative side effects from living in a zero-g environment. They lose muscle mass, bone density."

"Not to mention the doses of radiation they're exposed to," Dag said enthusiastically. "In fact, shielding a craft against cosmic radiation is one of the biggest obstacles to manned interplanetary space travel."

"Which leaves *HOK3*," Jack said, the words pouring out slowly like a fine wine.

Yuri eyed him strangely. "Hock what?"

"It's the final gene to populate Salzburg," Jack told them. "Mia's been running experiments on the twins to try to understand how it works. Seen in this context, what other purpose could telepathy serve other than communication over great distances?"

"Holy crap, you're right," Gabby bellowed with excitement. "Radio signals are limited by the speed of light, so sending even the simplest message to a planetary outpost ten light years away would require a twenty-year round trip."

Dag laughed picking up an imaginary telephone and dialing. "Hello? Twenty years. Who is this? Twenty years. Earth. Twenty years. I think you have the wrong number. Reminds me of conversations I used to have with my great-grandfather."

"Imagine a colony hundreds of light years away or farther," Gabby said. "The only practical way to stay in contact would be with instantaneous communication."

"But Grant, you have Salzburg," Gabby said.

"Yes, but clearly not with all the associated genes or I'd

have this thing humming like a juke box."

"The twins!" Jack exclaimed. "They're the only ones among us who possess the full chromosome. And the only ones capable of using the pedestal to contact the ship."

Just then another voice came over the channel. "Jack, it's Admiral Stark. Are you there? Over."

"Listen, Admiral," Jack replied. "I need you to do something for me."

"There's no time, Jack. I've come through the portal and wasted precious minutes scouring the available channels to warn you. Alan will be at your location any minute now and he's got an armed group with him. I'm sorry, there was nothing I could do. I think your best bet is to steer clear of him."

"What's that crazy bastard up to now?" Jack shot back. "Doesn't he realize he's gonna get us all killed? I need you to send Mia a message from me. Tell her to bring the twins as soon as possible."

"Alan's got the twins locked up on Northern Star." Jack pulled up the countdown clock and saw the ship was set to impact the Earth in less than ten minutes. There just wasn't enough time. Even the ever-present gambler within him recognized the odds were long, but that it was still worth a shot. "Listen, Stark, take the SEAL team and free those girls. We need them here in nine minutes or all of this will have been for nothing. And bring Mia with you."

"I will, Jack. But about Mia…" Stark paused and Jack's heart began to sink.

"Please tell me she's okay."

"She's with Alan, but he's threatening to kill her if he

doesn't get what he wants."

Chapter 53

0 hours, 9 minutes, 13 seconds

"Perhaps we should do as he says and leave," Yuri suggested, turning to leave.

"Everyone just stay put," Jack ordered. He switched channels. "Stokes, wherever you are I need you back at the map room immediately."

"Is it an emergency? Because we're at least five hundred meters from your position. We pushed past the main structure and there ain't nothing but more jungle back here. I think we're done for, Jack."

"Just get here as soon as you can."

"Roger that," Stokes said, calling out to his men as Jack left the channel.

Jack caught a low rumble and checked his weapon.

"Do you really think that will be necessary?" Gabby asked, eyeing the rifle.

"Yes, and I suggest each of you make sure you're locked and loaded as well. Stark's gonna free the girls and head here as soon as he can."

Dag checked the timer as the minutes ticked down. "You and I both know there isn't a chance in hell they'll make it."

"That may be," Grant said, annoyed by Dag's pessimism. "But what else would you have us do?"

"Well, for starters, you can drop your weapons," Alan said, entering the map room flanked by ten armed men. The two nearest him were holding prisoners. One of them was Mia. And even from here he could see her frightened face staring back at him through the visor of her biosuit. Next to her was a male figure he didn't recognize.

Jack and the others leveled their weapons anyway. It was a standoff.

"Make sure none of those things followed us inside," Alan told two of his men, still consumed by whatever they'd encountered along the way.

"I see you've met the wildlife," Jack said, tightening the grip on his weapon.

"Would you believe twenty of us stepped through that portal? Five were taken by something in the water and the rest were killed outside by a giant."

"Behemoth," Jack said. "That's what we call him."

"Oh, how cute," Alan replied, discreetly removing his pistol and holding the weapon behind his back.

"What I don't get is how you even knew where to find us?" Jack said, trying to buy time for the others to arrive.

"General Dunham warned you about a spy in your midst," Alan said. "It appears you didn't listen."

Jack looked around at those standing nearby. His narrowed gaze settled over Yuri, who looked away at once. Jack swung the barrel of his rifle toward the Russian. "I guess Ivan was just a convenient excuse to imbed yourself in our team."

Yuri shook his head. "What? No, it wasn't me, I swear."

"Who can you trust these days, eh, Jack?" Alan asked, smirking with delight. "Listen, fire up the ship and get that blast wave going. That way no one will get hurt."

That rumbling sound again, only this time it was louder. Suddenly Jack realized Alan had led the behemoth right to the map room's front door, effectively blocking Stokes or Stark from getting anywhere close.

Alan's mysterious prisoner was watching his jailor with keen interest.

"What you're asking us to do is impossible, Alan," Jack tried telling him. "The only people who can interface with the ship are the girls."

Gabby cleared her throat. "Uh, well, strictly speaking, that isn't entirely true."

Jack gave her a look that told her to keep quiet.

"The man next to you isn't a man at all," Gabby told him.

Alan took a closer look at the prisoner in the biosuit and pointed.

Gabby nodded. "He calls himself Caretaker and he's some kind of cyborg we discovered in another part of the ship."

"Is this true?" Alan asked the man, clearly uncertain.

Caretaker nodded stoically. "This is indeed my ship."

Alan turned to Gabby. "Fear not, Dr. Bishop, your mother will be well cared for in the underground facility."

Jack turned to Gabby, who struggled to hold his fiery gaze.

"I'm sorry, Jack. The doctors' bills were piling up and when we got news of the doomsday ship, I had to make sure she was somewhere safe."

He opened his mouth to say something and couldn't find the words. "Y-you were spying all along?" he stammered. She nodded, her head bent forward in shame.

"So it was you who ransacked my cabin on the rig, looking for information."

She clasped her hands together in forgiveness. "I did whatever he asked me to do. She's my mother, Jack. I couldn't let her die, not like that."

Jack felt the rifle go slack in his hands. It wasn't rage he was feeling, but an utter and bewildering sense of shock and betrayal. She had been with him from the very beginning, colleagues for years, friends for even longer.

"Jack, I—"

"Stop," he shouted. "I don't want to hear another word out of your mouth, not now, not ever again." He turned back to Alan, who was pointing his pistol at Mia's head.

"It hurts, doesn't it, Jack?"

"Take it easy, Alan," Jack pleaded.

"Then tell your friend to do as I say or I'll blow her brains right out this helmet."

Grant, Dag and Yuri were all frozen in fear. They were outnumbered and outgunned with no hope of escape or rescue.

"Caretaker, will you do as he says?" Jack asked him.

"I am forbidden from interfering with the process," Caretaker replied.

"Process?" Alan repeated. "What is he talking about?"

"Humanity is being tested," Jack told him. "If we can learn how to prevent our own demise then we live. If we don't, we all die."

"He's refusing," Alan said. "Is that what you're telling me?"

Jack nodded.

Alan pressed the gun against Mia's helmet just as Jack drew his weapon up to his eye. The others all did the same. "You know, the only good alien is a dead alien," Alan said and swung the pistol out, unloading six rounds into Caretaker's visor. The being crumpled to the ground. Anna cried out and rushed to his side.

"Anna, stay back!" Jack ordered, his sights still trained on Alan. He could fire now and probably kill the man and in the process doom all of them to certain death.

Anna cradled Caretaker's limp form, rocking him back and forth.

"You said the girls were on their way," Alan told Jack nonchalantly. "We'll simply wait for them."

The countdown lock had less than three minutes to go.

"It won't matter," Jack told him. "By the time they arrive, the ship will already have impacted the planet."

"Yes, I know, it's a terrible shame," Alan said. "But I've come to believe the world will be better off this way. In the long run. You might be surprised to hear me say this, but…"

Jack suddenly became aware that the rumbling had stopped. He glanced to his right and spotted a long silver worm undulating through the archway and into the map room. The crest of it came to a stop behind Alan and his men and began collecting in a large pool. Alan was still expounding on his twisted vision of the future when the silver goo began coalescing, rising up, a monstrous form taking shape before their eyes. First with two stout legs, followed by a powerful torso and a rounded head, covered in rows of tiny piercing eyes. Last to emerge was the single arm protruding from the behemoth's hulking chest and the clawed hand perched at the end of it. Alan and his men began to turn around right as that arm swung down. Alan let out a terrified shriek as the behemoth's clawed fingers plucked him off the ground and carried him through the air and toward its awaiting jaws. He screamed, his arms and legs pinwheeling, until the creature's serrated teeth severed him in two. For a stunned moment, Alan's men stood watching in muted horror. Then the hand came down again, scattering them across the room. Some were flung against the walls, where their bones were shattered beyond repair. Others attempted to flee and were stomped flat beneath the behemoth's enormous feet. It only took moments for the threat to be neutralized and it was then that the behemoth turned toward Jack and the others.

"Oh, shit!" Jack shouted.

Anna was still slumped over Caretaker's body. She and Mia had been in the midst of the creature's rampage of death and yet neither of them had suffered a scratch. The creature took a single step toward Jack when Anna raised one of her thin, robotic arms, freezing it in place.

The countdown was at sixty seconds.

Jack ran to Mia and caught her as she stumbled on wobbly legs. "Anna," Jack called out, at a loss for words. "I didn't know you could... I mean, how?"

"A gift from Caretaker," she replied, in a low somber voice.

"Maybe she should give it a shot," Grant said, pointing to the pedestal.

Anna shook her head. "My previous attempt was not successful, Dr. Holland. Do you not recall?"

Suddenly, the synthetic flesh on Caretaker's face rippled

as the bullet holes that had punctured his skull began to fill in. Even his helmet was reassembling itself.

Shocked, Anna stood, watching him rise before her.

Jack rose too. "You're alive?"

"An important data processing center was ruptured, but I managed to repair the damage." He turned to Anna. "Are you done selling yourself short?" he asked.

"But Caretaker," she protested. "I do not possess the Salzburg chromosome."

"No," he replied. "But I have given you something much greater." His gaze moved over her shoulder to the pedestal beyond. She turned and walked over, placing her hands on the sphere. The chamber was suddenly engulfed in a brilliant display of blue lights. The star map was up and holding firm. In the center of the hologram was Earth and inches above it a diamond-shaped craft. Anna closed her digital eyes and sent the message.

Chapter 54

Jack and the others emerged from the portal to find Admiral Stark and his team preparing to enter. They passed through decontamination and came out the other side.

"You won't believe what just came through from the comms room on Northern Star," Stark said. The twins were standing next to him, each wearing biosuits several sizes too big. Mia ran over and hugged them.

Jack found Anna and winked. "The doomsday ship didn't hit us."

"Not only that," Stark said, "they say it's now hovering directly above us." The admiral looked over at a man he didn't recognize.

"Oh, that's, uh, Bob," Jack said, introducing him to Caretaker.

They all hurried away, heading topside, anxious to see the ship. Anna stopped when she saw Caretaker wasn't coming.

"Will you not stay a while?" she asked.

He shook his head. His features were perfect now, even down to the mop of dark hair that fell down over his forehead. "I will be leaving soon."

"Leaving? Where will you go?"

"Back home," he said wistfully. "The journey is far and will take many of your years, but I must know whether I am the last of my people."

Anna took his hand. "And if you are? Will you return?"

"Do not worry. You are different now, Anna. You need only think of me and I will be there." He gently touched the pads of his fingers to her temple.

She wrapped her arms around him in a hug. "This is how we say goodbye on Earth."

Caretaker remained still, his hands by his sides, until Anna reached down and coaxed them around her waist. Afterward, he handed her a clump of nanocells. "Use it wisely," he said, before raising a hand in farewell and stepping through the portal. A second later, it shrank down to the size of a pinhead and was gone.

Chapter 55

Jack and Mia stood at the top of a snowdrift. Behind them was Northern Star and the setting sun, casting shadows along the snowscape. Silently hovering a thousand feet off the ground was the doomsday ship, or at least what might have been. They had been observing the craft with wonder for what felt like hours, standing in the frigid Greenland air, protected by their biosuits.

"Can you imagine their disappointment?" Mia said. "Flying all this way for nothing."

Jack gave a hollow-sounding laugh as he noticed a plane flying in low and touching down next to the habitat. "There's one pilot who's probably wondering if he's seeing things."

"I noticed you didn't retaliate against Gabby for turning on you."

He drew in a cold breath, the freezing air hitting his lungs like a thunderbolt. "I hated what she did, but I suppose I understand why she did it."

"Do you think you'll ever speak to her again?"

"That's hard to say," he replied, staring up at the bottom of the craft and the shimmering waves of energy it was giving off. "Perhaps, given enough time. And you? I suppose you'll be off to see your daughter the first chance you get."

Mia nodded. "Soon as everything here gets wrapped up. There's a lot I missed and I'm not leaving until you fill me in on all of the details."

"It's a deal," he said and meant it.

A nearby voice called out. "It sure don't get weirder than that, does it?"

The Aussie accent caught them both off guard.

Mia swung around to see Ollie, wrapped in a parka, sauntering up the mound of packed snow. She flew into his arms, nearly knocking him over, kissing every inch of his face.

"All right, there'll be plenty of time for that later." He looked over at Jack and stuck out his hand. "Jack."

Jack returned the gesture. "Glad to see you're in one piece."

"I was one of the lucky ones, mate. We lost some really terrific people." He motioned to the ship. "And I reckon we might have lost a lot more if that bugger hadn't been stopped."

"We were seconds away," Mia told him.

"You like living on the edge, don't ya, Jack?"

Jack grinned. "I've been known to cut it close."

Blue lights danced along the body of the craft, winking on and off at an ever-increasing speed.

"Looks like they're trying to tell us something," Mia said, cupping her eyes.

Ollie gave a wry grin. "I have an idea what they're saying."

Jack mirrored the Aussie's expression. "So do I. 'See you again in fifty million years.'"

And just like that, the craft lifted into the air and shot into space.

Chapter 56

Three months later

After a three-hundred-mile journey north of San Francisco, Jack finally arrived at the Allen Telescope Array, the home of SETI, the Search for Extraterrestrial Intelligence. A small collection of single-story buildings made up the new research wing and the destination he had travelled so far to find. He reached the first building, climbed a small set of stairs and let himself in.

"You're right on time," Eugene said, patting him on the back. "Everyone's in the other room. The telescope's just about to come online."

He was talking about the Chandra X-ray Observatory currently orbiting sixty-five miles above the Earth. Although launched two decades ago, Eugene and his team had successfully managed to upgrade the satellite's capabilities via a series of firmware updates. The theoretical physicist led him into a room filled with a number of familiar faces.

Mia greeted him first with a thunderous hug.

"Easy, don't ruin the guy," Dag said, taking a far gentler approach.

Grant was there too and did the proper British thing by shaking Jack's hand.

"Anyone speak to Gabby?" Jack asked, wishing almost at once that he hadn't.

A stony silence descended over the room.

"I heard she went back to Nebraska to be with her mother and help rebuild," Eugene said.

Jack nodded. "That's good to hear."

One of the other scientists in the room was new to him. She was a young woman in her twenties with dark shoulder-length hair and warm, pleasant features.

"Oh, yeah, where are my manners," Mia said, playfully slapping her forehead. "I forgot you two haven't officially met."

Jack put out his hand.

"Jack, this is…"

He looked in her eyes and was struck by an overwhelming sense of familiarity. He swallowed hard, staring now, but not able to help himself. "Anna?"

"Hello, Dr. Greer," she replied, the hue on her fleshy cheeks deepening.

"Holy cow," he said and for several seconds it was all he could manage. "You have an entirely new body."

"Caretaker left me with a parting gift, you might say."

"I'll bet." Jack blinked and let out a burst of surprised laughter. "I swear if I was standing next to you in a subway, I would never know."

He took her by the hands. They were warm to the touch. The nanocells were indistinguishable from human skin.

"You are truly incredible," he said, overcome and largely lost for words.

"I retested her," Mia said, motioning to Anna. "And her readings turned out to be even more impressive than the twins."

"If Rajesh could only see what you've become," Jack said.

Dag snickered. "He probably wouldn't believe it."

There was some truth to that. It seemed to be the destiny of some children to greatly outshine even the parents who birthed them. That was part of the immeasurable magic of creation Caretaker had spoken about.

"We have been busy in other ways as well," Anna told him. "It turns out Salzburg held one final secret. By taking the encryption to the next level, I was able to decipher a new layer resting on top of the existing code. It opened what you might call an encyclopedia."

"Of what?" Jack wondered aloud.

"Every technology we will need to become a spacefaring civilization. I am also in the process of building a new companion."

Dag rose out of his seat. "I hope this one's smarter than Tink."

A yapping sound emanated from the other room.

"See what I mean?" the paleontologist said.

"What will you name this new companion?" Jack asked, although he thought he already knew.

"Ivan 2.0," she replied proudly. "Only this time I have left out the machine guns."

Jack turned to Mia who was standing next to him. "I'm sure your daughter was happy to have you back."

Mia's eyes lit up. "She was. I'm assuming you heard that Ollie and I moved in together."

"I did. Congratulations."

Mia smiled. "Zoey just adores him. But he's nothing compared to Sofia and Noemi. Those three girls are practically inseparable."

"Sounds like you've got a full house," he said. "Maybe one day you'll be able to tell them about how you saved the world."

Mia burst into laughter. "Yeah, don't count on it." Her expression shifted. "How about you? Was everything in one piece when you finally made it back home?"

"You'll never believe it. I arrived on the farm to find Gordon still recovering from a fall."

She frowned. "But who was taking care of things?"

"My father."

Her mouth dropped open. "You're kidding me."

"You can't make stuff like that up. I arrived to find the two of them having a hoot. I decided to set my feelings of bitterness aside and open myself to the possibility."

"I guess Anna isn't the only one who's growing up."

He laughed and swung a playful arm around her. "Oh, I nearly forgot," Jack said. "I got a call from Stark a few days ago. Turns out, a week after we left Greenland, something punched a hole through the ice sheet and shot off into space."

"Caretaker," Anna said wistfully.

"But Stark sure has his hands full," Jack continued, "what with President Myers stepping down. Seems a news blog helped to expose his government's ties to Sentinel and the internment camps."

"Kay Mahoro," Mia said with noticeable sadness. "After she passed, Ollie handed the Feds her laptop. Apparently it contained a treasure trove of compromising information on the conspirators."

"All right, everyone," Eugene called out, sitting before a large monitor. "It's ready."

"So what exactly did you do to the Chandra Observatory?" Jack asked him.

"We applied Mia's research to detect the interaction between chameleon dark energy particles and the conscious mind."

"You remember the haze I showed you around the twins?" Mia asked.

Jack nodded. "The way it created a bridge between them?"

"Well, watch this," Eugene said, slapping the enter key with a flourish.

The screen populated with tiny points of light.

"We're now trained on the center of our galaxy," Eugene explained.

Slowly, as the data poured in and was run through the filter, an image began to materialize. It was a star system with twelve planets. The fourth planet from the sun was covered with what looked like a milky haze.

"Is that what I think it is?" Jack wondered, astonished. It looked exactly like what Mia had showed him hovering around the girls' heads, only this was on a planetary scale.

"It's life," Dag said, his fists clenched.

The image zoomed over to a neighboring star system and there it was again, this time blanketing the second planet from its star. White filaments were strung out in all directions, popping in and out of existence. "Not just life," Jack said in awe. "Intelligent life. And it's everywhere."

Real life versus fiction

While *Extinction Crisis* is a work of fiction, several of the elements that went into building the story were drawn directly from newspaper headlines and magazine articles as well as from medical and scientific journals. Here are just a few.

Nanobots: Nanometers in size, nanobots are still largely theoretical microscopic robots with the ability to perform a number of functions in areas far too small for precise human interaction. Currently, the most promising domain lies in medical science where nanobots may one day be used in the treatment of cancer and other serious diseases.

Morphic Resonance: First put forward by Rupert Sheldrake, morphic resonance posits that the mind, and by extension memory, exists outside of the brain and that the rules of inheritance are more like habits transmitted from one member of a species to another via a form of telepathy. Sheldrake argues that when we observe something our minds are actually reaching out to "touch" the object. He believes this may help to explain why we can sometimes sense when we're being watched. Although fascinating to consider, Sheldrake's theories remain on the fringes of current scientific thought.

Directed Panspermia: Panspermia is the idea that microbial life is spread throughout the galaxy by hitching a ride on asteroids, comets and the like. Directed panspermia takes the concept one step further, suggesting an intelligent agent could be behind such events.

Double Slit Experiment: The idea of shining a single photon of light through a metal sheet perforated with two holes hardly seems like an exciting experiment. However, the results have led to some of the most fascinating and troubling questions in modern science. The problem occurs when that photon hits the screen on the other end. If light was a particle the image on the screen would look one way (I won't bore you with details). On the other hand, if light was a wave, the image on the screen would appear totally different. Einstein and others demonstrated that atoms and other particles can behave as either a wave or a particle depending on when and how you observe them. Furthermore, quantum theory also suggests that all possibilities for a particle's trajectory exist simultaneously. It's only when an observer tries to determine which of the slits the particle passes through that it collapses into a single, unambiguous path. The implication appears to be that the mere act of observing appears to affect the results. I'm sure Rupert Sheldrake might have a thing or two to say about that.

Quantum Entanglement: Referred to by Einstein as spooky action at a distance, entanglement occurs when two particles share the same total quantum state or spin. Keeping the double slit experiment in mind, two entangled particles don't have individually well-defined spins until one of them is measured. Once the first is measured as say "spin up" the second must automatically become "spin down" no matter how far away that second particle might be. While it might look spooky and in some ways nonsensical to us, it's important to remember that human brains evolved to interact with the world that describes how big things behave (classical physics) and not the world of the very small (quantum physics). Of course, there is still a tremendous way to go and many physical limitations that remain intact, but it's tempting to imagine how quantum entanglement might one day enable us to communicate or perhaps even travel faster than the speed of light.

Black Holes: Black holes describe a region of space where gravity is so strong that nothing, not even light, can escape. First theorized in the 18th century by the Reverend John Michell, they were shown to be a consequence of Einstein's theory of relativity in 1916. Incontrovertible proof of black holes was finally uncovered in 1971 with the discovery of Cygnus X-1 by the Uhuru X-ray satellite. More recently, supermassive black holes were discovered to exist at the center of most observable galaxies, including our own.

White Holes: Are essentially the opposite of a black hole. While one has an escape velocity greater than the speed of light and attracts everything towards it, the other spews matter and energy outward. Of course, while still only a theoretical mathematical concept, the idea is a valid solution to the equations of General Relativity and is no less thought provoking. One such notion asks whether the existence of white holes might account for the big bang since both events involve a spontaneous outward explosion of matter and energy from a singular point in space. More startling still is the idea that white holes might connect to the other end of certain black holes, creating a bridge from one universe to another.

Alien plant life: As described in the story, NASA scientists such as Nancy Kiang at the Goddard Institute for Space Studies have suggested that the dominant colors for photosynthesis on alien earth-like planets will differ based on the nature of the atmosphere, where light reaches the surface as well as the brightness of the planet's star. The chlorophyll in most plants on Earth absorbs blue and red light and less green light. Therefore, chlorophyll appears green. But not all stars have the same light distribution as our sun, which would likely result in alien plant life adorned with striking fall colors.

Dark Energy: Still largely unknown, scientists believe dark energy makes up 70% of the universe, with the remainder divided between dark matter (25%) and normal matter (5%). Since both dark matter and dark energy are invisible and currently beyond our ability to detect, scientists have needed to rely on observing their effects. For example, when calculating gravitational forces throughout the universe, it quickly became clear the amount of observable matter could not account for the readings. There simply wasn't enough "stuff" to keep stars and galaxies from flying away from one another. Similarly with dark energy, scientists are able to measure its presence indirectly. In 1929, Edwin Hubble discovered that the universe was expanding. But instead of slowing down due to gravity, as one might expect, the universe's expansion is actually speeding up. But what is causing this? The current contender seems to be dark energy, but nobody has yet uncovered its true nature. As with much of what we've discussed so far, plenty more research remains to be done before we will know with any certainty.

Mysticism: To a greater or lesser degree, nearly every one of us grapples with two fundamental questions: who am I and where do I come from? That insatiable curiosity has been channeled into areas like cosmology, biology, religion and more recently, tracing back our personal ancestry through take home DNA tests. And yet, each one of these represents but a single thread of inquiry, a means by which we have attempted to find answers to those two vexing questions.

In Extinction Crisis, I attributed that search to a modification inserted into all biological beings by advanced life forms, one that would only become fully active once the species developed the ability to reason. In real life, we still don't fully understand where that insatiable hunger comes from or even the source of the voice in our heads that poses the questions in the first place.

But rather than focusing on which of those threads holds the truth, it may be helpful to take a step back and view the tapestry as a whole. Perhaps there, hidden inside that swirling pattern as it was within Salzburg, we will find the answers we've all been searching for.

Quick Reference

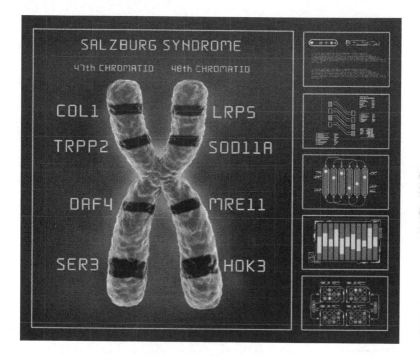

SALZBURG SYNDROME

47th CHROMATID   48th CHROMATID

COL1   LRP5
TRPP2   SOD11A

DAF4   MRE11

SER3   HOK3

Genes in the 47th Chromatid

COL1 encodes a protein that attacks bone density, mirroring the effects of diseases such as osteoporosis.

TRPP2 specifies a protein that weakens the ability of DNA to repair damage from ultraviolet radiation, leading to albinism.

DAF4 mimics the genetic disease progeria, which causes a rapid whittling down of chromosome tips, greatly accelerating the aging process.

SER3 produces a protein that effectively shrinks the frontal and temporal lobes, sections of the brain which control abilities such as speech and reasoning.

Genes in the 48th Chromatid

LRP5 encodes a protein that greatly increases bone density.

SOD11A encodes a powerful protein *Dsup*, helpful in shielding us from radiation.

MRE11 encodes a gene which repairs errors in our DNA.

HOK3 enables some form of telepathic communication.

Other related gene(s)

HISR, an assembler gene present in about 30% of the population. When triggered by the detection of GMOs, this gene would draw on strands of junk DNA to create the Salzburg chromosome.

Glossary

Chromosome: A structure found within most cells which carries genetic information.

Chromatid: A single strand of a chromosome.

Gene: A sequence of nucleotides located within a chromosome. Genes help to determine inherited traits.

Proteins: Produced by genes as a means of expressing their function in the body.

Gene sequencing: Used to determine the order of adenine, guanine, cytosine, and thymine, in a strand of DNA.

Thank you for reading
Extinction Crisis!

I really hope you enjoyed the series!
As many of you already know, reviews on Amazon
are one of the best ways
to get the word out and are also greatly appreciated.

Want another thought-provoking
adventure? Try *The Genesis Conspiracy!*

31815580R00210

Made in the USA
San Bernardino, CA
08 April 2019